Love of Mountains

Love of Mountains

Two Stories by Uno Kōji

Translated and Introduced by Elaine Gerbert

University of Hawai'i Press
Honolulu

These translations are based on the Chūō Kōron-Sha, Inc., editions of *Kura no naka* and *Yamagoi*, published in 1972. *Kura no naka* was first published in 1919 and *Yamagoi* in 1922 by Uno Kōji.
English translation rights arranged with Uno Kazuo.

02 01 00 99 98 97   5 4 3 2 1

Library of Congress Cataloging-in-Publication Data
Uno, Kōji, 1891–1961.
   [Yamagoi. English]
   Love of mountains : two stories by Uno Kōji / translated by Elaine
Tashiro Gerbert.
      p.   cm.
   ISBN 0–8248–1756–7 (alk. paper)
   1. Uno, Kōji, 1891–1961—Translations into English. I. Gerbert,
Elaine Tashiro, 1944–   . II. Uno, Kōji, 1891–1961. Kura no naka.
English.   III. Title
PL840.N6A24 1997
895.6'344—dc20   96–9711
                                                                       CIP

University of Hawai'i Press books are printed on acid-free paper and meet the guide-
lines for permanence and durability of the Council on Library Resources

DESIGNED BY LAUREN CHOI

In memory
of Uno Morimichi
and Uno Tomiko

CONTENTS

PREFACE

Uno Kōji (1891–1961) was a well-known and significant writer who is generally associated with an era in Japanese literature that began after the Russo-Japanese War (1904–1905) and lasted until the Great Kantō Earthquake of 1923.

He came to the fore at a time when the dominance of literary realism, established in the first decade of the century, was being contested by literature of a more aesthetic and experimental nature. Uno was one of those younger writers who challenged the orthodoxy of descriptive realism.

While he is generally associated with a group of men regarded as the second generation of naturalist writers (owing largely to his affiliation with Waseda University, the center of literary naturalism), his writing was marked by a playfulness and a critical self-consciousness that departed from the serious self-absorption that characterized the writings of many naturalists, including those of the Waseda *Kiseki* (Miracle) coterie.

Indeed, if the naturalists' contribution had been the attempt to describe phenomenal reality objectively, Uno's was to pull readers back to an awareness of the medium in which those writers worked. He reminded his audience that the reality they found in novels was one created of words possessing a different ontological status from that of the events purportedly described, and he thus confirmed the distinction between art and life at a time when many readers read novels as if the two were interchangeable.

The techniques Uno used to satirize the seriousness of modern Japanese literature are illustrated in the two well-known works translated in this volume: "In the Storehouse" (*Kura no naka*, 1919) and "Love of Mountains" (*Yamagoi*, 1922).

The reader of Japanese may notice that my translations do not always strictly follow the sentence order or even the paragraphing of the original texts. On many occasions I shortened sentences and broke up paragraphs to convey more effectively

what I believe to be the essential aspects of Uno's writing—
namely, its ludic, humorous, and especially critical quality.

There are a number of individuals whose answers to my
questions helped me along the way and whose help I acknowledge with gratitude. I would like to thank especially my editor,
Sharon Yamamoto, for her patience and promotion of these
translations and Gene Carvalho for carefully checking their
technical accuracy. And foremost I would like to thank Professor Edwin McClellan, who introduced me to Uno Kōji and the
literary culture in which he lived and wrote.

Work on this book was subsidized in part by a Northeast
Asia Council Research Travel Grant and grants received from
Gustavus Adolphus College and the University of Kansas.

Love of Mountains

INTRODUCTION

Of all the distinguishing characteristics Japanese critics have attributed to Uno Kōji (1891–1961), the one that is most often repeated may be rendered as "consummate and irreverent stylist."[1] This shoBuld not be surprising if we define Uno's style in the broadest possible sense: the way he lived before he wrote and while he wrote, the ways in which he used language, what he chose to write about, and the historical circumstances that shaped it all.

We may think of Uno's early life as having predisposed him, if not outright conditioned him, to see the world around him with a detachment not common among writers of his day. This detachment generated a skepticism that later developed into a relentlessly critical attitude toward much of what the literary establishment produced.[2]

Uno Kōji was born in 1891 to parents of samurai origin whose forebears had migrated from Shinshū (present-day Nagano prefecture) to Osaka, where, toward the end of the Tokugawa period, his paternal grandfather had served as a *yoriki* or police captain in the Osaka city government. Although they had lost their hereditary posts and stipends when the feudal system was dismantled in 1871, members of the former military caste *(shizoku)* still held pride of place in prewar Japan. The position Uno's father held as instructor of *kokugo, kanbun,* and calligraphy at the Fukuoka prefectural normal school in Fukuoka city in Kyushu may have been due as much to his family background as to his talents.

Uno's father, however, died of a stroke when Uno was barely four. Thereafter, whatever stability and security there had been in his childhood vanished. The family moved from place to place, living off the charity of relatives. They settled first with relatives in Kobe, until a brother-in-law, intending to make their small savings grow, speculated on the stock market and lost it all, including the funds earmarked for Uno's future education. When Uno was eight, he was sent to live with a grandmother and an uncle, and his mother went to work as a waitress in the countryside.

The uncle's house was located in Sōemonchō, a neighborhood adjoining the Dōtonbori entertainment district in Osaka and home to geisha, prostitutes, wig makers, gamblers, and others who made their living in the red-light district across the Dōtonbori canal. For the next several years, Uno lived in a divided world, at home neither among the *shitamachi* residents of Sōemonchō nor among the sons of military officers at the Rikugun elementary school, which he attended from 1899 to 1901.

Thus deprived of playmates, he relied increasingly, for pleasure and comfort, on the imaginary worlds created with his magic lantern slides and the many books he read. By the time he was a middle school student at the Tennōji middle school in Osaka, the world of those imaginary spaces was considerably expanded and enriched by foreign literature translated from French, German, and, especially, Russian into English (which he had by then learned to read) and Japanese. He had a seeming fondness for the poetry of the romantic and sometimes skeptical and satirical Heine,[3] but it was the quixotic view of reality in the stories of Gogol,[4] an odd being, like himself, ill at ease in society, that fascinated and delighted him the most.

Uno would not, like the writer Nagai Kafū (1879–1959), who was born into an economically and socially privileged family and who discovered the entertainment districts as an adolescent, elegize the world of the "gay quarters." Instead, he would focus on its unusual individuals as models for the characters of his stories, such as the sad wisp of a girl who had to practice her samisen every afternoon in preparation for her future calling as a geisha and vented her frustration in convulsive fits, and her geisha aunt who jumped into the canal on a December night to win a bet and pay her debts before the new year. His narratives would include glimpses of Dōtonbori denizens, such as the un-wigged, white-faced *onnagata* actor as he spat from his theater window, and portraits of the people of Sōemonchō, such as the oversized boy who hated school so much that his elderly parents had to carry him to the school yard or the gifted albino boy who released his grief by poking holes in the faces of playing cards.[5]

When he moved to Tokyo in 1910 to enter the English liter-ature department at Waseda University, Uno's inclination to as-sume the posture of the disinterested bystander was evident in his failure to follow the social conventions of the time and find a mentor in an older writer or to make his literary debut in the intensely group-oriented *bundan* by publishing in a coterie mag-azine *(dōjin zasshi)*.[6]

Literary naturalism was in its heyday in 1910, but Uno did not seek out Shimamura Hōgetsu (1871–1918), the naturalist critic who was then head of the Waseda literature department, or any of the other professors who were associated with the movement. His readings in Symbolist poetry made the prosaic language of the naturalists seem old-fashioned, much as his im-mersion in the portentous, melancholy, languid, weary worlds of the novels of the Russian modernist writers Andreyev, Artsyba-shev, Balmont, Kuprin, Sologub, and Zaitsev made the ebullient, self-affirming, Tolstoi-inspired idealism of the other significant literary movement of the time, the *Shirakaba* circle, seem fatu-ous and more than a little naive.[7]

Uno published his first important work, "In the Store-house," when he was twenty-eight, a relatively late age for a new writer in those days. Its fresh, colloquial style went far beyond anything the novelist Mushanokōji Saneatsu (1885–1976) had achieved with his highly publicized "write as you speak" *(hanasu yō ni kaku)* approach. As the critic Usui Yoshimi commented, "Today it is hardly unusual for a story to begin with the conjunction *and* [*soshite*], but at that time, when the average novel was strictly representational, it was highly unconventional."[8] There was nothing immature or green about Uno. Indeed, if anything, his writing seemed to parody and satirize the self-congratulatory effusions of writers like Mushanokōji, who, in his novel *Omedetaki hito* (An innocent), could pen such lines as "I am a man! I am a brave hero! My work is important!"[9]

But at the same time that Uno's stylistic facility was acknowledged and even admired, he was also criticized for his inappropriately "flippant" attitude. The literary establishment was quick to administer the corrective medicine of ridicule to one who deviated from its norms. Essays appearing in an August 1921 issue of the literary magazine *Shinchō* lampooned him. Lacking the sobriety associated with "pure [high] literature," he was called by less sympathetic observers a popular *(tsūzoku-teki)* writer, with all the condescension the word *popular* implied. His undecipherable oddness led some to employ unusual metaphors to describe him. The short story writer Akutagawa Ryūnosuke (1892–1927), known for his wit, called him "a spiritual chameleon";[10] however, later he acknowledged that Uno had been unduly criticized in the back rooms of the *bundan* for displaying a comic spirit that flew in the face of the decorum expected of serious writers.[11]

His standing within the *bundan* improved when he recovered from a mental illness that had led to a seven-year period of silence, lasting from 1927 until 1933, and began to publish more conventional kinds of novels. In the 1930s, he led a literary coterie, served as a judge on the Akutagawa prize committee, and counseled young writers. During the war, however, when colleagues and friends contributed their talents to the war effort, Uno quietly devoted himself to writing essays about life in the *bundan* during the Taishō era (1912–1926).

After the war, he was one of the first of the Taishō period writers to begin publishing again. He was awarded the Yomiuri shinbun literary prize for his long novel *Omoigawa* (Stream of remembrance), published in 1948, and was highly praised for his critical biography of Akutagawa Ryūnosuke (*Akutagawa Ryūnosuke*, 1951).

As an elder statesman of the arts, he tried to influence the future course of Japanese literature, and, as a judge on the influential Akutagawa prize committee, he could, to some degree, determine that course. He took a dim view of those who "followed literary trends."[12] When the committee came under pressure to award the prize to Ishihara Shintarō's flamboyant novel about the dissolute mores of postwar youth, Uno alone refused to promote the kind of sensual escapist fiction that the public hungered for, and he voted against *Taiyō no kisetsu* (lit., "Season of the Sun," but translated as *Season of Violence*).

His one departure from purely literary matters into the arena of politics occurred in 1953 when he joined with Hirotsu Kazuo (1891–1968) to campaign for the release of twenty members of the National Railway Workers Union and the Toshiba Electric Company's Matsukawa factory union who had been charged with sabotaging a Japan National Railways freight train. Named after the village in Fukushima prefecture where the accident occurred, the Matsukawa Incident *(Matsukawa jiken)* became the most controversial court case in postwar Japan. All but one of the accused were members of the Japanese Communist party, and demands for their release came from leftist governments and organizations around the world as well as from the liberal intellectual establishment within Japan. Uno contributed two novels to "prove" the innocence of the accused: *Yo ni mo fushigi na monogatari* (The strangest story in the world, 1953) and *Ategoto to fundoshi* (There's many a slip between cup and lip, 1954). In part as a result of his involvement in the case, he and his son Morimichi received personal invitations from Premier Chou En Lai to tour China with the writers Kubota Mantarō and Aono Suekichi in 1956.

Uno died of pulmonary tuberculosis in 1961. His collected works (in twelve volumes) consist of roughly 150 stories, novels, and essays.

The Taishō Bundan: A Society at Play

Probably few opportunities to assess the possibilities of "life following art" are as tempting as the case of life in the late Meiji/Taishō bundan.

As in the late Edo period (1600–1868), which saw the flourishing of gesaku within a "culture of play,"[13] the Taishō period was a time of change and uncertainty. The famine, rural unrest, urban growth, and economic dislocation that undermined the strength of traditional moral and ideological structures in late Edo were paralleled in Taishō by demographic shifts, inflation (leading to nationwide rice riots in 1918), and contradictions between publicly proclaimed morality for the group and cultural forms that appealed to individual private interest. And, as in late Edo, when contemporaries spoke of their society in transition as a world that had become "like the kabuki,"[14] Taishō was an age when new ways of mirroring the world about them created for some a keen sense of specularity and a sensation of living life on a stage.[15]

In contrast to the circumstances in which late Edo gesaku flourished, however, in Taishō the production of new forms of knowledge was more directly and extensively connected to a massive influx of foreign learning and art in the form of books, foreign teachers, and study abroad. Many of the leading members of the late Meiji-Taishō literary establishment (Natsume Sōseki, Mori Ōgai, Nagai Kafū, Shimazaki Tōson, Shimamura Hōgetsu, Osanai Kaoru, Arishima Takeo) had traveled and studied in Europe and America.

The bundan was a tightly knit and ingrown society. The private literary interests of its members were viewed as self-indulgent and nonproductive by the society at large, which still held to traditional prejudices against fiction writing. Their individualistic pursuits of self-discovery and self-affirmation ran counter to the mind-set that put the interests of the group first.

While in late Edo many of the leading *gesaku* authors were writing commercially for a general, urban audience, in the self-absorbed, Meiji-Taishō *bundan* the producers of literature were also the consumers, and writing took on a particularly self-reflective quality.

There were genres such as the *moderu shōsetsu* (model *shōsetsu*), wherein a writer peopled his novels with characters closely modeled on his *bundan* associates (most *bundan* writers were male). The most prevalent literary genre of the time, however, and the one that reflected the peculiarities of *bundan* life most closely was the *shishōsetsu* or *watakushi shōsetsu* (also referred to as the *watakushi wa shōsetsu*). This loosely organized narrative, a thinly veiled fiction under which a writer revealed his thoughts and feelings (often of an intimate, confessional nature), was a kind of writing that elicited interest in, concern over, and support for the writer himself from his readers, who identified the narrator with the writer, and bound the writer and his audience in a close relationship. The writer told the story of his life (proclaiming, as it were, "I am a novel," *watakushi wa shōsetsu*)[16] and received in turn reactions to and commentaries on his revelations from his peers, verbally (at literary meetings) and in writing (in critical articles and commentary and published transcriptions of group discussions [*zadankai*]). A writer could broadcast his problems with the knowledge that scores of readers would follow the installments in which he rehashed life crises in different forms and from different perspectives. He might speak in different voices (now first person, later third person, sometimes specifically as a novelist, at others more generally as an artist), but, in the end, the more he varied his voice and mode of presentation, the more aspects of the self he seemed to expose, and the more readily identifiable that self came to be. As a writer engaged in these self-revelatory writings, he had the emotional security of knowing that there would be solicitous, inquiring, speculative, and even probing reactions in the published commentary on his writings and in countless group discussions.

In this "literary hothouse,"[17] writers were also exposed to and stimulated by a constant flow of Western literature. Literary fads and "fevers" flourished, and a writer might be simultaneously a naturalist and a devotee of symbolism in an atmosphere where descriptive realism (and the underlying positivistic assumption that one could describe reality) was still widely practiced, although continuously challenged.

Foreign literature suggested not only a model for writing but also one for living. For some writers, so keenly aware of just how close at hand their reading audiences were, the style in which they conducted their lives was almost as important as the style in which they composed their sentences. Indeed, many young writers defined themselves largely through their playful deportment. If the writer and translator of Oscar Wilde's poems, Satō Haruo (1892–1964), created a stir by turning up at the Paolista café on the Ginza attired in a velvet suit and a red Turkish fez on some days, a bowler hat and flowing Bohemian cravat on others, Uno cut no less colorful a figure by going to the Paolista in a blue fez and a red cravat tied in a big bow. Having through his sartorial games acquired the nickname *oshare* (dandy), he played up to that reputation with an ostentatious display of his love of clothes: dressing up in finery just to go to the neighborhood bathhouse and showing up at literary banquets in the style of kimono worn by actors and with his face painted white.

Bundan writers looked not only to other writers' work for models; the circumstances of *bundan* literary production required that they also keep in mind the constructed images of the self that they had projected in their previous novels. Having created their identities and authorial voices, they had to continue to convince their readers of the authenticity of those voices by ensuring that subsequent writings (and life conduct) conform to the image of the personae they had created. Mimesis became an all absorbing activity for many.

In this highly performative world, it is hardly surprising that the Shingeki theater should have played such an important role in introducing new models of behavior from the West or that Uno Kōji should have associated with Shingeki actors and actresses or written novels about their society—and not so much about their plays as about the playacting that went on in their private quarters.[18] While *asobi* may function as a theme in a few late Meiji works (e.g., Natsume Sōseki's *Kusamakura* [Pillow of grass, 1906] and Mori Ōgai's short piece entitled "Asobi" [Play, 1910]), playfulness and performance in *bundan* social life become most apparent in mid-Taishō with writers like Tanizaki Jun'ichirō (1886–1965), Akutagawa Ryūnosuke, and Uno Kōji.

Asobi as a mood of leisurely detachment, exemplified in Sōseki's, haiku-like novel (*Kusamakura*) and in Sōseki's followers' advocacy of *yoyū ga aru bungaku* (literature born in a spirit of leisure and gratuitous play),[19] would seem to imply a rejection of naturalism's unrelenting focus on the epiphenomena of life. (To be sure, playfulness of a more vigorous sort is also to be found in Sōseki's earlier popular works, *Wagahai wa neko de aru* (I am a cat, 1905–1906) and *Botchan* (Little master, 1906), but Sōseki appears not to have sustained such a mood.) *Asobi* comes across as even more defensive in the detachment behind which Ōgai's protagonist maintains his critical view of society in "Asobi." Ōgai's alter ego, a bored official, fights back against a dehumanizing work situation by treating everything "as though it were a game."[20]

Tanizaki Jun'ichirō, whose early imagination was cultivated in a boyhood preoccupation with games, make-believe, and amusements, expressed what one might call play in a more positive generative capacity in his stories, beginning with "Shisei"

(Tattoo, 1910), in which the narrator begins by praising the "noble virtue" of foolish playfulness (a quality described as *oroka* in Japanese).[21] Akutagawa's literary sleights of hand included not only his unreliable narrators but also the literary hoax he played, pretending to have constructed the story "Hōkyōnin no shi" (Death of a martyr, 1918) on the basis of newly discovered documents dating back to Japan's Christian era of the late sixteenth and early seventeenth centuries.

Within this environment, Uno Kōji's playfulness was particularly ostentatious. He earned a reputation for being eccentric and strange and for reading, writing, and receiving *bundan* callers in his futon. His best friend, the writer and critic Hirotsu Kazuo, tells how Uno was self-deprecating and slouched around like a surreptitious lover in a kabuki play when he wore a threadbare kimono, but swaggered like a feudal lord when he put on a kimono with padded shoulders, and walked with the brisk step of a dandy when he wore a Western suit.[22] That he was, in short, ever ready to make a spectacle of himself and perform before an audience was documented by the writer Kume Masao (1891–1952), who reported how, on a lecture tour organized by the publisher Kikuchi Kan, Uno stood at the podium, stiff as a rod, arms folded and eyes closed, and refused to open his mouth when his turn to lecture came.[23]

Uno's writing was just as theatrical. The excessive garrulity, obsessive repetitiveness, and uncontrolled verbal disorderliness of his narrators called attention to the physical mechanics of speaking. His characters also perform: they laugh, weep, shout, and exert themselves with an egregious and immodest display of physicality that was rare in the "high" literature of the time.

His parodistic, self-reflexive, multivoiced manipulation of language and references to the body (on occasion he ventured toward the coarse, describing vomiting, menses, and urination) may have recalled for some the more ribald kind of *gesaku* literature. But, as the novelist Ishikawa Jun (1899–1987) observed, Uno seemed more like a Westerner in a kimono than a Japanese.[24] Borrowing Ishikawa's image, one might say that Uno at times used *gesaku*-like techniques to practice a criticism that was modern and basically quite rational. For example, the character Okkotsu the law student in Uno's "Yaneura no hōgakushi" (The law student in the garret, 1918) expresses a flippant attitude toward "civilization and enlightenment" *(bunmei kaika)* and its prioritization of instrumental reason and progress by skating up and down the corridor on sheets of waxed paper, eating breakfast, lunch, and dinner in bed, brushing his teeth in his futon and spitting out the window (he is too lazy to walk to the sink), and carousing with the maids.

Okkotsu's attitude toward "enlightenment" is further manifested in his preference for the traditional plebeian arts of *rakugo, gidayū* (performative narrative arts that featured vocal mimicry, including impolite sounds such as wailing, sniffling, sniveling, grunting, and groaning), and melodramatic Shinpa tragedy to the more emotionally controlled, cerebral arts of criticism, Western drama, and Western painting. He declares that he "hasn't the patience to try to re-create on paper the actual world the way those novelists of the naturalist school do," and to the honest but simpleminded uncle who expresses the wish that his nephew would write about something more dignified than the geta lying in the foyer—a subject of enduring fascination for Okkotsu—the young man replies offhandedly, "I haven't the slightest intention of saving the human race or contributing to the improvement of society," and, having said this much, tramps off to the bathroom.[25]

Kura no naka / *"In the Storehouse"* (1919)

Like Okkotsu, the novelist Yamaji who narrates this story dwells in the back rooms of society and has not kept up with the

times; forty years old, he is still in many ways a child. As he re-
counts episodes in his past life, he focuses attention on the physical manifestations of the body in a way that challenges the taboo
placed on such subjects by "polite" society (e.g., he speaks about
his naked body, lying in a futon, blushing, being sexually active
and then impotent). He conducts himself in a spirit of childish
play: appropriating the storehouse space gleefully, he criss-
crosses the room with the ropes he brings along and hangs up his
favorite clothes. He toys with his days, dividing each one into
three parts, and puts on a different outfit for each part. He
plays with his clothes, trying out different combinations, now
Western-style, now Japanese, and struts through the gay
quarters with juvenile pleasure, imagining how he might look
to others.

He not only revels in jumping in and out of his futon and lying in it but likens himself to a child when he is in it. In the protective folds of his (almost swaddling-like) futon, he retreats into
the far recesses of his imagination, and, stimulated by the prox-
imity of his favorite clothes (clothes with which he has developed a "skinship"), he daydreams about the details—the highly
personal details—of his love life. The physical closeness of Yamaji's world provides a protective space within which he can
play to his heart's content. In that close world, he can give vent
to his regressive tendencies by indulging in his passion for
smells. It is the sense developed before the sense of sight that
moves him the most.

At every turn, Yamaji's narration seems to embody an unre-
strained physicality, as if his irrepressible physical being itself
were projected into the text. There are uncontrolled emotional
outbursts (*Oya!* "Good gracious"; *Iyahaya!* "Dear me!") and
waggish exclamations (*sore wa, sore wa,* "well, well"). As he
babbles, he seems to take childish pleasure in the feel and sound
of words as they roll off his tongue. Polysyndetic verb pairs create a rocking momentum: "cut off by friends and cutting off

friends" *(tomodachi ni mikagiraretari tomodachi o mikagittari);* "forsaken by women and forsaking women" *(onna ni suter-aretari onna o sutetari).* Repetitions set up echoing rhythms as words are used to create sound impressions rather than to advance a line of thought. The alliterative "pawnshop" *(shichiya)* and its cognate "pawned good" *(shichimono)* are uttered ten times in the first few lines. He declares that he divides his day into "three parts" *(sando ni watte)* and goes on repeating "three times" as he explains how he changes his kimono "three times, three times a day . . . and not only does he change his kimono three times, three times. . . ."

The many indeterminate constructions *(to ka, to ka; yare; tari tari)* and rephrasings undercut the stability of what was just asserted: "already as many as ten or as many as twenty years" *(mō jūgonen mo nijūnen mo);* "I like women two or three times more than the ordinary man. . . . but as much as I like women, I like kimonos, no less and no more." The plethora of conjunctions *(soshite,* "and"; *sore de,* "so then"; *sore ni,* "moreover"; *sore kara,* "and then"; *sono ato,* "after that"; *sono ue,* "on top of that"; *sore bakari de naku,* "that's not all either") linking the sentences push the narrative along, creating the shifting, fluid quality of Uno's "slippery as eels" sentences.

While other writers adopted features of colloquial speech (e.g., Mushanokōji Saneatsu and Shiga Naoya [1883–1971] used the informal first-person pronoun *ore* and the self-reflexive *ji-bun*) to lend a greater note of intimacy to their narratives and close the distance between text and reader, Uno's "irresponsi-ble," "incompetent" narrator, who starts his tale in the middle of a sentence and then loses his train of thought, opened a space between text and reader and annoyed many a potentially sympa-thetic reader by frustrating the tendency to look for the *authentic* author in the text. Again and again, recalling that he has allowed himself to be swept away by the sound of his own voice, he pulls up short and struggles to regain control over the story and move it back onto "the main track." At times, Yamaji chucks aside authorial responsibility altogether by openly disparaging his narrative as a "sloppy, disorderly story" *(darashi-no-nai toritome-no-nai hanashi)*.

An effect of strangeness and alienation is created by incongruous combinations, such as the formal first-person pronoun *watakushi* and deferential verb forms (used to address the reader solicitously) juxtaposed with sudden addresses that demolish all sense of decorum: "Please close your ears!" His sudden insertion of a formal classical verb form or a quotation from the *Analects* produces a mock heightened effect, followed by a buffoonish effect created when he attaches the pluralizer *-domo* (normally used for animate beings) to his kimono (*kimono-domo*) and the epithet *aisuru* (to love) to his kimono (*aisuru kimono*, "my beloved kimono") and his futon (*aisuru futon*, "my beloved futon").

Outrageously loquacious in a society that valued reticence and allusive understatement, Yamaji calls attention to the act of narration (or narration about to begin) as he circles back again and again to the opening line: "And so I decided to go to the pawnshop." These shenanigans seemed to make fun of narrative modes that transported the reader unproblematically through the text, from event to event, and on to the end of the narrative.

The verbal mannerisms of the comic *rakugo* monologuist and the creation of the storytelling "stage" in the text (apparent most dramatically in the ending when Yamaji discovers that his "audience" of listeners has walked out on him)[26] highlighted the performative quality of the text and subverted the association that many *bundan* readers drew between first-person narration and sincere, truthful revelation in the *shishōsetsu*. While narrators who interrupt their narratives with chatty, discursive asides existed in late Edo *gesaku*, in the eighth year of Taishō it was decidedly unconventional, and its lightness and flippancy flew in the face of the dignity that so many writers had attempted to invest in the modern novel. At a time when many readers assumed that a narrative featuring a first-person speaker represented a verifiable, experiential reality drawn from the personal life of that speaker, who was coterminous with the author, Uno's narrative undermined the notion that language is something at the disposal of the writer to be shaped through intellect and will. Language in "In the Storehouse" neither mirrored an external order nor communicated an authorial self. On the contrary, through Yamaji's confusion, Uno suggested that language may possess a dynamism and momentum independent of the narrator's will. Language was slippery, and the writer not only played with it but was himself a plaything of its unpredictable force. Such a linguistic strategy was threatening to those readers whose psychic security depended on a one-to-one correspondence between the language of the novel and reality.

If the child-like self projected in the story undermined the idealized portrait of the self-aware, mature, emancipated "modern self" *(kindai jiga),* the very notion of progress and modernity was challenged by the story's digressive prose, which reflected the meandering pace of Yamaji's aimless existence and moved to the leisurely *(nonbiri)* rhythms of an "immature," bygone age.

The pawnshop setting with its cast of clerks and shop boys was reminiscent of the popular fiction and comic monologues of the Edo period, when pawnshops served as the common man's savings and loan institutions and were familiar features of the social landscape. The dim, shadowy world of the storehouse *(kura)* and the low-keyed exchanges taking place behind the hanging garments transported the story back into the dark back-alley world of Edo *jōruri*—an association made explicit when the divorcée likens herself and Yamaji to Osome and Hisamatsu, the oil shop dealer's daughter and the clerk whose love affair, ending in a love suicide in a storehouse, was celebrated in *jōruri,* kabuki, and songs. The multivoiced exchanges in the pawnshop also recalled the garrulous conversations of townspeople dramatized in the "funnybooks" *(kokkeibon)* of the Edo period novelist Shikitei Sanba (1776–1822), who situated his characters on "stages" such as a public bathhouse and a barber shop.

While literary attention had been lavished on the fabrics, weaves, patterns, and colors of clothing in Edo *gesaku* literature (in many cases such information had even been incorporated in the very titles of plays and novels), by Taishō that preoccupation had been supplanted by a focus on the interior life of the individual and had all but disappeared, except in the less reputable popular kinds of fiction. Yamaji's fussy concern about his clothes evoked an age when notions of the individuated self were yet to be born, when the color, shape, and patternings of clothing served as instantaneous signifiers of relationship, character, and fate in the kabuki theater, and when far greater care was lavished on the details of clothing in *ukiyo-e* woodblock prints than on the virtually indistinguishable faces of the women and men who wore them.

Stylistic reminders of Edo *gesaku* notwithstanding, "In the Storehouse" was a very contemporary piece in its critical spirit. Anecdotes about its origin reveal that the story was created in a spirit of high agonistic play.

Hirotsu Kazuo had heard from the head of the *Shinchō* publishing house how the novelist Chikamatsu Shūkō(1876–1944) loved clothes so much that he pawned his kimonos to raise money to have a new outfit made each season and then went to the pawnshop to visit his old clothes. Hirotsu passed the anecdote on to Uno and challenged him to "make something out of it." Uno rose to the occasion, wrote for "three days in his futon," and produced a story that he called "Aru oroka na otoko no hanashi" (A tale of a foolish man).[27]

In responding to Hirotsu's dare, Uno used not only the anecdote about Chikamatsu's love for his clothes but also well-known features of Chikamatsu's very own *shishōsetsu*. *Giwaku* (Suspicion), which critic Hirano Ken calls modern Japanese literature's first "true" *shishōsetsu*, had appeared six years before in 1913 and was well known by *bundan* readers as a work in which Chikamatsu's "narcissistically self-absorbed" narrator spun out "endless fantasies in the refuge of his bed" as he dwelled repeatedly on women in his past.[28] Uno wrapped his narrator in his "beloved futon" and set him to fantasize about the many women in his past life, called to mind by the kimonos hanging out to air before him. Chikamatsu's hero's obsession for a woman is transferred to the kimonos that "have left" Yamaji, "one by one," and made their way to the pawnshop," and his lachrymose confessional narratives are spoofed in Yamaji's confession of "shedding manly tears."

Other *bundan* personalities and icons were parodied as well. Yamaji's listing of "smells that excite me" and his insistence that he is not copying the novelist who wrote about the man who licks the handkerchief of the woman he worships pointed to Tanizaki Jun'ichirō's literary explorations of sexual adventurism: specifically, to the story "Akuma" (The devil, 1912), in which a young man steals the soiled handkerchief of the woman he loves, revels in its smell, and then proceeds to "lick it like a dog." The teasing pen flew out at Izumi Kyōka (1873–1939), a novelist known for the aura of mystery and the supernatural in his sensuous novels, in which white-skinned beauties had a way of materializing at just the right moment. And what *bundan* reader would not have read into Yamaji's greedy love of smells his exaggerated attachment to his futon, the "selfish dreams" with which he puts himself to sleep in it, and his hope that the beautiful divorcée sent back home will come to him while he is lying in it, a satirical gambit aimed at Tayama Katai's *Futon* (The quilt, 1907), that so-called naturalistic novel about a writer's sexual obsession with his female disciple that ended with a scene of olfactory fetishism that shocked many readers of the day (Katai's novelist-protagonist Tokio buries his head in the woman's soiled futon and inhales the scent of her sweat and body oil).[29]

Like Tokio, Yamaji is left alone at the end. Instead of the beautiful face of the divorcée, it is the fat, ugly face of the maid and the sour face of the head clerk that come to the fore of his consciousness. These faces—like the fat-cheeked, red-nosed face of Otafuku and the lopsided face of the clown Hyottoko raised aloft in festival parades—punctuate the story's end with a twisted grimace that points downward to the *chōnin* culture grounded in the material. "Love of Mountains," on the other hand, aspires upward to mountaintops and clouds, only to be undercut again.

Yamagoi / "Love of Mountains" (1922)

"Love of Mountains" is the last and longest of the "Yumega-mono" (Dream tale) cycle: five stories, putatively based on Uno's travels to the hot spring town of Shimo Suwa in 1919, that constitute in effect Uno's novelistic commentary on *shishōsetsu* writing.[30] All five stories address some facet of his trips to Shimo Suwa, his encounter with a young spa geisha whom he calls Yumeko, and his marriage to her older geisha sister Kotaki. The stories, which treat the same central events from different perspectives, contain accounts of the writer's many travels to and from Shinano, which do not cease with his marriage but continue as his longing for Yumeko draws him back to the mountains again and again. Desire for the unattainable, whether symbolized by the inaccessible Yumeko or the distant mountains of Shinano (Nagano prefecture), sets the emotional tenor of the stories.

Japanese critics have referred to "Love of Mountains" as "romantic," the product of a late Taishō period sensibility informed by the languors of late nineteenth-century European literature.[31] The protagonist's mountain viewing is indeed characterized by a kind of rapture that one may associate with a romantic turn of mind. But this product of Uno's "dream weaving room" (as he liked to call his rented study in the Kikufuji Hotel) is also parodic, satirical, and critical. Characterized by a constant movement between the inspirational and the reductive, it moves up and down the scale from the lyrical to the coarse.

Uno embodies the romantic artist's dream woman in Yumeko,[32] makes her remote and inaccessible, and then brings her down to earth by giving her, in addition to an expression of sadness and helplessness, dark skin, a misshapen face, a crooked hairdo, and a baby. He shifts register quickly, moving from poetic exclamation to buffoonish statement, sometimes virtually in the same breath. Like a circus clown on a tightrope, he pretends to be stylistically impaired, falling from lyrical heights into nonsensical hyperbole, but all the time is much more aware than his fellow acrobats, who take their feats seriously. Performing at two levels simultaneously—as a clown and as a tightrope walker[33]—he writes a *shishōsetsu* as he critiques its practice.

Uno was, in fact, credited with having coined the term *watakushi shōsetsu* and is said to have been one of the first to write about the genre. In "Tale of a Sweet World," the "author," Hanko Hanshirō, stops in media res to comment on his narrative and to call attention to the current practice of writing about oneself—a practice that has dire effects on his relationship with the geisha Yumeko, whom readers have mistaken for the geisha Yumiko in his story:

> I mentioned earlier that I'm a novelist. Well, when my novel *Human Heart,* which I wrote in Shimo Suwa in November and December, was published in the New Year's issue of a magazine, the publication led to some strange complications in that small town. Let me explain. One of the characters in my novel was Yumiko, a fictitious character based on the geisha Yumeko. You well-informed readers are undoubtedly aware of a peculiar phenomenon that exists in certain literary circles of our country today. I am referring to the character called "I" who appears so often and for no apparent

reason in so many contemporary novels. Typically, nothing is written about this character's profession or his personality; and nothing at all is said about his appearance. The only things related are his idiosyncratic musings and impressions. When we look more closely, we find that the "I" seems to be none other than the author himself. So naturally the "I" is a novelist. It's gotten to the point where the pronoun "I" is automatically taken to signify the author of the novel, and neither readers nor authors find this at all strange. I am not saying that we should end the practice of modeling the main character on the author or featuring a character referred to as "I," but we have reached a sorry state of affairs when readers equate all main characters called "I" with the authors and assume that the novels are about actual events. Because my novel *Human Heart* was an "I" novel [*watakushi shōsetsu*], the things I wrote about were all taken to be true, including the things I had made up about the character Yumiko. That didn't bother me, but it created considerable embarrassment for Yumeko, whom I love.[34]

Less than a year after the appearance of the story, critics began to use the term *watakushi shōsetsu (watakushi wa shōsetsu)* for what Uno had referred to as a "peculiar phenomenon" and those "idiosyncratic musings and impressions."

In time, various kinds of *shishōsetsu* were distinguished. Tayama Katai's *Futon* was viewed as the prototype for the confessional kind of *shishōsetsu,* and Chikamatsu Shūkō was regarded as having written "the most blatantly confessional" of confessional *shishōsetsu.*[35] The other main type was the *shinkyōshōsetsu,* or "contemplative" *shōsetsu,* a narrative about a state of mind.[36] The ultimate achievement in this "inner state" *shishōsetsu* tradition was, by general consensus, Shiga Naoya's short narrative "Kinosaki ni te" (1917).[37] Shiga's subdued meditation on death, written in clean, limpid prose, situated its first-person narrator in nature and, through a series of brief episodes, in which the writer looks closely at the deaths of a bee, a rat, and a lizard, arrived at a state of spiritual transcendence over the self and the fear of death.

The apprehension of nature in "Love of Mountains" marks a striking contrast with its careful focus in the narrowly framed scenes of "Kinosaki ni te." Uno's "I" *(watakushi)* takes in broad vistas, and entire mountain landscapes come to assume the aspect of scenes from a fairy tale, with neatly defined contours and miniaturized dimensions. As "Love of Mountains" lightly parodies the romantic novelist's search for a "dream woman," it gently spoofs the *shishōsetsu* writers' engagement with landscape through a playful interrogation of reality that critiques the reliability of perception.

The protagonist is a novelist who attempts to find and keep alive the inspiration he needs to write, and his search for inspiration is symbolized by the image of the dream, one of life's most aleatory phenomena. Like the poet Gerald de Nerval (whose life as described by Arthur Symons Uno had read about),[38] the daydreaming "I" is haunted by the image of a woman, and he returns compulsively to past events in which she figured. Time sequences revolve within time sequences as he traces the past, one memory conjuring up another. The first tale, "Tale of a Sweet World," for example, begins with the writer's second trip to Shimo Suwa in the winter, digresses back to the occasion of his first visit in the fall when he first met Yumeko, returns to the time of the second visit, then leaps ahead to the time of his third and fourth visits. The last visits, most recent in time, when Yumeko has been supplanted by the older geisha Kotaki, whom the writer marries, are treated summarily, even impatiently. Clearly, distant memories radiating from the figure of Yumeko are far more emotionally satisfying for him than accounts of more contemporary history that center about Kotaki. Memory gives rise to writing, and descriptions of essentially similar events in five different stories shift the focus from events to the recollection of events in writing, an emphasis further magnified by the many scenes where the writer is described sitting in his room, immersed in the daydreams that will eventually lead him to pick up his pen.

Dream provides the model for the meandering rhythm of the narratives and for the linkage between the events, which seem entirely fortuitous, as in a dream. It is a chance encounter on the street that takes the writer and his friend into a coffee shop, where on the spur of the moment they decide to take a trip and select a destination, Kami Suwa, at random on the map. It is chance that leads him to the café where he meets the "philosopher" Ichiki, who also loves mountains. Coincidentally, Ichiki happens to be a friend of Akagi Akakichi's, the inventor of the new fly trap that the "I" has gone out to purchase when he meets Ichiki; the café where he and the philosopher meet every night turns out to be a front for a gambling den; and one of the men arrested when the police raid the cafe is Akagi Akakichi.

Happenstance leads events to unfold before the eyes of the protagonist, who figures in the narratives not as an active agent but as a passive viewer who watches astonished as the world reveals its surprises. This passive viewer parallels the author who appears simply to follow the lead of his brush—a laughing brush that takes passing swipes at novelists who operate under the misapprehension that they can control their language and the impressions that their words create. Far from being a stable entity to be captured through "descriptive realism," backed by an ideology of *ari no mama* (the assumption that one can truthfully describe something "just as it is"), reality may turn out to be nothing more than an ongoing arbitrary succession of appearances and authors the playthings of fortune.

The descriptions of mountain landscapes provide an imagistic link unifying the narrative of "Love of Mountains." These descriptions proceed slowly, in a manner reminiscent of the leisurely pace of a hand scroll being unfolded. Seeing is akin to dreaming, both linguistically (the verb *to dream* in Japanese is *yume o miru*, lit., "to see a dream") and thematically (landscapes inspire "dreams").

The aleatory associations of the dream state are paralleled on the structural level in the sinuous patterns traced by long sentences that weave up and down the page and in the narrative windings impelled seemingly more by whimsy than by rational planning. The languorous dilations on mountain landscapes set to the pace of the writer's reverie give way to scenes of group activity organized in more intensely rhythmic form, in concerts, processions, and a raid on a café. Thus, the experience of vertigo ranges from the private rapture of mountain gazing to the communal ecstacy of *matsuri*. Musical activities often mark the climactic ends of sections of the "Dream Tale" narratives, where they synthesize and dramatize the emotions that have been accumulating, often with revelatory effects.

The "Dream Tales" are also distinguished by a constant interweaving of the lyrical and the playful in a way that destabilizes perception, making familiar objects strange and marvelous objects familiar. In "Love of Mountains," an ordinary inn room begins to take on a fantastic, alien quality as the writer magnifies the importance of its measurements and painstakingly details the disposition of its all-important windows. Conversely, a magnificent snowscape is turned into a miniature panorama, like a scene in a woodblock print, when viewed from a mountain path overlooking a valley.

Double visionings of nature and landscape created through the superimposition of traditional and modern associations further enhance the unstable, dreamlike quality of perception. Although the events of "Love of Mountains" took place a quarter of the way into the twentieth century, thirty years after the modern prefectural system had replaced the old provincial fiefdoms, the names used to designate the lands through which the writer travels are the old ones—Shinano, Shinshū, Kōshū, and Kai—names that appeared in medieval chronicles and in the travel diary of the Edo period Confucian philosopher Ogyū Sorai, referred to by his Chinese pen name, Butsu Sorai.[39] These poetic names evoke vistas of mountain ranges extending northward and of lonely, wild, and rugged terrain, far removed from the urban centers of civilization. They create a feeling of romance in the traditional sense of *fūryū*, which is also conveyed in the poem on mountains by Katsu Kaishū.[40]

These mountain landscapes are also refracted through the lens of a more recent literature shaped by Western influences. Appearing immediately after the title is a line from *Nihon Arupusu* (The Japan Alps) by the Meiji period writer Kojima Usui,[41] a Yokohama bank clerk whose four-volume study of the mountains was inspired by the writings and encouragement of Walter Weston,[42] the British geologist, alpinist, and Church of England missionary who was instrumental in establishing a tradition of Western-style mountain climbing in Taishō Japan.

Another example of this penchant for telescoped perspectives that point simultaneously to the past and the future can be found in the figure of Nishimukai Kanzan, a simple country fellow whose mountain viewing, music making, and seal carving recall the elegant pastimes of the *Edo bunjin* who devoted themselves to literary and artistic pursuits after the manner of Chinese literati. His name, *Kanzan,* written with the characters "viewing mountains," suggests the tradition of the *bunjin* who played up the conceit of being hermit-scholars living in mountain hermitages, removed from worldly concerns, by incorporating into their sobriquets the Chinese characters for mountains *(san)* and pavilions *(-tei).*[43] At the same time that *Kanzan* evokes a traditional literati ideal, *Nishimukai* is written with the characters "west facing," a reminder of the powerful attraction that the West exerted on the youth of Taishō.

The novelist's retreat to a mountain spa similarly recalls an ancient Far Eastern tradition embodied in poems, essays, and paintings, namely, the literatus' escape from the roils and toils of urban existence to rejuvenate his soul in nature. His gentle, expansive musing on mountains and, later, the pleasures of writing about his travels, collecting and viewing pictures of mountains, and savoring the memory of the landscapes he has seen, are all a part of the *bunjin*'s refined existence. But, although he follows the route to Kai traced by Butsu (Ogyū) Sorai in *Kyōchūkikō*, he does so riding in a sooty train—that metaphor for modernity introduced from the West. And the "western window" he gazes through looks toward the European West as well as toward Amida Buddha's Paradise in the West.

If sounds figured prominently in "In the Storehouse," it is the *asobi* of the eye that is privileged in "Love of Mountains." Windows provide the frameworks within which Uno toys with perception. In "Tale of a Sweet World," the first of the five "Dream Tales," the magical power of sight to transform and recreate reality is dramatized when the window through which the "I" looks freezes over and becomes "as frosted glass" and the landscape seen through the train window turns suddenly white the moment the train crosses the border and enters Shinano. In "Love of Mountains," the "I" looks outside the train window and sees a rugged mountain that towers motionless one moment, then in the blink of an eye appears to move like the kabuki actor Danjūrō,[44] stepping dramatically to the center of the stage. The "I" (= eye) takes in broad vistas and, from the high, framed perspective afforded by his room in an inn on the side of a mountain, watches as landscapes are turned into miniature panoramas, scenes in a magic lantern viewer. Shrine woods are anthropomorphized and endowed with an ability to put on makeup and move toward his window to "greet" him. Looking through a pair of old binoculars, he imagines turning himself into the Wind God.

To the confusion of spatial perception is added the psychological ambiguity of a state that exists between dream and waking, imagination and reality. In "Tale of a Sweet World," "A Dance," and "Dream of a Summer Night," the lines between physical seeing and mental visioning are deliberately blurred. The writer, often at a liminal time of day—late evening under a dark sky strafed by heat lightning or early, misty dawn on a hillside overlooking the town—has visual experiences of an unusual nature that present familiar persons within new contexts and shed new light on his understanding of their world. These revelations unfold with a suddenness and simple neatness reminiscent of fairy tales. Yumeko's hard-nosed aunt, the owner of a geisha house who makes her geisha offer morning prayers before a hilltop shrine to keep from becoming pregnant, reveals a maternal side of her personality as she croons a lullaby to Yumeko's child. Two old woodcutters coming down a mountain trail suddenly cut a caper that makes the "I" realize that the wizened crones before his eyes are former Suwa geisha.

The critic Katsuyama Isao once remarked that Uno, together with Akutagawa Ryūnosuke, rescued the novel from the dull state into which it had fallen under the influence of the naturalists, citing Kume Masao, who had referred to them as "the two members of the 'new fairy tale' *(shin-otogi-banashi)* school of Taishō period literature."[45] Despite its seeming levity, Katsuyama's description is in fact quite appropriate. Not only do Akutagawa and Uno write "interesting stories," but both writers share a certain quality of visualization that, one might say, tends toward the "fairy tale" in its simplicity and clarity of outline. Many of Akutagawa's stories possess a stylistic precision that yields visually sharp images within a clear-cut narrative progression. Uno's vision, on the other hand, mediated as it is by the "dream," tends toward fairy tale-like caricature. Most important, Uno uses the fairy-tale motif consciously, employing it as a critical tool to comment on the self-deception of the *watakushi shō-setsu* narrator, humorously called Hanko Hanshirō.

Through the fairy-tale motif, Uno critiques the notion that novels describe "truths" about a stable reality by underlining the play of language at the heart of literary mimesis. The modern-day *shishōsetsu*, he would say, may be little more than *otogi-banashi* spun by men whose self-absorption blinds them to the realities of life. Hanko Hanshirō thrusts himself to the fore with repeated use of the pronoun *watakushi*. His first-person narrative is subtitled "The New Urashima Story" *(Shin Urashima monogatari)*. It begins with lines that establish a parallel between Hanko Hanshirō and the *otogi-banashi* Rip Van Winkle-like character Urashima Tarō, who travels to the underwater kingdom of the dragon king on the back of a turtle, meets the dragon princess, loses track of time, returns home, opens the magic box given him by the princess to find nothing but white smoke, and instantly turns into an old man:

> It was just as Urashima on his turtle. . . . To be
> sure, it was a train of a railroad company operated by
> the imperial Japanese state, but the back of a turtle
> would have provided a more comfortable ride. The
> Chūō line train set out from Iidamachi station and
> lurched past Shinjuku, Nakano, and Hachiōji, shaking
> like a rickety horse-drawn cart. Where was it
> going? . . . There's no such thing as a Dragon Palace in
> today's world![46]

Characters in Uno's mock *shishōsetsu* "fairy tale" are near caricatures: a big country boy "as fat as Kintoki" leads Hanko Hanshirō to his room in the inn, and his friends in Shimo Suwa are a doctor with a cat-like face and a "Kaiser moustache" who studied in Germany; a bald, pink-eyed lawyer who looks like a rabbit; and a red-haired, round-eyed geisha with long eyelashes that open and shut like a Western-style doll's. Hanko invokes Emma, the King of Hell, the two-headed horse whose form Yumeko and her patron will assume because of their sin of adultery, and Kannon's white horse that will be sent to carry her out of hell. Kotaki, the famous senior geisha of Shimo Suwa whom Hanko Hanshirō eventually marries, has the neatly limned outlines characteristic of fairy-tale figures. She is "tall and stout with large cold eyes and a large black mole that adds no charm to the area between her nose and her mouth." With her heavy, lacquer-black hair piled on top of her head and two layers of patterned kimono skirts trailing behind her, she looks like "a thousand-gold-piece woman," so impressive that Hanko feels like clapping.[47]

In "Tale of a Sweet World," the protagonist's plight is echoed in the fates of the farmer from Ina and the obese salesman who, like the novelist, fail to get the women they love. In "Love of Mountains," the novelist's love of mountains is mirrored in Nishimukai's love of mountains, and his love of Yumeko is reflected inversely in Nishimukai's hapless marriage to a geisha who is as domineering and wild as Yumeko is submissive and demure. The repetitions, the polarizations of character types, and the neatly coincident dramatic ironies reveal the "fairy-tale" quality of the "Dream Tales," through which Uno deftly mocks the self-indulgent fantasies of *shishōsetsu* authors.

Games with names (e.g., the name of the rotund traveling salesman, Sasamaru Shihachi, contains the word *maru*, meaning "round," to reflect his shape, while *Shihachi* denotes the date of his birth, the eighth month—*hachi*—of the fourth year—*shi*—of the Meiji period) and the phonic rhythms of names like Hanko Hanshirō, Ichiki Naokichi, and Akagi Akakichi also contribute to the dismantling of an outlook on the world that claims a correspondence between language and reality.

As in fairy tales and dreams, the world of these stories is subject to sudden transformation. Physical change may herald psychological and ontological change. "Truth" in these *watakushi shōsetsu* breaks through suddenly, often shocking the protagonist, who stands paralyzed as the scales fall from his eyes. Hanko Hanshirō is stunned to learn about the pregnancies of spa maids whom he took to be innocent virgins, and he is completely immobilized by the events that overtake him at the end of "Tale of a Sweet World," when the smoke rises before his eyes and he finds himself frozen fast in his own wedding picture, next to his "thirty-year-old bride" (who "looks at least thirty-five"). In "Love of Mountains," learning that Yumeko is pregnant again, the hero "stands stock still in the middle of the room . . . as if he were imitating some actor when the curtain goes down at the end of the play."

Each of the "Dream Tales" brings its protagonist a surprise, and in each the ending is preceded by a comic round dance in which persons, events, and relationships merge, leaving the protagonist momentarily "out of control" before being thrown to a new level of perception. Uno does not permit these characters to settle into a fixed view. Attempts to attain the climactic, definitive ending are always undercut. At the end of the last of the five narratives, the writer who would arrive at transcendence through viewing mountains is blinded when his eyeglasses freeze over.

Readers accustomed to the *heimen byōsha* (flat description) of the naturalists or the *Shirakaba* writers' concerns with feeling and morality were caught by surprise by these prolix narratives that wandered into areas that were at times "exceptional to the point of being strange," as Katsuyama Isao says.[48] As for the truth content of the "Dream Tales," Uno himself coyly averred:

> At the time I published these stories, the *shishō-setsu* was very popular, and many said that my novels

were about events that had really happened to me. But my novels were a mixture of lies and truth, and the lies were more numerous than the facts (but while writing them I wrote with the intention of writing the truth). For example, in the first half of *Yamagoi* there is the scene of the Suwa shrine Pillar Festival. Readers said, "I've seen the festival, and it's not like the way you described in the novel." That is to be expected. . . .[49]

The saints do not laugh nor do they make us laugh but the truly wise men have no other mission than to make us laugh with their thoughts and make us think with their buffoonery.[50]

Notes

1. Uno's style is discussed in Ara Masahito, "Kisei sakka," in *Gendai bungaku sōsetsu*, vol. 2, *Taishō, Shōwa sakka*, eds. Nishio Minoru and Kondō Takayoshi (Tokyo: Gakudōsha, 1953); Funagi Shigenobu, "Uno Kōji ron," *Shinchō*, November 1919, 18–31; and Itō Sei, "Uno Kōji no sekai," in *Uno Kōji Kaisō*, eds. Shibukawa Gyō et al. (Tokyo: Chūō Kōron, 1963).

2. Two biographies of Uno are Minakami Tsutomu's two-volume *Uno Kōji den* (Tokyo: Chūō Kōron, 1971) and Shibukawa Gyō's *Uno Kōji ron* (Tokyo: Chūō Kōron, 1974).

3. Heinrich Heine (1797–1856): German poet and critic whose works were popular among young writers of the late Meiji period. After reading Onoue Shibafune's English translations of Heine's poetry, Uno attempted his own Japanese translations of Heine from his English sources.

4. Nikolai Gogol (1809–1852): Russian novelist and dramatist known for an unusual style that blended lyricism, grotesque humor, and satire. Gogol was not as widely translated into Japanese or read in Japan as the other major Russian novelists. In *Gogori* (Tokyo: Sōgansha, 1938), his long critical biography of Gogol, Uno suggests that it may have been because of the oddity of his temperament as well as the difficulty of translating his language. As an adolescent, Uno devoured

translations of Gogol into Japanese by Ueda Bin, Hirai Hajime, and Futabatei Shimei, but his favorite translator of the Russian writer was Nobori Shomu (1878–1958), the outstanding scholar and translator in the field of Russian studies in Meiji Japan.

5. Described by Uno in the 1935 essay "Empō no omoide" (Distant memories), in *Uno Kōji zenshū,* eds. Shibukawa Gyō et al., 12 vols. (Tokyo: Chūō Kōron, 1972), 12:60–101.

6. A number of the younger men studying at Waseda University at the time founded the literary journal *Kiseki* (Miracle) in September 1912. Although Uno never published in this group's *dōjin zasshi,* which numbered only nine issues, he interacted frequently with them and remained a close, lifelong friend of one of its founding members, Hirotsu Kazuo (son of Meiji period novelist Hirotsu Ryūrō). Other members were Tanizaki Seiji (younger brother of Tanizaki Jun'ichirō), Kasai Zenzō, Sōma Taizō, Funagi Shigeo, Negishi Kōsaku, Kobayashi Tokusaburō, Mada Hisakichi, Kawakami Kuni, and Waseda literature professor Sōma Gyofū. The members of the *Kiseki* group were regarded as heirs to the naturalist movement in literature. Whereas some of the earlier naturalist writers had tended to emphasize the outward aspects of life in their descriptions of characters, the *Kiseki* writers were more interested in exploring psychological states, frequently of an aberrant nature—as the title of Hirotsu Kazuo's 1917 novel *Shinkeibyō jidai* (The age of neurosis) may suggest. Kōno Toshirō finds the *Kiseki* men to be the true bearers of Taishō culture. They are "the ones who experienced before anyone else the languid, weary, melancholy world of the Russian modernist writers like Andreyev and Artsybashev. They are the so-called youths of pure literature" (Kōno Toshirō, *Taishō bungaku,* vol. 17 of *Shinpojūmu bungaku,* ed. Tanizawa Eiichi [Tokyo: Gakuseisha, 1976], 25; see generally 26–50). To some extent, the darker atmosphere of their works might be attributed to the financial and social burdens that they had to bear, which writers like Nagai Kafū, Tanizaki Jun'ichirō, Satō Haruo, and the *Shirakaba* writers, who were more financially secure, did not.

7. A coterie of young men who had attended Gakushūin, the peers school, and in 1910 founded the highly successful journal *Shirakaba* (White birch), which played a significant role in disseminating European art and literature throughout Japan during the Taishō period. The

group's spokesman, Mushanokōji Saneatsu, of aristocratic descent, was especially inspired by the humanistic ideals of Tolstoi.

8. Usui Yoshimi, *Taishō bungaku shi* (Tokyo: Chikuma Shobō, 1963), 184–185.

9. Donald Keene, *Dawn to the West: Japanese Literature of the Modern Era,* vol. 1, *Fiction* (New York: Holt, Rinehart & Winston, 1984), 443.

10. Akutagawa Ryūnosuke, "Jinbutsuki" (A record of characters), in *Akutagawa Ryūnosuke zenshū,* 6 vols. (Tokyo: Chikuma Shobō, 1958), 6:182.

11. Akutagawa Ryūnosuke, "Taishō hachinen no bundan," in ibid., 5:230. During the Taishō period, the *bundan* consisted of about a thousand writers, critics, editors, publishers, and translators devoted to literary pursuits. Two English-language studies that contain detailed information about the Taishō *bundan* are Edward Fowler, *The Rhetoric of Confession: Shishōsetsu in Early Twentieth Century Japanese Fiction* (Berkeley and Los Angeles: University of California Press, 1988); and Irena Powell, *Writers and Society in Modern Japan* (Tokyo, New York, and San Francisco: Kodansha International, 1983).

12. Satō Zen'ichi (*Uno Kōji* [Tokyo: Kawade Shobō, 1968], 103) discusses Uno's role as a judge on the Akutagawa prize committee.

13. The notion of a "culture of play" is central to H. D. Harootunian's discussion of the emergence of new forms of culture within the context of social transition in the late Tokugawa period (see his "Late Tokugawa Culture and Thought," in *The Nineteenth Century,* ed. Marius B. Jansen, vol. 5 of *The Cambridge History of Japan,* 6 vols. [Cambridge: Cambridge University Press, 1989], 168–177).

14. Harootunian, "Late Tokugawa Culture and Thought," 177.

15. The role of spectacle in public life in the Taishō period is discussed in Miriam Silverberg, "Constructing a New Cultural History of Prewar Japan," in *Japan in the World,* ed. Masao Miyoshi and H. D. Harootunian (Durham, N.C.: Duke University Press, 1993).

16. Robert Epp points out the identity between writing and life reflected in the formula "I am a story" *(Watakushi wa shōsetsu de aru)* in his introduction to *Rosy Glasses and Other Stories by Kazuo Ozaki* (Woodchurch, Ashford, Kent: Paul Norbury, 1988), 21. For detailed, book-length studies of the *shishōsetsu,* see Fowler, *The Rhetoric of*

Confession; and Irmela Hijiya-Kirschnereit, *Selbstentblößungsrituale* (Wiesbaden: Franz Steiner, 1981).

17. The term "literature of the hothouse" *(onshitsu no bungaku)* is used by Okuno Takeo *(Nihon bungakushi: Kindai kara gendai e* [Tokyo: Chūō Kōron, 1970], 87) to describe the literature produced in the fervid, self-enclosed atmosphere of the Taishō *bundan.*

18. Uno's novel about the society of Shingeki actors and actresses is *Ren'aigassen* (Love contest, 1920).

19. The notion of *yoyū* (lit., "excess play") took on the value of an aesthetic quality in Natsume Sōseki's expression "yoyū ga aru bungaku, yoyū ga nai bungaku" (literature with *yoyū* and literature without *yoyū*), implying a kind of literature born in a spirit of leisure and gratuitous play. The concept was taken up by the haiku poet Masaoka Shiki (1867–1902) and by Sōseki's literary followers. When the *shishōsetsu* developed by the naturalists became a commonly practiced genre, its advocates began to speak of it as *yoyū ga aru bungaku,* as opposed to the *honkaku shōsetsu* (conventional novel with a plot), which a writer composed to entertain readers and make a living for himself. For Sōseki and his followers, however, the notion of *yoyū* implied a certain freedom and lightness of spirit, such as might be found expressed in certain haiku, that was unlike the reality-bound aesthetic of the naturalists.

20. "Asobi," trans. James M. Vardaman Jr., in *Youth and Other Stories,* ed. J. Thomas Rimer (Honolulu: University of Hawai'i Press, 1994), 136–147.

21. Cited in Van C. Gessel, *Three Modern Novelists: Sōseki, Tanizaki, Kawabata* (Tokyo, New York, and London: Kodansha International, 1993), 75, 95.

22. Hirotsu Kazuo, "Hito no yoi furukitsune no kanji," *Shinchō,* February 1920, 21.

23. Later, backstage, he drolly exclaimed how easy it had been to appear in public and declared his willingness to repeat the experience any time (Kume Masao, "Insein no ippaku," in "Saikin no Uno Kōji, ningen zuihitsu," *Shinchō,* August 1924, 34–37).

24. Quoted in Minakami, *Uno Kōji den,* 2:224.

25. Uno Kōji, "Tenten," in *Uno Kōji zenshū,* 1:358.

26. *Rakugo* is a comic monologue delivered by a storyteller *(raku-goka)*, who sits on a cushion before an audience and with a few minimal props tells amusing stories combining pantomime and voice inflection as he assumes the roles of different characters. Uno's narrative style in "In the Storehouse" was dismissed as "nothing more than an Osaka *rakugo*" by the writer Kikuchi Kan (1888–1948), who reviewed it in the *Tōkyō nichi nichi*. Uno's sallying retort was transmitted by way of special delivery postcard (Kikuchi's own well-publicized method of registering disagreement): "If mine is an Osaka *rakugo,* there's the sound of the storyteller's fan in your 'Tadanao kyō no gyōjōki'" ("On the conduct of Lord Tadanao" was a historical tale of Kikuchi's, published the year before, that, Uno implies, could be recited in a *yose* hall to the beat of the storyteller's fan).

27. Hirotsu Kazuo, "Kura no naka no monogatari, Uno Kōji no shojosaku," in his *Dōjidai no sakkatachi* (Tokyo: Bungei Shinjū Shinsha, 1951).

28. Hirano cited in Fowler, *The Rhetoric of Confession,* 150–151.

29. Ironically, Uno's story satirizing *Futon* was published in the journal *Bunshō sekai,* which was edited by Tayama Katai himself.

30. The other four stories are "Tale of a Sweet World" ("Amaki yo no hanashi," *Chūō kōron,* September 1920), "One Dance" ("Hito odori," *Chūō kōron,* May 1921), "Dream of a Summer Night" ("Natsu no yo no yume," *Shinchō,* June 1921), and "The Heart of the Matter" ("Shinchū," *Kaizō,* September 1921). The five works were published together under the title *Waga hi waga yume* (My day, my dream) in 1922 by Ryūbunken and in 1927 by Shinchōsha. Most of the "Dream Tales" also reappeared in the separately published volumes collectively entitled *Yamagoi* that were issued in 1933 by Kaizōsha and in 1944 by Kyōritsu Shobō.

31. Yamamoto Ken'kichi wrote that Uno's "romantic bent is most obvious in the 'Dream Tales'" (*Watakushi shōsetsu sakkaron* [Tokyo: Shinbisha, 1966], 93). Usui Yoshimi referred to the stories as "a string of romantic novels about Yumeko," of which the most representative is "Yamagoi" (*Taishō bungaku shi* [Tokyo: Chikuma Shobō, 1963], 188). Kataoka Yoshikazu saw the cycle of stories as "the expression of a longing for an eternal woman" and also found "Yamagoi" to be the

"most romantic" among them (*Kaisetsu, Gendai nihon shōsetsu taikei,* 65 vols. [Tokyo: Kawade Shobō, 1950], 33:440).

32. The "dream woman" was a Taishō period emblem that was given pictorial form in the many popular paintings and sketches that the artist Takehisa Yumeji (1884–1934) made of his own dream woman, "Yumeji." The images of the thin, consumptive-looking, slope-shouldered, sad-eyed young woman seemed to give visual symbolic form to the mood of world-weary sadness expressed in many popular songs written in a minor key at the time.

33. An image appearing in D. C. Muecke, *The Compass of Irony* (London: 1969), 129, cited in John J. MacAloon, *Rite, Drama, Festival, Spectacle: Rehearsals toward a Theory of Cultural Performance* (Philadelphia: Institute for the Study of Human Issues, 1984), 124.

34. Uno Kōji, "Amaki yo no hanashi," in *Uno Kōji zenshū,* 2:442. Uno's first-person narrator who stops in the middle of the story to call attention to the act of narration and his narrator who raises doubts about the soundness of his state of mind predated by several years the *shishōsetsu* of Kasai Zenzō, who similarly focused attention on the narrative frame (Fowler, *The Rhetoric of Confession,* 261), but without the self-conscious playfulness that Uno displays in "Tale of a Sweet World." Uno's contributions to the identification of the *shishōsetsu* genre are described by Shinoda Kazunori in "'Yume miru heya' no kōzu," in *Shishōsetsu nihon bungaku kenkyū shiryō sōsho,* ed. Sekiguchi Yasuyoshi (Tokyo: Yūseidō, 1983), 162.

35. Fowler, *The Rhetoric of Confession,* 154.

36. The *shinkyōshōsetsu* was discussed by Kume Masao, Nakamura Murao, and others in their debate on the pros and cons of the *shishōsetsu* vs. the *honkaku shōsetsu* (a newly coined term for the traditional European-style novel) in a special June 1926 issue of *Shinchō.* In his own article on the *shishōsetsu* ("Shishōsetsu no shiken" [A personal view of the *shishōsetsu*], appearing in the same issue of *Shinchō*), Uno also discussed the *shinkyōshōsetsu* as the ultimate Japanese novel form. He traced the first appearance of a "*shishōsetsu*-like *shishōsetsu*" (*shishōsetsu-rashii shishōsetsu*) to the novels of Mushanokōji Saneatsu, whose simplicity and forthrightness called to mind the free painting of schoolchildren. Uno stated

that "the Japanese genius is most suited to the *shishōetsu*," and, as an example of the extreme form that the genre might attain, he cited Kasai Zenzō, whom he placed within the "spiritual lineage" of Bashō (*Gendai bungaku-ron taikei*, 8 vols. [Tokyo: Kawade Shobō, 1956], 3:296).

37. Shiga Naoya's "Kinosaki ni te" (1917) was translated by Edward Seidensticker as "At Kinosaki" (in *Modern Japanese Literature*, ed. Donald Keene [New York: Grove, 1956]).

38. See Arthur Symons' *The Symbolist Movement in Literature* (London: William Heinemann, 1899), which Uno read in English.

39. Ogyū Sorai (1666–1728), an important figure in Confucian thought and letters of the Tokugawa period. In 1706, Sorai made an official mission to the province of Kai to inspect the land thereon behalf of his lord, Yanagisawa Yoshiyasu (who had recently had his Kawagoe fief exchanged for Kai province). He wrote two travel diaries in which he described his trip: *Fūryūshishaki* (A record of elegant emissaries) in 1706 and *Kyōchūkikō* (Travel through ravines) in 1710. *Kyōchūkikō*, written in *kanbun*, is a shorter, condensed version of *Fūryūshishaki*. The care with which the writer in "Love of Mountains" notes the measurements and placement of the windows seems almost a gentle parody of the exact notation of measurements of things in Ogyū Sorai's travel diary. For example, in describing items in a Zen temple, the Confucian scholar writes:

> On the right side [of the image] was a staff, I do not know of what kind of wood. It was very light in weight and of a deep black colour, and showed cracked patterns. It was 7 *shaku*, 2 *sun*, 3 *bu* long, and both ends were very thin. At two places, 3 *sun*, 7 *bu* from the upper and 6 *sun* from the lower end, there were pearl-like shapes. Four *shaku* from the upper end there was a water-measuring mark. A fan made of palm tree leaves and a duster were tied to it. The fan was 7 *sun*, 2 *bu* wide and 1 *shaku* long. The handle was 6 *sun*, 7 *bu*. Of the duster only the handle remained; it was 8 *sun*, 5 *bu* long. (Olof G. Lidin, trans., *Ogyū Sorai's Journey to*

Kai in 1706, Scandinavian Institute of Asian Studies
Monograph Series, no. 48 [London and Malmö: Curzon, 1983], 100)

A *shaku* is equivalent to .994 foot, a *sun* to 1.2 inches, and a *bu* to .12
inch. Buildings, bridges, and gates receive similar careful attention to
size and shape.

40. Katsu Kaishū (1823–1899), a Meiji period statesman and
naval officer who studied naval technology in Nagasaki and captained
the *Kanrin-maru,* which carried the Iwakura embassy to America in
1871. He later served as minister of the navy in the Meiji government.
In addition to writing histories of the Japanese navy and army, he composed Chinese poetry and travel essays.

41. Kojima Usui (1875–1945) was a key figure in the populariza-
tion of Western-style mountain climbing in Japan in the Meiji period.
He began climbing the Japan Alps and Mount Fuji in 1888 and in 1907
founded a mountaineering club, which was later known as the Japan
Mountain Association. Inspired by writings such as Shiga Shigetaka's
Nihon fūkei ron (On the landscape of Japan, 1894) and Walter Weston's *Mountaineering and Exploration in the Japanese Alps* (1896)
(part of which Kojima translated into Japanese), he wrote numerous
travel essays about mountains, in which he combined a poetic feel for
his subject matter with an objective scientific eye. His best-known
work is *Nihon Arupusu* (1912).

42. Walter Weston (1861–1940), the "father" of Japanese mountaineering, was an English missionary who climbed Mount Fuji and
other peaks during fourteen years of residence in Japan. He popularized the name "Japanese Alps" through his *Mountaineering and Exploration in the Japanese Alps* (1896).

43. Might not Nishimukai Kanzan also recall the bushy-haired
figure of the legendary T'ang dynasty (618–907) poet of Cold Mountain, Han-shan (lit. "cold mountain"; Kanzan in Japanese)? Seeing in
Nishimukai and Horita traces of the eccentric, free-spirited "buffoon"
monks Han-shan and his companion Shih-te (lit. "the foundling"; Jit-
toku in Japanese) may not be so farfetched if we consider the traditional literary practice of *mitate,* finding analogies between unlike
things. In Zen paintings, Han-shan is always laughing and Shih-te is

depicted holding the broom with which he gathers up leftovers in the kitchen of the Kuo-ch'ing-ssu monastery to give to his companion. See Yves Bonnefoy, *Asian Mythologies,* trans. Wendy Doniger (Chicago and London: University of Chicago Press, 1991), 133.

44. Danjūrō (Ichikawa Danjūrō, IX, 1838–1903), an actor associated with the *aragoto* or "roughhouse" style of kabuki acting, which was characterized by bombastic declamation, dramatic and expansive body movement, and exaggerated costuming and makeup, for the purpose of portraying large-scale, fantastic deeds.

45. Katsuyama Isao, *Taishō watakushi shōsetsu kenkyū* (Tokyo: Meiji Shoin, 1980), 18–19.

46. Uno Kōji, "Amaki yo no hanashi," in *Uno Kōji zenshū*, 2:410.

47. Ibid., 440, 443.

48. Katsuyama Isao, *Taishō watakushi shōsetsu kenkyū*, 19.

49. Uno Kōji, preface to *Waga hi waga yume* (Tokyo: Shinchōsha, 1927).

50. Octavio Paz, *Marcel Duchamp or The Castle of Purity,* trans. Donald Gardner (London: Jonathan Cape, 1970), 41–42.

In the Storehouse

Kura no naka

And so I made up my mind—I was going to the pawnshop. I don't mean that I was going to the pawnshop to redeem something I had pawned. I don't have that kind of money. And I didn't want to go there to pawn something. I don't have anything to pawn anymore—not even a kimono. In fact, the kimono I'm wearing is already in hock.

What do I mean?

I've already borrowed money against it, and that isn't all. Every month I have to pay a fee for wear and tear on this kimono—which is three times the interest I have to pay every six months for the money I borrowed against the other things I pawned.

As for my decision to go to the pawnshop. . . . Please forgive my rambling. . . . Sort it out—any way you please, only hear me out.

I had been thinking about it ever since this year's summer airing. "This year's summer airing" makes it sound as if I do it every year. The truth is—it's the first time it ever occurred to me. When I still had most of my kimonos, I never bothered. Other people aired theirs, it never occurred to me to air mine. You might say I was too slovenly.

But when my kimonos had all left me for the pawnshop, and I saw from my room, in an open room on the second floor of the house across the way, a matron's kimono with a plain red silk lining, a girl's lined kimono with an old-fashioned arrowhead pattern, a man's striped kimono, and many other garments, too numerous to enumerate, hanging side by side from ropes extending in all directions as in a used-clothing store, I remembered with painful nostalgia my own dear things (certainly of far better quality) and ran straightaway to the pawnshop and told the clerks that I wanted to air my clothes myself. I promised that I wouldn't bother anyone, that I wouldn't get into anybody's way, and I repeated this several times, but all the head clerk had to say was that all the goods in their keeping were well cared for and that he himself had a hand in their care and did not hesitate to air them when it was needed. . . . And he refused to grant my request.

I don't need to tell you outright. As I go on talking, you'll realize that I'm not the most trustworthy person.

Indeed I frequently failed to return money I borrowed from friends and never vacated a rooming house without leaving behind an unpaid bill. Yet I am past the age Confucius describes as beyond indecision and vacillation—I am forty years old.[1]

Is there anyone who would lend me anything for putting my seal to a pledge? No publishing house, no magazine or newspaper publisher (I earn my living writing novels and am still single) would advance me a sen unless I have a publishable manuscript to give them.

How about my pawnbroker?

Yes—you may have guessed it—he's the exception, probably the only person in the world who still trusts me—and for good reason.

I've come close to being evicted from my lodgings for not paying my rent, but I've never failed to pay the interest on money I owe my pawnbroker. Indeed, I pay my dues on the third of each and every month as a peasant has to pay a tyrannical landlord.

You see, the interest is payable every six months, but I have pawned so many things, at so many different times, that some interest becomes due every month. So, each and every month I pay interest together with the monthly rental fee (actually a compensation for wear and tear) for the kimono I'm wearing—as I mentioned earlier.

Yes . . . and as I go on talking you will gradually understand how really strange I am.

I'm still paying interest on the money I borrowed on a one-yen or eighty-sen machine-spun kimono and *haori* that I wore in my student days and pawned some fifteen or twenty years ago. It's foolish, I know, but I can't stand the idea that the kimonos that misfortune has removed from my keeping are not mine anymore.

Although I may not immediately recall some of the clothes I haven't seen in ten or more years, I can say that I haven't forgotten any of the many I owned. And all during those past fifteen to twenty years while I lost many friends, men and women, they left me or I left them, I was never really separated from my kimonos. I always remained close to the pawnshop in which they are kept. And if the pawnshop storehouse caught fire and my kimonos all burned to ashes, it is I and only I who would really bear the loss, and that despite the notice displayed by the pawnshop that says: "In the event of a loss due to fire or theft or any other cause, that loss is shared equally between the borrower and the pawnshop." And this is so because the interest alone that I paid the pawnbroker over all those years amounts to several times his original investment; he wouldn't suffer any loss whatsoever. In other words, I'm an unusually dependable customer, and so they trust me (I mean the pawnbroker, the clerks, and the shop boys) and eventually made an exception to the rule and granted my request, the request I mentioned earlier.

It was after the rainy season sometime in early summer that one of the shop boys led me up to the second floor of the pawnshop storehouse.

As I passed the shelves where bundles of kimonos neatly wrapped in old paper were stacked on the shelves, layer on layer in perfect order, I was overcome with a feeling almost, but not quite, like the joy I felt when I entered, accompanied by a professor, the library reading room of my alma mater. It was shortly after I had left that school—and my eagerness to study had never been keener. What a joy; I can't describe it. My heart was thumping as if it wanted to leap out of my chest.

On the other hand, the area next to the door provoked a pretty disagreeable feeling. Violins were dangling from the ceiling as if they were brooms, and wall clocks were lined up like masks hanging on a museum wall. Pianos and organs were left there as if to be forgotten, and pots and pans were scattered all over as in a junkyard.

Mine indeed is a strange nature. . . . From my earliest childhood I've had a peculiar liking for smells, no matter the kind (there are of course exceptions): lamp black, soot, carbolic acid, phenol, even night soil in the fields and the smell of plain dust. I like each one of them for its own particular qualities.

You know, there is among us novelists someone who recently wrote about a man who delights in licking mucus off handkerchiefs;[2] it may sound as if I am imitating him. Not so. What I say about myself is the truth, and that can't be helped.

Now I have to tell you what struck me, or rather my nose, first when I entered the room where the kimonos wrapped in old paper were shelved. It was an inexpressibly lovely odor, a mixture of the smells of the camphor and naphthalene kept in the kimonos and the dust that was all over that room. That was really pleasurable. (It would probably be unbearable if I had to smell it every day.) And then there was the discovery of my best kimonos in a chest of drawers (some of my less valuable ones were wrapped in paper, as were those of so many other customers). They had the whole chest all to themselves. Oh what a pleasure that was!

I have lived mostly in rooming houses and have never owned a chest of drawers, and so I have never had so many of my clothes with me at one and the same time—and for a man I have a lot of clothes.

I had been told by the head clerk that they were kept in a chest of drawers, and at the time I didn't know whether I could or should believe him, but when I actually saw my dear kimonos so well cared for, I felt like a parent must feel when he learns that the son he gave up for adoption or the daughter he gave away in marriage are really well off.[3]

And, respected listeners, I believe that, as I go on with my story, you will agree with me that this is not an exaggeration.

What I felt when I and my dear kimonos, some of which I hadn't seen in over ten years, were brought together again was actually not that unusual for me—although it may seem a bit strange from the point of view of more settled sort of people. That is why I'll take a moment to tell you what happens to me each and every season, when summer turns into fall, fall into winter, and winter again into spring.

As you know, each season requires its own kind of clothing.

I could, of course, redeem some of my old clothes from the pawnshop, but as it is, I prefer to buy new ones, and at times I have to go to great lengths to raise the money I need. But one thing I always do at the end of a season is take to the pawnshop the clothes I used during that season and use the money I get to buy new ones, and I repeat this every season, and that is why, over the years, the clothes I keep at the pawnshop have multiplied at such an amazing rate.

Well now, I got the shop boy to fetch me some hemp rope, which I strung like a spider web, from the bars of the small storehouse window to the post supporting the shelves holding the pawned goods, from the post to a peg on a pillar, and so on, and then I proceeded to hang up my clothes, one by one. And while they were airing, a few hours at a time, I stretched myself beneath them and, using my arm as a pillow, took a nap. And this way it took four days to air everything.

And so my decision to go to the pawnshop again—no, how I got the idea after the airing. . . . No, that's not the proper order; I've been sidetracked again. . . . Please feel free to change, to rearrange . . . as you listen.

One may say that in general I lead a rather slovenly existence. Yet I never fail to get up about six in the morning, make my bed, clean my room, and wash my face before eating breakfast. But then, after sitting at my desk for a couple of hours not doing much of anything, I usually go back to bed and, while leafing through a magazine, fall asleep again. Around noon the rooming-house maid wakes me, and again I wash my face and then eat lunch. (Whether I make my bed and pick up my room at that time depends entirely on the mood I'm in on that particular day.) After lunch I go back to my desk for an hour or two, then go back to bed, do a little light reading, and doze off again. Comes evening the maid wakes me once more. I put away my bedding, wash my face, and sit down to supper.

After that. . . .

Now this may seem particularly foolish to you . . . but please listen to it anyway.

I take a stroll through the nearby geisha quarters, and I do this every day, rain or shine. I can't settle down to work unless I take this walk.

I usually enter those quarters, where the geisha houses are aligned with the houses of assignation, using a special passage with a special name ending with the words "New Lane."[4]

I not only love to look at the faces of the geisha and apprentice geisha[5] walking about, I take in every detail that I can put my eyes on, from their hairdos to their obi, and from their obi down to their geta. And I am often fascinated to the point of following them, so that it's not unusual for me to walk up and down that lane at least three or four times of an evening.

But isn't it so that, no matter what, there is always at least one thing about a geisha that is attractive? Not only the young ones—so gentle and seductive—I mean all of them, all those who are still in the bloom of their womanhood—I exclude not one.[6] It may be her figure or her face or her hairdo, and even if her hairdo is unbecoming and she has no pleasing features whatsoever, her kimono is bound to be attractive—at least to me.

This stroll takes me roughly two hours or more, and then I go back to the rooming house, write if I feel like it, or read until three or four o'clock in the morning, then go to bed, and while leafing through a magazine or simply daydreaming, fall asleep.

When I think about it, I'm really surprised that my life is so regulated, that all of my God-given days are so much alike, all divided into three parts. . . .

To go back to the kimonos: when I had a lot of them (I told you earlier, I never had all of them with me at the same time), as I divided my days into three parts, I used to change kimonos three times a day. I also mentioned this earlier, yet it's still embarrassing to say: although I like women a lot more than most men (to say "love" wouldn't be quite right), I'm no less fond of kimonos; in fact, I find them irresistible.

At times I not only changed kimonos three times a day but changed all of my clothes three times within the very short period I spent at my desk. I changed obi, *haori*-kimono combinations, underkimonos, and all my underwear.

Someone watching might have thought that I suddenly had to go somewhere and would certainly have been surprised seeing me in the nude, stripped of my clothing, as if my extreme sensitivity to drafts and cold air had suddenly vanished.

Sometimes, and just as impulsively, I changed into Western clothes and sat in the wicker chair (there was only one, by the window) watching the sky while smoking a cigarette. On other occasions I went as far as spreading newspapers on the tatami, and putting on the appropriate geta or straw sandals—which I got from the shoe cupboard in the foyer—walked back and forth swinging a walking stick.

As I listen to myself telling you all of this, I have to admit that it sounds more than a bit strange. And as I go on it may become stranger still.

By no means do I think that my looks are extraordinary; and I would say this even if I were really handsome, even if I were flattering myself. Neither would I reproach the gods or blame my parents had I been born without any good features. Blaming them wouldn't help anyway.

Please don't laugh at me; be patient, and continue to listen.

To put it in a nutshell, I am grateful for having been blessed with a slender, fairly well-proportioned, medium-sized body.

I have an acquaintance who has a handsome enough face—some go as far as to say that he looks terrific when seated—but to me he looks terribly ill proportioned standing up or sitting down, and he's not even five feet tall. I can't understand why some people are taken in by the looks of a face to the point of not being able to see the figure of a person as a whole.

'Tis true, seen naked I am hardly more than skin and bones, and even I can't call that handsome. But put a kimono on me, one of my dear kimonos, and I look striking. And that is why I say, as Westerners would, thank God for my figure, my taste in clothes, and especially my love of kimonos.

The story is getting more and more involved. . . .

Anyway . . . many men spend all their energy trying to gain fame and fortune. I spent most of mine sorting out troubles I've had with women. And the novels I have written are mostly complaints, complaints I couldn't keep to myself, about the many unpleasant experiences—there were very few joyful ones—all those affairs brought about.

(How insincere can you get? . . .)

Well, a number of my stories were made up, and I embarrassed and lost many friends because of the wild stories and sometimes outright lies I told about them. I also lost some on account of the mixture of truths and lies I used to get money from them.

But no matter what happened there was always a woman in my life to write about. And the gods willing, I'll continue to complain and even rejoice sometimes because of those women until the day I die.

Last year I had a strange experience, though.

I, who have known women since my teens and have enjoyed them much more than most men, suddenly, without warning, became impotent.

I can't express in words what I felt.

And to cap it. . . . There was this aspiring student of literature who said to me, "Well, Sensei, since an ordinary person's day is three days for you, when he ages one day, you must age three," and he guffawed as if it were a big joke.

I had told him that I divide my days into three parts to use them more efficiently and that the only time I could see him would be at night.

I felt as if cold water had been poured down my back.

It could be true . . . couldn't it?

After all. . . . Anyway, so the story goes, some scientists using light and sound waves to increase or decrease the time spent sleeping had turned baby chicks into full-fledged chickens and piglets into full-fledged pigs almost overnight.

As I mulled this over I broke out in cold sweat . . . and went to see a doctor.

I took medicine . . . to no avail. I saw more doctors. They were no help. They all told me, more or less, the same thing in the same noncommittal, standoffish tone of voice: "Yes, it is possible, it happens. . . . No, you'll get better. . . ."

I felt as if I were losing my mind completely . . . and let my feet guide me. . . .

They led me to a place where women are available for money.

The woman with whom I had been on very intimate terms for a while didn't want to see me anymore, and I believe that the problem I just mentioned was the reason—indeed.

How could such a thing happen to me? I asked myself again and again—I was barely forty years old.

And in this manner I kept on . . . and on. . . .

Then too, I was almost buried in debts, and all I had left were a few kimonos, and I had to have new clothes each and every season. So I had to pack off, one by one, those dear kimonos to the pawnshop.

This made me so miserable and irritable I couldn't work. I left the rooming house every evening not to return before dawn the next day.

Then I tried to count, on my fingers, all the kimonos I lost, but by that time my heart was so heavy I invariably broke down. Slumped over my desk I couldn't hold back my tears. . . . I cried . . . as only a man can cry.

Please don't laugh!

Those were wretched days and nights. It took me three, perhaps four months to recover . . . somewhat.

For all that, my routine—getting up at six, being awakened at noon, then again at supper time—didn't change, but bereft of my dearest clothes, I spent most of my time in the futon. I read and wrote in the futon and didn't leave my room until evening for my walk. Those walks I couldn't give up.

I'm going to digress again . . . but you really have to listen to this. . . .

It's about a certain futon, and it happened three or four months after what I just finished telling you.

Cooped up in my room I couldn't help thinking about it.

And friendless, without women, without the kimonos almost dearer to me than my very life, I had no choice, I had to write. And I wrote. I wrote feverishly, page after page, story after story. I had never worked so hard in all my life.

And as I wrote I tried to figure out how much I would be paid. I finished each page by writing, in place of the page number, in very small numbers, the amount of money I thought the page would bring me.

You know, by now, that most of the time I spent in my room I spent in my futon. I still have to tell you that, until this year, though worn thin as it was, I wrote two-thirds, no, three-fourths of what I had to write to make ends meet tucked in that futon, as a turtle in its shell. In short, you may say, I depended on it for my living. And for the last ten to fifteen years I had been thinking about getting a more suitable one. I was trying to be as carefully choosy as a soldier is when he gets his horse, or a geisha her kimonos, or as the literati of old were when they chose their inkstones. But it was only at that time (the time I mentioned earlier) that I decided to get one. And I wrote ceaselessly, page after page, until the fees I collected for my stories amounted to what I thought I needed to make the final arrangements—it took me two months.

When the new one was ready, I knew I'd be loath to use it while the old one was still around (because I'm miserly, miserly to a foolish degree), so I quickly sold the old one to the ragman.

Of course, people who can afford better may not think much of this futon I went to such trouble to get, but to me it was more valuable than anything else. I was as happy as a child.

The top part was of *Yūzen* crepe, showy but in a subdued sort of way and set off by a red-bean-colored border. The bottom part of the futon was an egg-yolk yellow of the sort used in guest rooms in many ordinary homes.[7] And to cover it I had a sheet made that was narrower by several inches. I also wanted very much a second top part, but my money didn't go that far. And as I was afraid to soil the underside, I had a muslin night jacket made with the money I got from the ragman.

I know that this is not the kind of story mature people enjoy listening to. . . .

But when all of these things were finished and ready, I was as deliriously happy as a child on a holiday.

I would have loved to show off this futon to my friends, had I had any.

Anyway, I spread it out, got into it, got out, admired it, then got in again and, eventually drowsy, dozed off.

When I woke up, I remembered at once that I was in that wonderful futon and jumped out to inspect it again.

I rearranged the sheet I had spread over the bottom pads to make sure that it revealed evenly—a strip of two or so inches on either side—the egg yellow beneath. I smoothed out the top part, pushed down its four corners, and went back to curl up under it. I felt as if I were in the maw of a lovely, soft monster.

Reading in it was also very comfortable, but when I tried to write, the top part bulged and got in my way, so I asked a carpenter to make me a desk about four inches high so that I could write by getting out of the futon just a little.

And now that futon is gone. Gone to the pawnshop as well.

Once it was gone I couldn't stand the sight of the four-inch-high desk any longer and took it to the pawnshop too. "Is that an ironing board?" they asked me. I told them that I would accept anything if only they took it off my hands. "How about thirty sen?" So now it is probably buried in dust somewhere in that awful pile of household furniture on the first floor of the storehouse.

You know, when I say I rent my clothes from the pawnshop, since they are my own, all I do in fact is exchange some for others, and this without a second thought; but I can't do that with a futon. So I'm renting one from a futon shop at twenty sen a day. A futon that is several times inferior to the one I sold to the ragman.

Now why did I pawn a futon I loved so much?

The story will stray off course again . . . make a big detour . . . but please don't pay any attention to that. I have to confess the loss of that futon I loved so much—the shame of how I lost it! . . .

I had had it a little over a month when that woman came into my life (if it hadn't been for her, I would still have it).

It happened like this: one day I received a letter from an unknown woman in which she told me in great detail how she fell in love with my novels and how she hadn't missed reading a single one of any that bore my signature, from way back up until the present, and how she longed to meet me face to face.

It was because of this that I lost my futon.

At first I thought nothing of it. Women—who by the way are seldom beautiful—sending such letters to writers, that's an old story. And, at forty, even men like me have lost interest in such chance encounters. Not to mention that I didn't have a single kimono to go out in and that I spend most of my time in my dear futon.

So I made sure not to answer her, thinking that she wouldn't have the nerve to write a second time. But she did write; what's more, she started sending presents: first a keg of pickled turnips she said she received from relatives in Kyoto, then pickled winter sparrow in sake lees—a special product of her home province that, if not all that tasty, was at least unusual. Moreover it was supposed to keep you from catching cold.

Not three days went by without a gift or a letter from her, and being the man I am, I finally gave in. I answered her. I answered her once, twice, and then we arranged to meet. (Since I'm going to write about this in greater detail in a novel, I'll just give you a sort of summary here.)

What kind of person do you think that woman was? Judging from her handwriting, which was quite beautiful, I was convinced that she couldn't be some artless young girl. And the presents she sent with her letters suggested the taste of a forty-year-old—rather good taste, in fact. She couldn't be nineteen or twenty years old, of this I was sure. But for all that, I couldn't imagine who she really was.

Well, I found out. She was someone's kept mistress, thirty years old, and quite a beauty. It was because of her that I pawned my precious futon in exchange for three or four kimonos. I saw her perhaps five or six times in all.

Once she asked me to meet her at the Tokyo railroad station at around four o'clock in the afternoon. When I got there, she told me that her patron had just left for Kyoto, that is, she had come to see him off and, ten minutes later, to meet me at the same place. Not only that, she suggested that we take the next train to Kyoto, the very place her patron had gone.

My heart skipped a beat. How can a woman doing what she did be so lighthearted about it?

Our relationship lasted about a month. Yes, she soon tired of me. And I don't believe that I'm conceited when I say I'm convinced that my strange lapse in health was the reason. . . .

In the house in Hama-chō where she was kept, the signal for whether I could safely call on her was the presence or absence, in the foyer, of the patron's shoes.[8] After about the second or third visit, each time I went to the house I saw his shoes lined up in the foyer. And so for days on end, each time I walked through her gate I returned home disappointed. Then one day as I was on my way home I ran into her maid. "The master comes around a lot these days, doesn't he?" I ventured. "No," she answered casually. "But every time. . . ." The words had barely left my mouth when the maid, visibly flustered (but only for a very brief moment), put in, "Oh, the master? Yes, he comes just about every day now." (I'm sure she stuck out her tongue the moment my back was turned. Well, what can you expect from the servant of a kept woman? "Like mistress, like maid.") Yet I went back the very next day. This time because I was angry. I crept close to the entrance and peered into the front hallway like a thief. Just as I expected, there were the same shoes with quite a layer of dust on them (in such a house the maid is indeed just like the mistress—just as slovenly).

Now, would a man who keeps a mistress wear the same shoes every time he goes to see her? Those shoes must have been sitting there for more than two weeks. If one picked them up, chances are their outline would be left behind in the dust. In other words, the shoes were a kind of talisman for warding off evil, that is, for chasing away undesirable callers.

That was the end.

Oh, what a fool I had been. How could it have been so brief and so unsatisfying? Well, it's all over. What do you suppose I think of that woman now? One thing is certain. Whenever I think of my futon, I have to think of her.

Now then, at the beginning of this story I told you that I had decided to go to the pawnshop . . . but could you please wait a little longer and let me tell you another story before I go back to that?—

So, having lost, as I finished telling you, my darling futon (oh, I get so sentimental when I talk about such things . . . one wouldn't think I'm forty years old) . . . I made up my mind to change rooming houses. I needed a new lease on life: a fresh start, peace and quiet, and (I know this sounds crazy) to shake off an evil spirit that I had come to believe wanted to possess me.

So I rented a room in a rooming house that had the shape of a blown-up carpenter's square. This room was located in a corner of the building and, therefore, had a sliding door somewhat less than three feet wide.[9] The doors of the other rooms facing the same corridor were over twice as wide, and they had one large window, whereas mine had two, nice enough, smaller ones at right angles to one another, and the maid assured me that it and the room above it were the best in the house.

Alas, once I had moved in, it didn't take me long to realize that instead of the best, mine was probably the worst room in the house.

Every day, for at least four hours and at times as much as six hours straight, without a break, the lodgers, their guests, and the housemaids kept walking back and forth in the hallway in front of my room, making slapping and thumping noises as if they were soldiers parading about in slippers.

As I said before, the other rooms along the corridor had sliding doors six feet wide—twice as wide as mine—so their occupants should have heard twice as much of the noise I was tormented by, and no matter how thick-skinned they might have been, they couldn't have taken it, they would have complained. . . .

In all those many years I spent in rooming houses, I had never experienced anything like it. This house must have been especially badly built. You know, some of those noises were as loud as the stampings of sumo wrestlers before a match. I couldn't settle down to work, and after a while I felt my face muscles twitching as I racked my brains for an explanation.

Then it occurred to me that in most other rooming houses the rooms form a horseshoe around an interior garden as in certain brothels (please forgive the vulgar example). This rooming house, however, was more like half a horseshoe with a right angle. So that all the lodgers whose rooms were farther removed from the entrance than mine had to pass in front of my room to go to the washroom, to go to the toilet, and to go out. This meant that their guests and the housemaids too had to pass in front of my room. Moreover, on the opposite side of the entrance was the stairway to the second floor, so that all the upstairs lodgers and the people who visited them had to pass in front of my room.

Worse yet, every passerby had to take an extra step right in front of my room because that's where the corridor came to the aforementioned right angle. (Now, you may think that I am overly finicky, but please bear with me a little longer, and hear me out.) It sounded as if all those people with whom I had no business whatsoever were about to come into my room or had just left my room. And to top it all off, the staircase that people used to go upstairs or come downstairs was right next to my room.

For a time I had been able to calm myself with the thought that I might be mistaken, but as soon as I had determined the source of those terrible noises, I couldn't stand it another minute and went to complain to the rooming-house mistress.

Until then I barely knew her by sight, but I found out soon enough that talking to her was a sheer delight. She was young, rather pretty, and five or six months pregnant; she wore her hair combed back and up in a sort of pompadour style and had a way of curling her lips ever so slightly when she spoke that I found darling. (I must be an incorrigible fool.)

Well, it was finally decided that the maids would be moved into the four-and-a-half-mat room[10] next to the vestibule, and the lodger who had occupied that room would be asked to take mine, and I would move into the maid's room next to the kitchen. That was almost a month ago.

It's not that I didn't hear footsteps from my new room, but since they were the ones of the maids on their way to the kitchen, and no others, I associated them with sounds made by the straw sandals of the one-night call girls in the gay quarters. (What a foolish man I am. . . . Come to think of it, what I said earlier about wanting peace and quiet may have been a fib.) And so I not only tolerated them, but even enjoyed them, although, when the mealtime preparations got under way, there were unnerving clatterings of dishes, and the voices of the maids—their chatting and singing—were much louder.

When they ran out of things to talk about, they sang popular songs, and when their stock of popular songs was exhausted, each in turn sang a song of her home province.

When they talked, their voices were subdued, and I couldn't follow what they were saying, but when they sang, I could hear every word. At first, compared to the sound of footsteps, it was not only quite bearable, but even pleasurable. Lying on my hard pallet, I listened to the maid from Tsuchiura in Hitachi province sing her hometown boat song, and I took pleasure from secretly learning it. And so, in no time, I also learned the boat song and the rice-planting song sung by the maid from Yuzawa in Ugo province. But after I had listened with a fair amount of interest and had learned the Echigo ballad from the maid from Suihara in Echigo province, all of their songs began to grate on my ears, and in the end I became quite exasperated when they came to the parts they didn't sing well. But by then I had even learned to imitate the Sendai accent as well as the mistakes of the artless maid from Sendai, the one who boils the rice, when she sang "Hello, Hello Turtle."[11]

Isn't it like this with everything? It's fun while you're trying to learn it and turns into a bore as soon as you know it.

Now I've come to hate this former maids' room next to the kitchen. But I still have a month's rent to pay before I can move out, and even after I finish paying it's not likely that I'll find paradise wherever I go.

And so I thought about going to the pawnshop. As I said earlier, I thought of it after this year's summer airing. . . . At last my story has come back to its beginning.

Isn't that a way to lend it importance, though? To make it seem as if what will come next will really be interesting?

Don't be misled. It's little else but the woman in me, whining, complaining, and bumbling on from behind a manly mask.[12] Anyway, please continue to listen.

And then I went to the pawnshop.

"Welcome, it's been a long time."

Five or six heads in a row, from clerks down to the shop boy, turned toward me simultaneously and greeted me. I was greeted with a chorus of hellos as bands of revelers are greeted when they lift the curtain to enter one of those houses in the gay quarters.

As I ducked my head under the curtain to enter the shop, something (or rather someone) caught my eye. It was a woman sitting in a dimly lit spot at the counter behind the row of clerks and shop boys. I had never seen her before. She was about thirty and had her hair done up in a butterfly chignon. She had an oval face, with a high nose; she was fair skinned, and she had attractive eyes with a strange glint in them . . . all in all a beautiful woman. I guessed right away that she was the shop owner's younger sister. Though her facial features were far more refined, they resembled his closely.

"I would like to air my clothes," I began, addressing Inokichi, the clerk with whom I was on especially friendly terms and called Ino-kun.

"Air your clothes?" screamed several voices in astonishment. "At this time of the year?"

"I realize that it is not the proper time for it, of course, but I am concerned. It would be regrettable if my futon should mildew, and I would also like to see to my woolens."

This brought about a unanimous outcry and an enumeration of all possible reasons why they could not grant my request. Each and every garment was properly cared for; moreover, airing them now would be bad for the clothes, etc., etc. But since business was slow and there wouldn't be any more customers for a while, I decided to press my demand, moving from one subject of conversation to another while managing not to lose sight of the counter. After about twenty minutes she got up and went into the back room. And with most of the clerks and shop boys busy at their respective tasks, I approached Inokichi.

"Say, that woman who was at the counter, isn't she the younger sister of the owner?"

"Really, Mr. Yamaji, your eyes are as sharp as ever," laughed the clerk. "She's quite a beauty, isn't she?" But then he added in a way that suggested that not all the shop employees sympathized with her, "She's been divorced, you know. She always quarrels with the master and with us too. She's not only ill tempered, she's hysterical."

"When did she come back?"

"Three or four days ago."

"Is she home for good?"

"I wonder . . . probably for a while anyway."

Then I changed the subject and returned to my request. But all I got from them was a promise to talk to the owner that very day and to inform me of the outcome. Reluctantly I returned to my lodgings. A whole day went by without word from the pawnshop. Need I say it? I was as curious about the owner's sister who had been sent home as I was eager to get their permission to air my clothes. So I set out again for the pawnshop.

"I tried to talk to him about it, but. . . ." With these words, as soon as he saw me, Yokichi tried to dismiss me before I could open my mouth.

The wretch, I thought to myself, and deliberately shut my ears to whatever else he had to say and sat down across from where Inokichi was sitting while looking in the direction of the dimly lit counter.

She was not there that day. And, as usual, there were no other customers in sight. So I took a cigarette from my sleeve, and turning my head toward Inokichi, I said quite loudly, "I wonder how much interest I have to pay you this month." At that Yokichi fell silent in the middle of what he was saying.

Later on, after we had been chatting for a while, Inokichi, lowering his voice a bit, said, "Mr. Yamaji, you owe me a treat, you know. Listen, that divorcée checked out your name and said that you're a famous novelist. Miss Hysteria is a great reader of novels, you know."

"That's promising," I answered as casually as possible, and then resumed negotiating to air my clothes. But in my heart,

truly I felt very happy. It had been a long time since I had had a
close relationship with a woman. Not since the time I pawned
my futon. But Inokichi, being Inokichi, evaded my request and
carried the conversation back to the hysterical beauty.

"And then . . . then she went over your account, and she
asked all kinds of questions. I told her that you are a very
important customer. She smiled, ever so sweetly, and said,
'He's different, after all, he is a novelist.' We shouldn't make
light of it, should we, Mr. Yamaji? But you owe me a favor,
Mr. Yamaji."

"Well, I am an important customer, am I not?" I said with a
smirk. Deep down I was really happy. I felt like a seventeen- or
eighteen-year-old—a mature person can't feel that way—and I
was all the more determined to get permission to air my clothes
so that I could come back to the shop every day.

When I said "a mature person can't feel that way," I meant
I was fantasizing that while I was hanging up my clothes she
would come to the second floor and . . . you know, that reckless,
selfish, conceited adolescent kind of daydreaming . . . and I felt
so good about it—I hadn't felt that good in a long time.

When Inokichi stopped talking, I reopened my negotiations,
moving my head from right to left, facing one clerk after the
other, addressing them all.

I came to the pawnshop to see my favorite kimono after a
long separation, and there was this beautiful, divorced
woman. . . .

Somehow this story is too pat, I really feel uneasy about it.
Yet everything happened exactly as I am telling it to you. So
please be patient and continue to listen, won't you?

It was then that the beauty quietly made her way to
the counter.

This may sound like something out of a novel by Izumi Kyōka, but it isn't.[13] Its inspiration is quite different.

I blushed when I saw her, then felt the wind go out of my argument. I imagined she was thinking something like, "That man, here he is again, stubbornly trying to get his way." I felt terribly self-conscious, but thought that the worst thing that could happen would be for me to lapse into complete silence. So summoning up whatever courage I had left, I managed to put my proposal to them once more, but interlaced with jokes and all sorts of lighthearted talk. And this went on for about fifteen minutes, until she interrupted with a clear, sharp voice. "Yokichi!" she called, summoning the head clerk to her side. I pretended not to notice and resumed talking to Inokichi and was still talking to him when Yokichi returned from the counter and said to me, "Since you have gone to so much trouble you may as well come tomorrow afternoon if the weather is good. . . . If it rains, please come the following day." Needless to say, Yokichi was simply passing on her orders.

My world had suddenly brightened. My plan to entertain myself by seeing my clothes again had succeeded, and to boot I had the pleasure of making the acquaintance of a beautiful woman. I stayed on, talking for a while longer, then returned to my lodgings. I felt as if I had been drinking sake, I was drunk with happiness.

When I came back the next day, the first thing I did was to look in the direction of the counter. She was not there. Worse yet, Inokichi wasn't in the shop either. I could, however, ask where he was without arousing suspicion. So I asked the shop boy. Yokichi answered instead, curtly informing me that Inokichi was out on an errand.[14] Then motioning with his chin, he ordered the shop boy to take me to the second floor of the storehouse.

I entered the dim interior with my thoughts still on the shop below. But when I got to the second floor, to the place that reminded me of a library reading room, and I saw the heaps of clothes all wrapped in old paper—oh, what a sight!—I forgot about everything else and reveled in my newfound happiness. It mattered little that the clothes inside the old paper packages had belonged to others. The fact that they were clothes was enough for me. Oh, happy sight. And the odors that came from those packages. . . . What nostalgia!

I stood before the dear familiar chest in the corner, the chest I hadn't seen in over half a year.

The shop boy had gone back downstairs. He probably knew that even the kimono on my back belonged to the shop and had no reason to worry about me.

And I, as if I were opening the secret drawers of some hidden treasure trove, stealthily and carefully opened the first drawer of the chest, then closed it and opened the second, then closed it and opened the third . . . for a while I did nothing but repeat this motion. Ah . . . the feeling of opening and closing those full, heavy drawers, to say nothing of the sight of their contents. The sweet, whispering sounds they made as I opened and shut them, and the feel of the air expelled, roundly, firmly against my skin. Please don't think I exaggerate! Far from exaggerating, I'm exasperated because I haven't got the words to describe it!

Most people, when asked what happiness is, can't give a straightforward answer, but I can tell you that this feeling is at least part of what happiness is all about. And I fully understand women who part with their most precious possession for the sake of kimonos.

Should I be mistaken, surely that can easily be forgiven. Anyway, who would care to contradict the likes of me? And if there were such a person, I would have to say that that person doesn't know how much women love kimonos.

As I said earlier, I like women. I can't say that I love them. Deep down I may even despise them. Please don't laugh, this is no wisecrack. And though it may sound like it, I am not trying to hold forth as some sort of philosopher, but in this matter I have to take their side, I have to defend women, all women.

I don't believe that women leave men because of money, but I do believe that they will leave men, any man, any time, for kimonos, and we have to forgive them for that.

What am I trying to say anyway? This doesn't even make sense to me.

Please don't think about it too much—be patient—and continue to listen.

So then I moved away from the chest, took the rope I had tied to my waist when I left the rooming house, and strung it up in a straight line, from the lattice of the window to the pillar, and from the pillar to the pegs in the wall, and so on, and hung up the contents of the first drawer. That took up almost the whole line.

Of course, I hoped that this airing would go on for quite a while—at least four or five days. I was tempted to put the machine-spun kimonos and the cotton kimonos of my student days, which were wrapped in paper, on the remaining free section of the rope, but I thought, What if she came? . . . What if she saw them? . . . and I gave up the idea.

Then I called the shop boy to get my futon. As I spread it out—I hadn't seen it for such a long time—it seemed almost too precious to put that body of mine in it. But I couldn't bring myself just to sit while I waited for my clothes to air; and there would be no need to feel ashamed if she were to see me; indeed, I much preferred that she see me sleeping in the futon than sitting in the kimono I had on.

What a difference between the rented futon I had been using of late and this one! As I slipped into it, clad only in my under-kimono, I felt as if my body had suddenly become strangely

small, and I thought that my neck sticking out of its ample
swellings must look ridiculously scrawny.

I put aside the magazine I had brought along to read and
gazed at the clothes dangling over my head.

Oh, yes—I meant to talk to you about those kimonos and
the memories they hold. But you know, even if I were to talk
straight through a whole day and night, I couldn't tell it all. And
remember, I warned you in the beginning that it would be a foolish, rambling tale . . . please forgive me.

Now back to those kimonos and the memories. . . . I don't
want to sound pretentious, but the truth is, even if I were forbidden to remember, there's not one kimono on this line that
wouldn't make me think of at least one woman. Take, for example, that combination hanging over my head—the fine hemp
kimono with the splashed pattern made from cloth woven in the
fashion of old Echigo, and the striped Takajima crepe with the
indigo pattern black as night against a navy blue ground, and the
dark grey gauze *haori,* and the Satsuma linen outfit.[15] The serge
hakama that also belongs to it is not on the line because it's kept
in a different drawer.

At last I'm on track. This is going to be my last aside (I've
reached the point where I can hardly distinguish the main story
line myself), and since one of these days I'm going to write about
this in a novel anyway, I'll be as brief and to the point as possible.

This happened over ten years ago. I was still around thirty
at the time, and my dear aunt, who had been widowed when she
was twenty-seven, was forty-five or forty-six and was living in a
country town in a nearby prefecture. I went to visit her. It was
summer, and I wore the Echigo linen kimono and the loose-
weave *haori.* (A loose-weave *haori* doesn't sound very attractive,
does it? But in those days they were anything but common, even

on trains in Tokyo, so I was very proud of mine.) I also had on the serge *hakama* (I don't like those serge *hakama* anymore). And it was there at my aunt's house that I met this girl.

She took koto lessons from my aunt. She was twenty years old, and except when she laughed, her face was as expressionless as a doll's; even her hair was done up like a doll's wig. Her family was in the restaurant business—somewhere downtown, which may explain why she yearned for the Yamanote type of refinement.

My aunt not only gave her koto lessons but, with her refined features, looked quite the part of the Yamanote matron. So she came to my aunt's house practically every day, dressed in Yamanote-style finery. And whether she simply took a walk in the small town where she lived or went to Tokyo, she was always dressed as if she wanted people to turn around to admire her. And when she talked with me, she had a habit of blurting out *Hazukashii!* at almost every word and then covering her face with her large kimono sleeves, as bashful young girls do.[16]

Who do you think she was? I'll tell you right off. She was a kept woman.

Such discoveries do not really shock me. As you will learn, if you continue to listen to me, I have known many women, women of all sorts of callings, and this from my earliest childhood on, but when I found out what she did, I must say, I was surprised.

She was raised by an older sister, having lost both her parents at an early age (the restaurant I mentioned was managed by that same sister). At seventeen she was made to take her present patron and since then had known only that one man. How that could be, I don't know, but it may explain her girlish ways. She wasn't given a place of her own but remained in the house she was born in and greeted and entertained her patron in the room that was hers when she went to kindergarten and later to elementary school, and. . . .

Speaking of her patron: he was the second wealthiest man in the prefecture—an important taxpayer, it was said.

She received a monthly allowance of one hundred yen, and twice a year she got a thousand yen, and in those days the yen was worth a lot more than it is now.

Isn't it amazing?

Some men joke about it when they say they wish they were women. To me this is no joke. In fact, in those days, in my heart of hearts, I often, and for quite some time, wished I hadn't been born a man.

Then one day the three of us, she, my aunt, and I, went to Tokyo together. Of course, we didn't tell her patron about it.

Our train passed through an out-of-the-way area so that we had a whole second-class carriage to ourselves. (Did that give her the idea?) All of a sudden she blurted out, "How nice it would be if this were our honeymoon trip and your aunt were our mother."

Taken by surprise and bashful as I am, I turned brick red. Then it occurred to me that an ordinary woman couldn't have said that—kept women must lack a certain sense of shame. But I was very happy, in fact, my chest expanded with pleasure.

And that's not the end of it. . . . There's more to it yet.

As soon as we arrived in Tokyo we went to the Mitsukoshi department store, and there without any further ado she bought the Satsuma kimono hanging there, and, mind you, I was thirty years old already. And in the evening, after we had returned to my rooming house and were talking about going to a play the next day (my aunt must have gone out shopping), she abruptly took a ring off her finger and told me to try it on. When I had done so, she took my hand and looked at it. "It fits well," she said. "I'm giving it to you."

The next morning she received a telegram from home and returned immediately, accompanied by my aunt. My aunt probably felt somewhat responsible for her. Then several days thereafter she sent word that our affair had been discovered and that I should not write to her until she gave me the go-ahead. At about the same time I received a letter from my aunt, in which she told me with great indignation that the patron who had found out about the expedition to Tokyo was blaming her for our misdeed and was making her life miserable. Why did he blame her and she blame us? Whatever the answer may be, we, the girl and I, parted for good. And all that remains is the Satsuma kimono and the ring, which is in hock too, tucked away in the pawnshop safe.

What is the matter with me anyway? Well, let's try to get a little sleep for now.

And so I dozed off curled up in my darling futon, on the second floor of the pawnshop storehouse. And I dreamed a strange dream.

A large horseshoe-like shape appeared before my eyes. Then, just like those new electric advertising lights that change color as you watch, in the twinkling of an eye it turned into an aerial view of a rooming house, and then into the blueprint of a brothel, and then, the basic shape unaltered, it turned into my elementary school badge.[17] (The insignia of the elementary school I attended was shaped something like a horseshoe.) The badge split asunder, right down the middle, without a sound, as sometimes happens in movies, and the left side disappeared. And I watched in amazement as the remaining half first assumed the outline of a key and then became the aerial view of a rooming house different from the first, in fact, half the first (it was the rooming house I'm living in right now). And then I had the sensation of a shadowy presence moving in front of me. After the long, harrowing experience of noisy footsteps in the corridor, this was a gentle feeling, a feeling of quiet, as if the person passing had no feet.

At that point I had the sudden urge to open my eyes. I did. And who do you think I saw? Yes . . . it was the hysterical beauty. A bit shaken, I cried out, "Oh, please excuse me."

"Did I wake you? You look so comfortable," she replied smiling. (I may have mentioned it before, but she certainly was a beautiful woman.) "You really have a lot of clothes, don't you?" she added. "You lead a carefree life. I envy you."

I replied, "What's carefree about it?" (By that time I had collected myself.) "As you can see, even my futon is in your shop."

"Yes, but all you have to do is put forth a little effort and write something, and everything will be fine."

"But that 'little effort' doesn't come that easily."

At first, feeling that it would be rude to remain in the futon, I sat up, but before I realized it I was back in my former position—lying down.

At that moment there were footsteps on the ladder, and in a moment Ino-kun's good-natured face appeared.

"The master will soon be home, and so. . . ." He seemed to address no one in particular. "We acted on our own, without consulting the master, so. . . ."

In other words, they acted on their own in giving me permission to air my clothes; but the expression on Ino-kun's face seemed to signify that he had something else on his mind. At any rate, when I answered, "All right, all right. I'll clear it all up and leave," she broke in shrilly: "I don't care even if the master is coming back; I was the one who told Yokichi to do it in the first place."

"Yes, that's so, but. . . ." Ino-kun scratched his head uncomfortably and seemed at a loss for words.

"All right, don't worry. I'll put everything back in its place, so please go back downstairs."

Ino-kun went downstairs. But she stayed behind and helped me put my clothes away. I returned home feeling many times more satisfied than I had the day before. (I might add that the owner of the pawnshop went to the stock exchange in Kabuto every afternoon.)

When I came back the next day, the woman was not at the counter. I briefly greeted the people in the shop and made a bee-line for the second floor of the storehouse. Ino-kun followed me.

"Mr. Yamaji," Ino-kun called after me, and, smiling, held out his hand. He had not yet reached legal age and could not smoke openly.[18] The outstretched hand was his way of asking for a cigarette. I gave him one from a pack of Shikishima—with an embarrassed look on my face.

"Did she go out today?" I asked.

"Go out? Not when you're coming!" he answered. "Thanks for the cigarette. She's coming now. She's in the back." (I forgot to mention that Inokichi had a slight stutter, not that it matters. . . .)

He finished smoking his cigarette, asked for three more, which he tucked up his sleeve, and went downstairs.

That day, I decided to air half the contents of the paper packages of one-yen, fifty-sen kimonos and half the ones in the second drawer. When I had hung out the clothes, I took out the futon and curled up inside it as I had done before. Need I say that I was expecting her to appear at any moment? It may sound conceited, but I was sure she didn't dislike me . . . and even if it was conceited, that's what I wanted to think. But she didn't come, even after I was in the futon.

The clothes from my student days hanging over my head included some old garments I had worn when I was in middle school; among the assortment of spun-cotton and splashed pattern kimonos was an unlined silk kimono from Morimura and a matching kimono and *haori* of ordinary Ise silk. At the time I was a third-year student in middle school.[19] (It was a time when I had an irrational hatred of navy blue cotton kimonos with white patterns and thought that any garment with a sheen to it was attractive, and these were the sort of clothes that we were ordered not to wear in public, but did so secretly.) And I wore one of the two, the unlined silk in the summer and the Ise silk in the winter, with a bit of white collar showing at the neck (around that time I shunned Western-style dress shirts) on many an evening when I went to listen to a certain woman *gidayū*.[20]

I went to middle school in Osaka. And in Osaka in those days it was customary for fans to give congratulatory gifts to the *gidayū* such as one or two one-yen bills inserted between the tips of a pair of bamboo chopsticks stuck in an orange, when oranges were in season, and placed on the dais in front of the *gidayū*'s reading stand in full view of the audience. After a while I managed to scrape together what it took for such a gift (not all that easy for a middle school student such as I was) and took a pair of bamboo chopsticks, stuck them in an orange, put two one-yen notes between them, as I had seen done, and took the gift to the reception desk. (I didn't know that the orange and chopsticks were provided by the theater and that all the guests had to give was the money—can a middle school student be expected to know that?) The old woman at the reception desk first stared at me wide eyed, then smiled and said, "My, how correct you are." At that, the people standing around her all snickered, and I thought, here you go again, and I blushed. (I am sure I was wearing the Ise silk.) Yes, I must have been infatuated with that woman *gidayū*. The other day I blushed again when I unexpectedly saw her performing in the lead spot at a *yose* hall in Tokyo.[21]

Her name?

Had she been prettier, I would tell you. As it is, I can't. I can't tell.

It was also around that time that I needed money very badly, and I began to think of such things as pawnshops, with which, as you know, I became rather too well acquainted later on.

(I had no friends, not even close companions; in fact, as middle school students go, I was sort of a loner.) And there was this silver dish. I don't remember whether someone suggested it to me or I came to the conclusion that it must be quite valuable all by myself. It was used for sweetmeats and candy whenever guests came to the house. At any rate one evening I slipped it into my kimono and ran down to the pawnshop some blocks from my house. And after pacing back and forth in front of the shop to get up my courage, I finally dashed in, bowl in hand—only to be turned down.

I can imagine that this story about mostly my first love pangs may be quite tiresome, so I'll tell you as little as possible; just enough to round out the picture—

I was out walking one day when a ricksha coming from a sidestreet suddenly dashed by me, and behold, in it was the woman *gidayū* I was infatuated with; for a while I just stood there looking. Then I made up my mind to run after her and did so for about a block. I wanted to know where she lived. But the ricksha stopped in front of a restaurant, and she went inside. I was crestfallen, and when I saw the empty ricksha as it passed on its way back, I didn't even have the courage to question the ricksha man.

Eventually, though, I found out where she lived. I had taken a different way to school that day, through back streets passing rows of houses still shuttered, for it was early morning, when all of a sudden I saw a nameplate with her very name on it right beside the plate of a carpentry shop. Was her husband, or her brother, a carpenter? No matter, the house was in sorry shape.

About that time too, a famous female *gidayū* moved in next door. I became acquainted with her when she asked me to address a letter she was going to send abroad, and although it was hard to find an appropriate excuse each time, from then on

I went to visit her often. As you guessed, it was the longing for the other *gidayū* that drove me.

And so I learned, and this also quite by accident, that the woman I pined for had been a student of my neighbor's. I ran into her on one of those visits. She looked rather surprised. How could she have expected to meet again in her former teacher's home that strange middle school student who had given her two yen? She greeted me with barely a look (it may not have been a greeting at all) and said nothing. I was flustered and speechless as well.

About a week later I ran into her—literally—and of course I blushed again. I passed in front of her door as she left the house. Since I knew where she lived, I never failed to pass by her house on my way to and from school. At times, as I approached the house, my whole body became as stiff as a rod, and I didn't dare look up. And later on, even though I had visited her on several occasions, when I saw her, from as far as a block away, with another man, or even saw a man approaching her house, I ran away.

I won't go into greater detail; anyway, before I knew the joys of love fulfilled, we parted. And what is left are these kimonos.

And the next person I was romantically involved with was a geisha I had known since childhood. And after that . . . and then . . . after that . . . I have no intention of giving you a history of my love affairs. All I want to do is give you an idea of the kind of uncommon women I've been involved with these past forty or so years, without taking into account the prostitutes I bought, lived with, or made love suicide pacts with, or the undiscriminating geisha[22] I eloped with . . . all that is hardly worth mentioning. What is important is that all that's left from consorting with those unconventional women are these kimonos, and that what I've said about women does not concern ordinary women, and that I'm obviously not qualified to talk about ordinary women.

Now, may I tell you one more story? . . . I won't force my-self on you. . . . Those of you who can't stand listening any longer, please close your ears.

It's from the time of this Yoneryū pongee and the serge hang-ing to the right of my head and the Western clothes that are not among the things I'm airing today. In other words, it happened between the year I left a certain private university at age twenty-four and the following year.

The other party was an unknown actress, so unknown that today I don't know where she is or what she's doing. I know she was a graduate of a girls' school—but then, can a woman be relied on to tell the truth even about a matter such as that? Any-way, whatever brought us together, some incident or other, didn't keep us together more than three months. At first she thought she would write, then she thought she would paint; but she never wavered in her desire to lead the life of an artist. Alas, she didn't have the talent to write, or the talent to paint, so she became an actress. Of course, I don't mean that acting doesn't require talent. But all the while she was living with me this woman told me that I was a writer without imagination and that my ideas were so outdated that I couldn't write anything besides mushy love stories. To which I used to reply, "Granted you are knowledgeable about a certain kind of love life, but what kind of life is that anyway?" But that didn't faze her. And she gave me to understand that whatever I knew about her was quite super-ficial, and that in fact her life was devoted to ideas. . . .[23]

Oh well, what are ideas after all?

Well, this much is clear; she walked out on me with more aplomb and finality than any other woman I have ever known.

"I'm going to take off the doll's clothes," she said, and that was that. Of course, I recognized it as a line from Ibsen.[24] But I wonder what sort of merit a woman has when she's stripped bare? It may be all right in a play, and then again . . . Ibsen may not know what he's talking about. At any rate, no matter how I look at it, I believe he popularized a very bad idea.

And then before I knew it, I dozed off again in my dear futon on the second floor of the storehouse, which had become almost as dear to me as the futon itself.

"Mr. Yamaji, Mr. Yamaji." It sounded as if someone were calling me in a dream. And when I opened my eyes, she was standing at my bedside. (That was the first time she had called me by my name!)

"You really sleep nicely, don't you?" She went on talking as I rubbed my eyes. "You hardly make any sounds at all."

"Well, as you know, as one gets older, one loses energy." I was already so used to her that I fell easily into a bantering tone.

"Old? Old? You have no reason to talk about being old. Isn't a man your age in his prime? It's I, at my age, who have nothing to look forward to," she replied, in a familiar tone as well.

(By and large our conversation that day was most ordinary. But to me it was a delight beyond words.)

"If one has money as you do, doesn't one usually find a reason for living, though?"

"You must be joking. If I were a man, I'd want to be a writer. Please write about me sometime in your novels. I'll tell you everything. May I visit you? Where in Hayashi-chō do you live?"

She had probably found my address in the account book.

"I used to live in Hayashi-chō," I answered, and in the process of giving her my present address, I complained about the rooming house where I live now.

"It's funny," she said, "that we should be talking about so many things on the second floor of a storehouse when we've only just met. We're just like an old (excuse me) Hisamatsu and Osome, aren't we?"[25]

Then she laughed aloud for the first time. I laughed too. And so the day came to an end.

The following day, I had barely begun getting my clothes out of the drawers when she came to help me, and despite my objections, got the futon and laid it out. "Have a good rest," she said. I continued to protest for a while but eventually gave in. As I crawled into it, she took up a crouching position leaning against the pillar. Then she moved, and when I changed the position of my head on the pillow, her face was hidden by the clothes hanging from the ropes.

"Have you ever been married?" she asked suddenly.

"No," I said, as I turned toward her. She was still hidden by the hanging clothes. "No, I've always lived alone as I do now."

"Oh? According to the account book you redeemed them all, but some three or four years ago you had a lot of women's clothes in here."

"Ahh . . . yes, please forgive me, I forgot. There were those two years I didn't live alone." I tried to look at her as I spoke, but that white face of hers remained in the shadow of the hanging clothes.

"Did you separate?" At last she emerged from behind the screen of clothes and faced me.

Oddly enough those very clothes that served her as a screen were a constant source of irritation for the other woman. "Why do you, a man, need so many clothes?" she used to harp at me whenever she was dissatisfied with her own. Strange, isn't it?

"Why did you leave her? Why are men so cruel?" she continued.

"Oh, I wasn't cruel, on the contrary. As my friends used to say and criticize me for, I was too kind. She was hysterical. She was. . . ." I was about to say that she was uncontrollably hysterical and had been sent home for that reason, but the words got stuck in my throat. I suddenly remembered that the woman I was talking to had been divorced and sent home because she was hysterical. This time I used the silk crepe kimono hanging from the line to hide my face as I said, stammering, "She was really very hysterical."

Had I hurt her feelings as I feared? She didn't say anything at all. And I got all the more flustered, and took off on a clumsy defense of hysteria.

"Of course, you could call a man such as I am a male hysteric. Moreover, I always felt that in today's world whoever is not hysterical is either insensitive or plain stupid. What I was going to say is that the woman was not as hysterical as she was absolutely crazy."

"What on earth did she do?" she finally asked.

"Well, for example, without warning she would thrust some of her kimonos at me and tell me to take them to the pawnshop at once. My pleadings to her to give me a little time to raise the money she needed—if she needed any—had no effect. So often in broad daylight I, a man, carrying a big *furoshiki* bundle, took off for the pawnshop. I had no choice once she had made up her mind. When I came back with money, I had to take her to the Ginza or to a movie, and she became so lively, in so weird a way, that I didn't dare show my dejection. And if she detected the least expression of disapproval on my face, she exploded in a rage. And it didn't take her more than two days, or at the most three, before she started all over again with complaints such as, 'You have all the Ōshima silk and other nice kimonos that you want, and I have nothing but this common silk that I'm wearing. How can I go out with you, so elegant, when I'm dressed so miserably? And it's all because of you. You forced me to pawn my best clothes.' (She had already conveniently forgotten that I had done all I could to convince her not to pawn them.) Then out of a sense of fairness, I pawned some of my own kimonos, and as long as the money I got lasted, she was cheerful. Alas, the money lasted but a very short time. She spent it as quickly as a straw fire burns. How could I work under those circumstances? I couldn't."

"My goodness," she exclaimed.

"But, in comparison, even that was tolerable. The worst was when she discovered and was offended by the mention of a love affair in one of my novels, a love affair that had nothing to do with her—or did she read it when she was waiting to be offended? At any rate, it fanned the fire of her hysteria to the point where—and this is embarrassing to say—she beat me mercilessly. It was so bad I ached all over. I could hardly get up in the morning. I felt so weak. And if I forgot myself and groaned with pain when she was in a bad mood, she not only let me have it again, but beat me three times as hard."

"Good heavens!" she cried.

By then we had moved away from the screen of clothes that hung between us and were facing each other. And again I forgot myself. I kept repeating the word *hysteria* over and over again. She too was quite moved by my story, but managed after a while to ask me, "Did your wife come from the country, or? . . ."

"We were a common-law couple," I answered. "She was a third-class geisha."

Strange as this may seem, I was putting a good face on the situation; she was, in fact, what they call an unlicensed prostitute.

"And where is she now?"

"I hear that she's in Akasaka. I never see her."

This too was a lie to put a good face on it. She was in a third-class red-light district in Yokohama, far removed from fashionable Akasaka.

And so it was, perhaps to hide the embarrassment I felt for telling such lies—yes, even I feel uncomfortable at times for telling such blatant lies—that I began to chatter, and that was a big mistake.

"Four or five days ago I read in a newspaper that according to a court decision hysteria is now considered a ground for divorce."

I didn't notice it right away, but when I saw the expression on her face, I sensed that these words may well mark the beginning of the end. I was alarmed.

That very moment—it was probably past three o'clock—without warning the shop boy came up from below, telling her, "The master has returned and wants to see you." All these happenings one on top of the other at the wrong time seemed to spell disaster. She was quite shaken and went downstairs without another word, and I didn't have the courage to look her in the face again.

And so I was left once more, my small head sticking out of the futon and my kimonos dangling over my head. For a while I stared vacantly into space. Then I closed my eyes. I wanted to sleep but couldn't. I was too upset.

It would, would it not, have a corrupting influence on the servants to know that their master's younger sister, a divorcée, had gone up to the second floor of the storehouse to meet and talk to a man there?

But even if that were not the case, she was probably deeply offended by the way I talked about hysteria and divorce.

As I thought of all that, how I had hurt her feelings, and how maybe she was being scolded by her shop-owner brother that very minute, it wasn't so much pity for her that I began to feel as concern for myself lest in a blind, hysterical fit she come charging in on me.

This may be a good place to stop. Otherwise who knows where all this folderol will lead and how it will end. Yes, let's bring it to a close.

Well, then . . . quite a bit sooner than I would have otherwise, I put everything away as quickly and quietly as I could. And surveying the scene from the second floor as a thief would, I waited until the shop was nearly empty and very quietly climbed down the ladder and slipped away.

The next morning at about ten o'clock (for me, an ungodly hour) the housemaid called out something like, "An Ikeda here to see you." (Ikeda was the name of the pawnshop.) For a moment I thought that it might be her, and I jumped out of the futon. "Is it a woman?" I asked enthusiastically.

Derision was all over the maid's face (a face like Otafuku's),[26] her lips, her fat cheeks, even her red nose.

"No, it's a clerk. . . ." She sounded as if she wanted to say "a bill collector."

Now, if I'm going to exaggerate a bit, I have to say that I was weak kneed with disappointment but deliberately affected an air of composure.

"Have him come upstairs," I replied.

"Excuse me," he said, before entering the room.

Oh, that voice . . . made me feel worse. I had half expected Ino-kun, and here was that Yokichi, the head clerk, with his sullen, sour face that I disliked so much.

"Excuse me for calling while you're resting. . . ." Even his manner of greeting repelled me.

You can guess why he came.

"Beginning today, and for some time to come, I shall have to take care of certain things in the storehouse myself, and I shall take particularly good care of your belongings, and so. . . ."

He was telling me—in his "polite" way—that I could not air my clothes anymore.

What really nettled me was the barefaced lie he used to tell me so. However, I managed to control myself. "Very well, very well then. I won't."

Having said this, I abruptly rolled over—in my rented futon—and so dismissed him.

And so did the joy of the visits and hoped-for visits and the unanticipated special pleasures come to an end—in less than three days.

Did the shop owner put an end to it because we talked in the storehouse as if we didn't care what the employees might think?

In that case, I'm still hopeful.

Or is it because the last thing I said to her offended her? If that is so. . . . I wonder whether all I'll have to look forward to, in my room next to the kitchen, are the boat songs, rice-planting songs, and Echigo ballads. . . .

Where is everybody? . . . Isn't there one single person left—still listening?

Notes

Kura no naka was first published in the April 1919 issue of *Bunshō sekai* and again as a separate book by Shūeikan in December 1919. It is one of Uno's best-known works and appears in many collections of his writings.

1. The reference to *yonjū fuwaku* (forty years old and beyond vacillation) is from *The Analects* 2.4. In James Legge's translation, the full passage reads: "1. The Master said, 'At fifteen, I had my mind bent on learning. 2. 'At thirty I stood firm. 3. 'At forty, I had no doubts. 4. 'At fifty, I knew the decrees of Heaven. 5. 'At sixty, my ear was an obedient organ *for the reception of truth*. 6. 'At seventy, I could follow what my heart desired, without transgressing what was right.'" (*The Four Books: Confucian Analects, The Great Learning, The Doctrine of the Mean, and The Works of Mencius* [New York: Paragon, 1966], 13–14).

2. An allusion to Tanizaki Jun'ichirō's "Akuma" (The devil, 1912), in which the narrator revels in the odor of a woman's soiled handkerchief and then moves on to discover the piquant taste of the snot smeared on it.

3. The importance of ensuring the continuity of the household in Japan has led to the practice of adopting an heir to continue the family line when there is no suitable candidate within the family. Conversely, families with several children might give up a child for adoption to enhance that child's prospects in life. The adoptee is usually but not always a male child. Sometimes, often through marriage, an adult male will be brought into a household that lacks a male heir.

4. The area referred to would appear to be the Asakusa entertainment district in the northeastern sector of Tokyo, where many of the cheaper geisha houses and bars were located.

5. ·Young apprentice geisha (*hangyoku,* lit., "half [*han*] a geisha's fee [*gyokudai*]") were thirteen- and fourteen-year-old girls who accompanied their older geisha "sisters" on their rounds.

6. The Japanese text refers less obliquely to a woman's menstrual period, and the phrase *are no aru aida no onna* (women while they still have "it") is repeated a second time for emphasis: *Are no aru onna ni suteru onna wa hitori mo arimasen* (Among women who have "it," there's not a one I'd cast aside) (*Uno Kōji zenshū,* ed. Shibukawa Gyō et al., 12 vols. [Tokyo: Chūō Kōron, 1972], 1:65).

7. A Japanese bed or futon consists of two parts: the lower part is constructed of a pad or pads *(shikibuton)* of cotton stuffed in a cloth envelop (Yamaji's is made of pongee, a soft, thin silk with a knotty weave), and on the top, covering the sleeper, is placed the thick, quilt-like *kakebuton,* often sewn from more elaborately decorated cloth.

8. It is customary to remove street shoes before entering the living quarters of a Japanese home.

9. A *fusuma,* a sliding panel door covered with thick paper; used as a room divider in Japanese inns and homes.

10. The size of a room in a traditional Japanese building is measured in terms of the number of tatami on the floor. A room of four and a half mats *(yojōhan)* is a small room, approximately ten feet square.

11. The localities named are in areas of northern Honshu associated with long, cold winters and rough living conditions. The feeling of rusticity conveyed by the old provincial names is reinforced by the use of the Tōhoku dialect to render the well-known children's song sung by the maid from Sendai: *mosu mosu kame yo,* as opposed to *moshi moshi kame yo,* as it would be sung in standard Japanese.

12. The image of a womanly Yamaji speaking from behind a "manly mask" is a comic twist on a famous passage in *Tosa Nikki* (Tosa diary, ca. 935), in which the author, Ki no Tsurayuki, adopts the transparent conceit of pretending to be a woman writing like a man.

13. Izumi Kyōka, whose fantastic romantic plots featured white-skinned seductresses of enchanting beauty in supernatural settings, was still publishing prolifically when Uno composed "In the Storehouse." Whereas a bit of the fantastic associated with Edo period literature was still to be found in Kyōka's tales of mystery, Uno undercut the mysterious ambience surrounding his white-skinned beauty by making her "hysterical."

14. As the head clerk *(bantō)*, Yokichi is displeased at being countermanded by the owner's younger sister. The pawnshop appears to be a rather large, prosperous establishment, organized along traditional lines, in which the head clerk functions as the manager of the clerks *(tedai)* and apprentices *(detchi)* and acts as an agent for the shop owner.

15. In Japan, cloth is often named after its place of origin or the person who first produced it.

16. The word *hazukashii* (lit., "to feel bashful, shy, ashamed") is an interjection expressing maidenly modesty and embarrassment, as does the gesture of holding the sleeve before the mouth.

17. Neon signs *(denki kōkoku)* were a great novelty in 1919. The influence of motion pictures can also be discerned in the description of Yamaji's dream.

18. Then, as now, the legal age was twenty.

19. Cotton kimonos with white splashes on a navy blue ground *(kongasuri)* were often worn by students. They had no sheen, in contrast to *meisen,* which were of silk. As a third-year middle school student under the old educational system, Yamaji would have been about sixteen years old.

20. In the latter half of the Meiji period (1868–1912), Osaka-style idayū (dramatic narrative recitations accompanied by samisen) performed by pretty young women *(musume gidayū)* was a rage among rudents. As a child Uno had firsthand contact with a *musume gidayū* when one such entertainer rented the second floor of his uncle's house in Sōemonchō.

21. The *yose* was a popular entertainment hall featuring a variety of shows, including *rakugo* (comic monologues), *kōdan* (historical tales recited to the beat of a fan), singing, and magic acts. The *shinuchi,* or the last spot on the program, was reserved for the star attraction, in this case, the *musume gidayū.*

22. Yamaji uses the expression *mizuten-geisha:* a geisha who rolls *(ten)* into bed with a partner without looking at *(mizu)* his face—most undiscriminating indeed.

23. At the time, the "philosophy of idealism" *(risōshugi no tetsugaku),* "democracy" *(minponshugi),* "socialism" *(shakaishugi),* and other partially digested -isms imported from the West were much in vogue among intellectuals.

24. A reference to Ibsen's *The Doll's House,* which was translated into Japanese by Shimamura Hōgetsu in 1911 and staged numerous times in the Shingeki theater. It stimulated great interest with its radical social views.

25. Osome was the daughter of the owner of an oil shop; Hisamatsu was the young clerk with whom she committed love suicide in a storehouse. An article of clothing—a livery coat—figures in the plot of the story of their tragic love affair, which was dramatized in *jōruri* plays by Ki no Kaion (1663–1742) and Chikamatsu Hanji (1725–1783), staged in the kabuki theater by Tsuruya Namboku (1755–1829), and taken up in *shinnai, tokiwazu,* and *kiyomoto* ballads during the late Edo (1600–1868) and early Meiji (1868–1912) periods.

26. The characters *ta* (many) and *fuku* (wealth) in the name *Otafuku* are matched pictorially by the "full storage" of the swelling forehead and fat cheeks of her moon-shaped face—the image of a plain woman. Otafuku masks are borne aloft at festivals, often together with masks of an ugly, comically distorted man's face known as Hyottoko.

Love of Mountains

Yamagoi

P A R T   1

*Far in the north
Snow-white mountains.*
—*Kojima Usui*

I cannot say when my great love of mountains began. Yet when I stop to think about it, it's clear that I've had a predilection for mountains from my earliest childhood; then again, on second thought, I vaguely remember that it all began somewhere when I first saw a certain mountain. Still, my friend may be right when he says, "It grew out of your excessive longing for the mountain country Shinano, where she lives—what was her name again?—that geisha you have been in love with for the last three or four years—a platonic love so rare in this world."

Yumeko, yes, Yumeko!

Who could have known then that I would find such a woman there? Who could have foreseen it? . . . That early autumn day when I chanced to run into a friend, and we happened to talk about taking a trip, and entered a café, and put our heads together over a map, hunting for a good place to visit, and eventually selected that small hot springs town in Shinano.

At that time I truly felt like seeing mountains, those mountains of which Katsu Kaishū says in his poem:

The highest mountains
in the Land of the Rising Sun
are in Shinano
Shinano where the bamboo grass grows.

Their peaks are beyond the clouds
deep in the sky
Birds straining their wings
cannot reach them.
And beasts treading their ore-laden crags
are fain to run.

Their rivers flow at dizzying speeds,
cut deep ravines and
forever threaten their banks
There is no way to ford them.

They mark the place where many
a path must end.

That evening when I boarded the train with my friend my head was filled with visions of a town of bubbling hot springs on the shore of a lake brimming over with blue water, surrounded by high mountains.

As it turned out the real mountain lake didn't hold half the charm I had anticipated. The lake basin was as narrow as a cat's forehead, and the lake itself and the mountains were like an ugly woman, without a single redeeming feature.

"Can't you see the Alps from here? It looks like you can't see the Yatsugatake mountain range either. Can you see Ontake?" I asked the inn clerk. "No, this place is surrounded by mountains, and those beyond are not visible," he explained matter-of-factly.

The scenery was indeed not what I had expected, but then heaven blessed us in another, unexpected way.

The heat had continued oppressively into early fall, and for about a week before our departure we sweltered under a steady spell of temperatures well exceeding those of the height of summer. "What's happening? Usually the heat doesn't bother me much, but this heat! I can't get anything done," I remarked to a friend. And we came to wonder whether it weren't high time to take a trip to a cooler place. And so we did.

It was eleven o'clock at night when our train left the station at Iidamachi.

As you gentlemen know, that line[1] is one of our nation's third-class railroad lines, and the passenger cars are barely more comfortable than freight cars, so we came to regret the reckless-ness of our choice in no time at all. We suffered not only from the lingering heat of the day, but also from the press of the people, and most of all from the smoke, especially when we passed through a tunnel.

We talked about getting off at the next stop each time the heat roused us from the stupor into which we had fallen. And we did go down to the platform each time the train stopped and got a breath of fresh air, but it was so chilly outside after the stifling heat in the coach we were afraid we would catch cold.

The train moved on, southeast to northwest, across Kai province, and at every stop black mountains towered before us as the Milky Way flowed by smokily in the heavens above. And we talked about how hot it was in the coach and yet how cold it felt outside now that we were in mountain country and how it might turn hot again come dawn.

It was still dark when the train passed through Kōfu, but we had endured about all we could, and had made up our minds to turn back at the very next stop, when an unexpectedly large crowd got off, leaving enough room for each of the remaining passengers to lie down. So we decided to stay after all. Exhausted, we slept for several hours.

Dawn broke. It wasn't the light but the sudden chill that woke me.

"It's really cold, isn't it?" I turned to my friend, who was lying on the seat across from me; he too seemed to be wide awake, for he sat up abruptly and said, "What do you mean cold? It's freezing!"

The train stopped. I looked out the window wondering where we were and saw affixed to a pole a white placard with FUJIMI. 3135 FEET ABOVE SEA LEVEL written on it; I felt an indescribable shiver of excitement as I announced this to my friend, who said, pulling at the collar of his kimono, "Yes, it's really mountain country, isn't it? This is mountain country cold. It's certainly different from Tokyo."

The lines dividing the seasons are clearly marked on a calendar. For instance, today may be winter, but turn one page, and spring begins. On a given day of a given month summer ends, and the next day fall begins. In nature, too, it sometimes happens that one single day separates two seasons.

Could it be that the night we left Tokyo, crossed Kai, and headed for Shinano was the beginning of such a day? At any rate, summer seemed to have changed into autumn overnight. But we could hardly imagine it; we thought that the air was so cold simply because we were now in the mountains.

The starry sky that we had seen from our train window the night before was gone. The lake surrounded by low mountains was a picture of gloom; low dark gray clouds were hanging over it.

"It's really cold, isn't it? It's like winter. We'd better find ourselves a good inn."

The cold wind almost froze our lips as we stood talking in the square in front of the station.

True, the mountains and the lake didn't hold half the charm I had expected, but the frosty autumn air, the mountain air, or, at any rate, the unexpected weather was certainly more than welcome.

The drizzling autumn rains kept me indoors most of the two weeks I remained there. My friend had to return to Tokyo, unexpectedly, ahead of time, to take care of some business. So, all alone, I spent the days leaning against the window, looking through the misty rain at the hot springs town below where smoke rising from the many bathhouses wound its way into a boundless gray sky. I could also see the lead-colored lake on the other side of the town, but the nearby mountains were almost invisible.

My inn was located on a hill in the eastern part of the town. And the room I occupied on the third floor was its only eight-mat room. It was a strange room with a window on the west side that framed a panoramic view of the town and the lake. It was five feet high and as wide as the room was long, about twelve feet. Indeed, this window was so unusual, it would have been unusual for the stage setting of a modern realistic drama.

Surely the gods[2] must have wanted me to enjoy this town, the lake, and the mountains all around to have led me to a room with such an extraordinary window through which to view them.

On the south side of the room there was a seven-foot alcove[3] and, in the remaining three feet of wall space, built-in shelves below yet another fairly large, round window. Four papered sliding panels[4] covered the entire east side of the room, separating it from the corridor. A large round window occupied the three feet of wall space at the southern end of the corridor. On the northern side a three-foot wall adjoined the west side, and the remaining three feet of the north side opened onto the outside corridor with two sliding doors. There was in the north corridor yet another, this time rectangular window measuring six by three feet and fitted with sliding glass panels. A diagram illustrating the relation between that room and its windows would look like this:

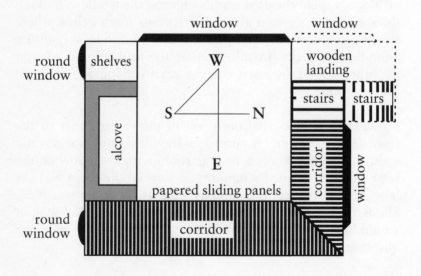

I'd like to add that to go from my room to the second floor I had to open the sliding doors and take a staircase facing west. Five or six steps down was a wooden landing, about three by six feet, and on the west side of this landing another window fitted with glass panes. In other words, the window was located at a height midway between the third floor, where my room was, and the second. That is to say, the second-floor corridor was located six steps down the staircase from the third-floor landing.

As I mentioned earlier, the inn itself was built on the highest ground in town, so my room in this three-story building was in the highest possible spot. In fact, the alarm bell hanging from the top of the fire lookout tower, which was no more than twenty yards away, was no higher than eye level when I sat at the west window.

You gentlemen may get a better idea of the location if I say that my inn was located on the side of a mountain and the watchtower was built on a hill that was the foot of the mountain. But more important than this sort of detail was the influence that this room on the third floor with the many windows had on my life.

Who but the gods could have foreseen it!

For the week or so that I was alone following my friend's departure, the days all began and ended with rain, with one exception. On that day the clouds vanished, and from each and every window, as far as the eye could see, the sky looked as if it had been dyed, it was so bright. As soon as I got up I opened the west window and looked out, opened the round window over the shelves on the south wall, then surveyed the scene from the round window in the corridor on the same side, then from the railing of the east corridor, then peered through the glass panes of the north corridor window, and in this manner made the round of all the windows to take in the whole landscape.

As I said before, the high mountains in that part of the country were blocked from view by the low mountains that surrounded the town; not a single one was visible. As a matter of fact, until recently, even the low mountains had been hidden from view by the rain and were either completely invisible or looked hazy and very far away. But on that day those mountains really surprised me, they appeared so close.

Bedecked with grasses, trees, whole woods, they rose against the blue sky as if they had dressed up expressly for this fine autumn day and had come to my window to pay me a formal call.[5]

Less than a mile from the round window, on the south side, washed in the rain for several days, stood the woods of the Gracious Deity of Suwa—a luxuriant green against the blue of the sky.[6]

"You can't see it from here because of those woods, but on the other side, Mount Fuji, though a bit squeezed in, can be seen peeking through a gap between the mountains that surround the lake." Even the impassive inn clerk seemed to be moved by the fine autumn weather as we stood side by side looking out one of the round windows.

"That mountain. . . ." He spoke leaning against the railing of the east corridor. "As a matter of fact, we're standing on part of it right now, and over there, those terraced fields are another part of it. . . . It rises to the east, and that mountain behind this one, the one covered with evergreens that seems to be leaning to the right . . . between those two mountains. . . ." And then, pointing at a mountain with a round shape that showed a bit of its head, "All the mountains in this region are low, but over

there, in the back, hiding on the other side, are some that are
about five or six thousand feet high, and since this area is already
over two thousand feet above sea level. . . ."

"Is it the Yatsugatake mountain range?"

"No, the Yatsugatake range lies in the opposite direction;
you can't see it from here, but if you go to the train station platform, its peaks are completely. . . ."

Then, looking through the north window, he said to me,
"You can see about two-thirds of the town from here. . . . The
red smokestacks, about two hundred of them, are from the silk-
thread factory. Those stones on the roofs are special to this region; Suwa is famous for them—as well as for its bossy women
and its prostitutes. See that large wood at the foot of the mountain across from us? There are a lot of prostitutes living over
there. And you see that big round mountain above it? That's
Wada pass, one of the passes on the old Nakasendō highway.
There's also a road that goes to places like Ueda and Komoro."

But no matter what he told me, the view from the west window pleased me most. From there Shiojiri pass was also visible. The clerk explained that the Tenryū river, which flowed to
Ōmi, originated in a spot below that pass where the sparkling
lake narrowed. The mountain range on the west end of the
lake did not look quite so high, and Kiso was probably on the
other side.

I had no difficulty imagining the mountains beyond those
mountains, and no matter how often I saw them, I never tired
of looking at them. And as I kept looking, I caught sight of two
peaks shaped like crooked cubes pushed into the sky above the
screen-like range of lower mountains on the west side of the
lake. They were obviously not part of that mountain range.
Not only did they appear to be over three times farther away
and five times taller, but geologically speaking, they seemed to

belong to a different category of mountains. They also seemed to be lined up right next to each other, though they were obviously quite a distance apart. And to say that they were visible behind the mountains surrounding the lake from their shoulders up would not be quite correct. If one wanted to compare them to human figures, it would be more appropriate to say that while all the mountains visible from the six windows of my room were either dark green or dark blue, or green or yellow, those two mountains, or at least their crooked-square peaks, were draped in silver. And they appeared to me—and of course I am not an expert—to be at least ten thousand feet high. When I pointed them out to the clerk and asked him about them, all he could do was tilt his head and say, "Well now, what were those mountains called again? They certainly seem high, don't they? . . . I suppose . . . they're probably part of the Japan Alps."

"Is that Kiso over there?" Then, pointing in the direction of the tall mountain on the left, I asked, "Isn't that Ontake in Kiso?"

"Let's see now . . . it may well be." He tilted his head again. "But I've heard that Ontake can't be seen from here. . . ." And when I asked him, "Are you from another province?" and he answered, "No, I was born in this town," I felt indignant. This man was born here and lived here all his life and didn't even know the names of mountains he had to look at every day.

Later, when I was alone again, I sat motionless for several hours on the sill of the west window and gazed at the lake, and the mountains on its western shore, and the two snow-covered peaks beyond those mountains, and my irritation vanished, and my heart felt cleansed. I felt an indescribable nostalgia welling up, an emotion of the sort a traveler might experience after many years of wandering in strange lands when unexpectedly he sees once again the place he was born.

Actually, I was born in the city, am now thirty years old, and have never lived elsewhere for more than a month. And to say that these past five or six years I well nigh starved is no lie.

But then, isn't it so that many a young man in his twenties or thirties, whether born in a city or not, is interested in little else besides city life, that is, romance and money? And that is my case. And I believe that those among you gentlemen who are my age must feel as I do. Even if I were reduced to living in a garret or even a hovel and eating two instead of three meals a day, I would prefer living in the city: enjoying myself, working, suffering in the city. And the devil take the countryside, all of nature—mountains, lakes, fields. . . .

And yet, what strange things mountains are. Why do they seem to possess such charm, not only for those born in villages surrounded by mountains, but even for people like myself, born and raised in a grimy city? And I believe that I am no exception, either.

Who do you think could walk, on a clear autumn or winter day, in the Yamanote district of Tokyo without stopping and gazing with astonishment at the Chichibu and Nikkō mountain ranges or at the purple slopes of Mount Fuji and Mount Hakone emerging suddenly between the houses and the flatlands? Few indeed!

According to a certain European scholar whom I read recently, this feeling stems from the intimacy with mountains that our primitive ancestors knew and passed down to us through the subconscious from generation to generation.[7]

Seen in this light, you see, I do not mislead you gentlemen when I say that the pleasure of looking at the snow-clad mountains across the lake from the western window in the inn was akin to the nostalgia of seeing one's home village again after a long absence.

Later, I was surprised to learn that those mountains, which seemed to be at least ten thousand feet high, were, next to Mount Fuji, the highest mountains I had ever seen.

On that occasion I also saw, for the first time, a geisha called Yumeko who had a one-year-old child.

Two months later, this time alone, I boarded the train at Iidamachi at eight in the morning. The preceding two months my feelings were in a ferment, and I was intoxicated with love for mountains and for her.

To tell the truth, I had seen her no more than three or four times and all in all hadn't spent more than ten hours with her; and since she was a woman of few words and I was by no means what you would call a talker, we would certainly not have needed more than two phonograph records to record all the words that passed between us.

Her skin was dark and her hair so curly that her chignon was always crooked; her face was misshapen, and to top it all she had a baby, and so on, and so on. Were her defects enumerated, they would probably outnumber her good points three to one. But as my elementary school teacher used to say, "A person's face and figure, no matter how ill formed, always reveal the heart within."

The mood that her tall, slender figure and bowed head inspired in me was, in a word, romantic; but if there was one feature that could have undermined this overall romantic effect, it was the shape of her mouth.

Ye gods, have pity on her and me!

Later I came to realize that of all the men and women I have known since the day I was born or, as the saying goes, of all the people in this world born of women, I have never met anyone who so refrained from talking about herself and gossiping about other people. She appeared to be silence itself—silence that is the poet's ultimate form.

Some people may say, Given your feelings, what you say about her is no surprise. And they may be half right since, as another old saw goes, love lends the lover the eyes with which he sees his beloved.

The gods are my witnesses: I had no designs on her when I made that second trip. I wasn't wondering how I was going to redeem a woman who was not a bonded geisha but the daughter of a family that operated a geisha house; nor was I wondering what kind of man fathered her child; far from it, I simply wanted to see her. Her and the mountains!

And that is why I chose to take the 8:00 A.M. train. And this time, the thought of the land that lay on the other side of the pass made even the discomfort of having to inhale the smoke when passing through the many long tunnels at Kobotoke and Sasago enjoyable.

However, when we emerged from the Sasago tunnel, the smoke inside the train was so thick that I could barely make out the faces of the people next to me. Suffocating, I raced the other passengers to open a window to let it out. . . . And there before my eyes, in between the wisps of white steam that hung suspended in the air before gradually disappearing, stretched out under a high, perfectly clear, and boundless autumn sky, lay the broad Kōfu basin shaped like the bottom of a dredged pond. Behind the mountains enclosing the basin on the south was Mount Fuji with its familiar peak visible from the shoulders up. And when I looked to the west toward the mountains that bounded the land of Shinano toward which I was heading, I let out a second cry of delight.

What looked exactly like a folding screen was surely the so-called Kaigane mountain range of Kai province. I didn't know their names at the time, but they certainly caught my eye before anything else, those three snow-capped mountains that towered above that screen-like range. They were lined up from south to north in ascending order of height. I was especially impressed by the resemblance they bore to a picture of the European Alps that I had purchased at a bookstore on the Ginza and pinned on the brown wall of the room in my rooming house about a month before. In the photo, Jungfrau, Eiger, and Mönch were lined up from right to left like the panorama before my eyes.

What was the name again of the mountain that looks like Eiger?

In "Travel through Ravines" Butsu Sorai writes, "Nōuma, Nōushi, Hōō, Jizō, and Komagatake stand in a row. The first two, higher than the rest, are called the 'white peaks.' Just to look at their rugged slopes fills one with awe. Each winter snow falls on their tops, whitening their forests and so hiding them from view."[8] Is it not this very scene that he describes? If so, then are those mountains Nōuma, Nōushi, Hōō, Jizō, and Komagatake?

Later I found that the three mountains were, from south to north, Nōtoridake, Ainodake, and Kitadake. Kitadake, also called Kaigane, was after Mount Fuji the highest mountain on the Japanese island of Honshu.

After that, in the three or four hours that remained before we reached Fujimi, I went to the companionway of the coach and opened the doors on both sides to look at the passing landscape so often that the conductor had to admonish me several times.

The train passed Kōfu, and as it approached the region around Hinoharu the scene outside the left window sent me into ecstacy. A dizzying ravine dropped at a steep angle on the left side of the railroad tracks; that is, the train was running along the top of a natural dike (it could not possibly have been man-made) that bordered a large ravine. A stream rushed along the bottom of the ravine where the slope of the dike ended. According to the map, it was the Kamanashi river. The steep slope that plunged from the railroad tracks to the Kamanashi was covered with fields and a scattering of small villages. But the bank on the other side of the river was no mere slope, not even a large dike, but literally a perpendicular cliff that stood on its end, straight as a stick or, if you prefer, an upright folding screen.

As I said, the train was high up. Even the Kamanashi river at the bottom of the valley, if measured from sea level, could hardly be thought of as low; but that mountain on the opposite bank was something else. It shot up as straight as can be, something like ten thousand feet.

It was Kai-Komagatake, and Kai-Komagatake is 9,780 feet high.

From the train window one could see to the left, behind Kai-Komagatake, several mountain peaks that, while not as high as Kai-Komagatake, were by no means low. They were probably Hōō, Jizō, and Okusenjō. I also spotted behind them, outlined in black against the evening sun, stretching far away to the south, what was probably the highest mountain range in Japan.

Although my eyes wandered over other peaks, they were invariably drawn back to the astonishing Kai-Komagatake thrusting its full figure right before us, as Danjūrō would, stepping onto the kabuki stage. Indeed, it seemed as if the other mountains were totally eclipsed, as if they were literally hidden in its shadow.

At any rate, Kai-Komagatake was closer to us than the other mountains, and it stood there baring its grotesque shape to our view, showing off the nearly ten thousand feet of its fantastic mass from the bottom up, bathing its foothills in the Kamanashi river as its distorted top, draped with snow down to its shoulders, peered over the heads of the other mountains and down at the land of Shinano next door.

It was evening, and on our side of the Kamanashi river lavender smoke rose from the solitary houses that dotted the bank in the gathering dusk. Only the swiftly flowing river was visible, an undulating trail of white against black. From where we sat, facing the setting sun, the greater part of Kai-Komagatake, as well as the other mountains, was stained by dark shadows, but its snow-hooded peak rising above all else caught the rays of the setting sun and was mottled red, violet, and blue. To the left, in the direction from which we had come, Mount Fuji, which was at an angle to the sun, glittered gold against the towering pale purple peaks of the screen-like range marking the border of Suruga.

That evening I arrived in the town that I had already come to consider my second home, though I had spent but ten days there, and was once again a guest on the third floor of my favorite inn. Led to my room after the sun had gone down, the first thing I did before changing my clothes was stand at the large west window and look into the darkness where both the distant lake and the screen of mountains surrounding it were black shapes under the starry sky.

The fitful flickering of lights like fireflies (yet not a fifth or even a tenth as many as there are in Tokyo) engulfed in the pitch black made me feel so lonely that I felt like crying. And then those lights, and the scattered sounds of musical instruments, and the singing and the din from the entertainment quarters near my inn, and the clamor from the public baths, brought to mind the goings-on in all those lively, crowded places.

And then I wondered what the geisha Yumeko was doing. . . .

This time I ended up staying in that town for nearly two months. It was my intention to restrain myself as best I could during that period and to meet with Yumeko only once every two days. I hesitated to call on her in the morning or the afternoon, even though she was a professional geisha, for even a geisha under contract needs her morning sleep, and time to herself to relax, and have her hair done, and visit the bathhouse. And how much truer was this in the case of a geisha like Yumeko, who had to take over and manage an independent geisha house when her stepmother was absent. I was even more loath to impose on her time when I thought about her one-year-old child, whom she had to nurse once in the evening and again when the child woke up before midnight. Surely it was more convenient for her not to go out in the evening. And yet, on the nights I did not call her, I found it difficult to settle down to my own work and read and write. I don't know how often I got up and circled my room looking out each of the six windows, in the east, west, south, and north.

Cloudy nights and clear nights alike, the black mountains and the lake outside my window bore the same expression. And on the days when I rewarded my patience of the day before and called her, I spent the afternoon looking out each of the six windows in turn because from the time lunch was over I was too nervous to sit down. The cold was gradually becoming very severe, and when I got chilled standing at the windows, I jumped into the bubbling hot springs bath, and from the bath went back to the windows. At that time of the year the sky was clear practically every day, and from the east window the tall forms of two mountains were always visible on the other side of the folding-screen range that bordered the lake. I had prepared a rough map of Shinano, which I kept on my desk, and after studying the positions of the various mountains in relation to the location of my room, I came to believe that the higher of the two mountains on the right was Ontake of Kiso. After some more checking, I decided that the mountain to the left was probably Komagatake, also in Kiso, although its location was a little different from what it should have been according to the map. And so I concluded that the two mountains were Ontake and Komagatake. The peaks of Ontake and Komagatake visible from my windows were completely covered with snow, as they had been before, but as the days passed they came to gleam like ice. They seemed to be not mountains of ordinary earth and rock but mountains of ice polished at night by an unseen hand as day by day they turned bluer and brighter than a sword.

One day an unfamiliar young man came to visit me. Though I say a young man, he was no more than two or three years younger than I, a man of about twenty-seven or twenty-eight, with a moustache. Evidently he had read stories of mine that had been published some time ago in magazines, and hearing that the author of those stories was in an inn in the same town, he had come to meet me. The calling card that the maid brought in when she announced that I had a caller bore neither address nor title, nothing but the strange name Nishimukai Kanzan.

"How do you pronounce your last name? It's rather unusual, isn't it?" I asked.

Embarrassed, he put his hand to his head of thick unkempt hair parted carelessly down the middle and said, "Yes, it's pronounced Ni-shi-mu-ka-i. . . ."

I thought that Nishimukai was probably his artist's name, but didn't question him any further about it. Moving on to other matters, I learned that he was a professional engraver of seals, that he had been born in Kōfu, that his father was operating a seal shop in Kōfu, and that he had worked there until three or four years ago. But when business fell off and his father's shop could no longer support both of them, he had joined an electric power company and, after spending six months in a training school, was now working at the transformer substation located in that town.

A large, square foot warmer[9] was sunk into the floor in the middle of the room according to the custom of the region. I was seated in my usual spot on the east side of the foot warmer, warming my feet and hands. The large west window was fitted with four sliding paper panels with large glass insets, and from where I sat I could enjoy the scenery outside as I warmed myself.

When the maid led Nishimukai Kanzan into the room and I invited him to sit across from me, on the west side, he modestly declined and seated himself formally on the north side, several feet away from the foot warmer. As I mentioned earlier, he spoke briefly about himself, then asked me about my novels and talked about his own work. When I say his work, I don't mean his job at the power company, but the seal engraving that he had done since he was a child and that he did even now whenever he had any free time. It was something about which I knew little, but I admired his earnestness and joy when he talked about it. Indeed, he reminded me of myself, of the way I felt when I talked about literature or art. But if I were to say what impressed me most, it would be the general madcap effect created by his thick brows and short nose.

More than an hour had passed since he came, and I had urged him repeatedly to come closer to the foot warmer. "I could talk to you more easily if you were not so far away. Won't you come closer and warm your hands and feet? How about it? You won't be able to reach your cup from there when we have tea." Finally he bowed his head politely and crawled on all fours to the north side of the foot warmer. "Well, then, if I may. . . ."

At the time, although there was not yet much snow in the town, the nearby mountains, including the low-lying ones, were covered with a heavy snowfall, and as he seated himself, he reacted with sudden astonishment to the spacious scene visible through the glass of the west window. "Oh, we are higher than I imagined," he exclaimed in his small voice. Turning toward me, he excused himself and started to sit down, then got up again and moved toward the window. I rose and accompanied him.

Since, as I have said repeatedly, it was a large window with a western exposure, the sun came streaming in every afternoon. And to ward off the summer rays there was an awning that could be lowered by releasing the rope of the pulley attached to the left side of the window frame. I had lowered the awning little by little as the sun moved toward the west. In general, I dislike it when the sun shines in my room, even on a cold winter day. But now, so as to take in the view together with my guest, I pulled the awning with the rope. The pulley squeaked as the awning moved up under the eaves, and the town, the lake, the screen-like mountain range on the western shore, and, behind it, two tall mountains rising steeply and with icy sharpness emerged under a blue sky with a glittering radiance that pierced the eye.

"I can see Ontake!" Nishimukai shouted unexpectedly.

"So that is Ontake of Kiso?" I chimed in joyfully. "It must be that one on the left. And the mountain on the right, is that Komagatake?" "No, it's Norikura." Nishimukai's eyes were blinking under his thick brows at the dazzling sight.

His expression was so blissful that I asked him, "Do you like mountains too?"

"Yes, I love them. I'm rather unusual that way. No matter how irritable or even angry I am, all I have to do is look at a mountain for those feelings to vanish completely."

"Yes, your name is Kanzan—'Mountain Gazing,' isn't it?" I observed.

"Oh, that?" He scratched his head in embarrassment.

"I too like the sight of mountains, in fact more than food." And as I said this, like him, I too was blinking to shield my eyes from the light. "The people around here are really something. They don't even know that the mountain over there is Ontake. Then again, it may be just the inn clerk who is so ignorant. I had to find out on my own what it was by consulting maps. But I feel twice as happy now that you've confirmed it for me."

"Do you really like mountains that much?" Pleasure rang in Kanzan's voice. "If you like, I'll take you to the generator station about two miles up the mountain behind us, where my friend is on duty. You can see those mountains far better, clear from the shoulders up."

"Is that so? By all means, please take me there."

Eventually we returned to the foot warmer and were exchanging opinions on a variety of topics when he suddenly asked me, "Are you interested in music?" What was he thinking of?

"By music do you mean the violin, or the koto, or songs? That sort of music?" I asked. "I can't play anything myself, but I like music very much. Do you like it?"

"I don't know why, but that sort of pastime is the only thing I care about. Especially instrumental music. I like it more than eating." Nishimukai spoke as though he were confessing to something shameful. "I'm often mocked by people for liking strange things, like literature, painting, and seal carving, things that they say lead nowhere. When I think about it, it seems they may be right, but then I like each in its own way. The engraving of seals that I mentioned first is an art I inherited from my father, and while I by no means dislike it, one might say that I like it the way one likes a young woman to whom one has been betrothed in childhood or, perhaps worse, the way one likes a wife one can't get rid of. Now, if I had to say which, I seem to have come to dislike it more than I like it."

"But didn't you say that you still sometimes engrave seals?" I asked.

"Yes, and therefore it would seem that I like it after all." He scratched his head (this was evidently a habit of his) and looked embarrassed. "I can't get by on the monthly salary the company pays me, so I engrave seals on the side to earn extra money. . . . Actually, though, I much prefer literature. But no matter how much I like literature, a person like me could not even hope to give it a try. I enjoy reading anything that I can get my hands on, but I'm poor and can't buy books the way I'd like to, and so it's really a case of unrequited love."

" 'Unrequited love,' that's an interesting way of putting it."

I was becoming more and more interested in what this visitor had to say. "How about mountains? That too is a kind of unrequited love, isn't it?" Though he was now speaking more informally with me, at times his tone was curiously formal and reserved. "In spite of my love of mountains, I'm lazy, and my legs are weak, and living as I do, I haven't any free time, so I've never climbed a mountain that can really be called high. Is that your case too, Sensei? As I said, every other day I visit the electric generator station on the mountain behind us and spend the day looking at the mountains, but that's about all the climbing I do. And unlike you, Sensei, I have never traveled outside my homeland of Shinshū, so I don't know anything about the mountains in other places. . . ."

"Well, but you play a lot of music, don't you?" I asked. "What kind of music do you play? Do you play an instrument? Or sing?"

"Oh no. I wouldn't say that I can play. . . ." He looked bashful again. "As for singing, as you can see, I have a short nose; my ear is not so bad, but because of my nose I can't carry a tune. Well . . . I can sing a little bit after a fashion, but . . . on the other hand, I've tried my hand on a variety of musical instruments. I've played the samisen, and I put in a few years on the koto. I also play the violin and the *shakuhachi* flute, though only a little. . . ."

That evening I invited Yumeko to join us, and after the three of us had eaten dinner, I asked, "Mr. Nishimukai, won't you play something for us? You don't have to sing, we'll have Yumeko sing something." But he had been unusually quiet ever since Yumeko joined us, and no matter how often I urged him, he adamantly refused and would not even look at the samisen. It may have been because I had fallen silent after Yumeko came and my speechlessness had infected him. As for Yumeko, she sat looking down at the floor as she always did, and when I urged Nishimukai to play and Yumeko to sing, while he wouldn't even pick up the samisen, she said in a barely audible voice, as a very young girl would, "I can't sing anything. . . ."

Eventually Nishimukai got ready to leave.

"Well then, Sensei, how about it? Will you try going up the mountain with me the day after tomorrow?"

"Yes, anytime is fine with me, but what about you? Will it interfere with your work?" I asked.

"We're on the relay system, and I'm due for time off the day after tomorrow," he said. "I came to see you today instead of going up the mountain, so the person up there is probably waiting for me."

"There's a woman on the mountain?"

"No, a man," he said, scratching his head again.

On the day we had agreed to meet, shortly after noon, Nishimukai Kanzan came to take me up the mountain. As it often is in the highlands, the winter sky was so clear that sounds echoed for miles around. Yet I was concerned because it had snowed, even if only lightly, two nights ago, the evening he had left for home.

"How are the mountain roads after a snowfall?"

"Above the generator station no one but hunters and post-men dare walk, but below it a little snow doesn't make much difference," Nishimukai said. In spite of what he said, however, he was wearing a pair of snowshoes, the kind used by most of the people in the area.

"Does one have to wear that kind of shoe?"

"No, your everyday shoes are fine. I assure you."

We walked down the path in front of the inn and came out on a street; turning right we passed a restaurant, a geisha house, the town's sole photography studio, and a notions shop all in a row. When we had gone about a block down the fairly lively street, we came to a fork in the road. From that point on, the road to the left, an extension of the street we had been walking on, sloped downhill. There were but a few houses on the road to the right; the road to the left seemed to be more a part of the town; there were stepping-stones running alongside it. The road to the right, which we took, climbed almost imperceptibly; that is, it led up into the mountains.

I had heard, five or six days before, that Yumeko's house was on the left side of that road, where it branched off from the main street, and I now tried to see if I could identify it. As we reached the high grounds, an old house on a stone foundation and a gate lantern with the inscription "House of Dreams" on it came into view. Without thinking, I tugged at the sleeve of my companion walking beside me.

"That house," I said gesturing with my chin. "That's the house of the geisha who was with us the day before yesterday."

"Yes, I know, the House of Dreams." He sounded as if he had known it for the past ten years, which after all was only natural. He was a resident of the town, and there was no reason why he shouldn't have known it.

I felt myself blushing.

What must he think of my flustered behavior? Worse yet, what if Yumeko had seen my obvious embarrassment from inside the house? Instinctively I began to walk faster.

From that point on, the road was covered with snow that had accumulated over a number of days; it wasn't snow that had frozen and turned to ice but snow that had simply failed to melt and that had remained as it was, pure white, like a white cloth spread on the ground.

I knew well how snow looks in the city. It may be piled up half a foot on the roofs and remain three weeks in the corners of gardens and in hollows where the sun doesn't shine, yet the morning after a heavy fall, even if it is a foot high where people haven't walked, it is always full of mud and trodden to slush in the streets. One may also see it as transforming the city into a sort of woodblock print, with the white parts being places where the snow is piled up and the black areas where there is none, such as fences, pagodas, and chimneys. But here, though in a sense it was the same snow, it was completely different. It was packed hard, as in the streets in town, and sharply marked by wheel tracks, yet the entire surface was pure white without a speck of dirt or even the shadow of a speck. It felt as if we were walking on refined sugar. The mountains above the valley as well as the cliff beyond the valley were the same immaculate white, as if they too were covered with sugar.

The road we were walking on was, as I said earlier, actually a mountain path used mainly by children who lived in villages higher up and who day after day walked to and from the school at the foot of the mountain.

Tired, and already wanting to go back to the town we had left behind, I stopped climbing and looked back about every ten paces, and each time we came to a bend in the road, and each time we approached a rise with a good view.

The road passed along the top of a cliff flanking the valley so that we never lost sight of Suwa at the bottom of the valley, or the lake, or the mountains that surrounded the lake.

That landscape too was altogether unlike even the outskirts of a city, which on a morning after a heavy snowfall tends to look like a dark-skinned girl with a coat of white makeup.

The snow in Suwa was like the pure white skin of a maiden. There was no pattern of black and white. There was nothing but pure white. And so while the sky above was a stunning blue and as clear as can be, the world below was the muted color of a city in the middle of a snowstorm. The hundred or so smokestacks, standing like a grove of trees, were ash gray, and the color of the water of the lake about to freeze was gray.

The mountains on the other side of the lake were more heavily laden with snow than the snow-capped mountains of miniature landscape trays, and they sparkled under the blue sky with a whiteness that gleamed whiter than white. But what immediately caught my eye were the shapes of two tall mountains across from the mountains by the lake.

No, Nishimukai had not lied. Those mountains began to reveal more of themselves with each step I took. It was just as he had said; I could see twice as much as I could from my room on the third floor of the inn. I had never imagined such beautiful mountain scenery. It was magnificent, no, sublime beyond description. It was so splendid that, unable to take my eyes off it, I turned around after each step and, finally disregarding the slippery footing of the snow path altogether, began walking backward the way children sometimes do. When the path turned in a direction from which the view was blocked, I ran to the next bend, where I would be able to see it again. At last the two mountains came into view, revealing not only their peaks of polished ice, exposing themselves not only from their shoulders up, but showing everything, from their sides, bare of snow, to their very tops. I even became conscious of the twenty or forty miles of air separating the two mountains from the mountains encircling the lake. I don't know how many times I exclaimed aloud, "That's Ontake! That's Ontake of Kiso!" as I looked in their direction. "And that's Norikura!"

"Yes," Nishimukai answered. "And to the right of Norikura, too far from here for the likes of us to go, you can see Hotaka and Yarigatake and other mountains of the Japan Alps all in a line, if you climb another mile and a half from the generator station to the path that leads to Wada pass."

"You mean we can't go there now?" I asked.

"No, we can't. We would have to plan it carefully. We would have to have a good guide, snow leggings, and snowshoes as the people around here wear. . . ."

"Which means we can't go at all," I sighed.

At last Nishimukai said, "We're almost at the station—one more turn after this next one coming up. There's a splendid view sitting at the foot warmer in the caretaker's quarters. The air is warm because of the engines, and there's a fire in the hearth too, so we'll go in and warm ourselves."

The station gate consisted of nothing but two black poles, not even a fence. As we passed through it, a small man emerged from a building and approached us from the far side of a broad expanse of flat land that was probably a vegetable garden in the summer.

"This is my friend Horito," Nishimukai introduced him to me.

"I have heard your name often. It's good of you to have come." I couldn't tell how old Horito was; he was strangely withered, yet his face was quite childlike.

"Please come this way." He led us toward the generator station.

Incessantly churning engines that made an unearthly racket took up half the building. "Quite a busy place," I said.

"Oh no, since the silk-thread factories in the area are idle, only half of these machines are in operation." As Nishimukai was explaining this to me, Horito bustled about, checking the fire in the fireplace and making tea. "As a matter of fact, as you saw on your way here," Nishimukai explained, "when winter sets in, most of the mountain creeks freeze over, so naturally there is less water in the waterfalls, which makes them freeze more easily, so that we have quite a time managing here. The electric lights in your room at the inn, Sensei, are dim because of reduced hydroelectric power in the winter."

I barely heard his explanation, for I was peering here and there through the glass window looking for Ontake of Kiso, but I couldn't see anything that resembled it. "Where is Ontake?" I asked, unable to control my impatience any longer.

"You can't see it from here," Nishimukai answered, "unless you go to that residence hall over there. . . ."

Then he turned to Horito and said, "He would like to see Ontake. How about asking Nakao to come and watch things while we go over there?"

"I was just thinking the same thing," replied Horito, and he set out for the Japanese-style house that stood at a right angle to the station. Soon Horito's associate Nakao came over to greet us. He was a pale youth about the same age as Nishimukai and Horito.

"Horito is tidying up over there right now, so please wait a minute," he said, sitting down by the hearth next to us.

"Excuse us for calling you over during your break," Nishimukai said to Nakao.

"Don't mention it. I wasn't doing much of anything anyway."

Eventually, led by Horito, Nishimukai and I set out for the Japanese-style residence hall. It was one half of a duplex; the other half appeared to be vacant, for the door was shut. The bare, shabby apartment consisted of a small room and a tiny entryway with the cheapest of straw mats on the floor. Welcoming teacups had been laid out on a white cloth that had been spread over the dirty quilt covering the foot warmer. Horito, who was small and slender, boiled water and prepared tea with the graceful, attentive gestures of a kabuki female impersonator. So, in the beginning, while Nishimukai and I sat across from each other at the foot warmer and talked, he did not join us but hustled and bustled all about the small apartment. I left my seat and opened one of the sliding screens. A deep valley stretched out into the distance: at one end was the town of Suwa, and on the far side of the town were the lake and the mountains bounding the lake, and beyond those mountains, jutting boldly into the blue sky, Ontake and Norikura.

"Sensei, can you see the mountains?" Nishimukai called from behind.

"I can see them well."

For a long while I was so enraptured that I forgot the cold. The valley, the town, the lake, the mountains by the lake, even Ontake and Norikura, all lay beneath my feet. There were other mountains too that appeared to be even taller, but no matter; these two mountains could not be described any other way than as reaching beyond heaven itself.

"Did you bring the flute today?" I heard Horito's voice behind me by the foot warmer. He was addressing Nishimukai.

"I brought it," Nishimukai replied in a low voice.

At last I turned toward them and walked back to the foot warmer. "By flute do you mean a *shakuhachi?*" I asked Nishimukai. "Did you actually bring such a thing with you?"

"Yes," answered Nishimukai, with typical embarrassment.

This brought to mind his: "I like music more than food." It also reminded me of what I saw when I entered Horito's lodgings. There was practically no furniture, only a secondhand desk and an old-fashioned bookcase; but musical instruments were everywhere: a koto leaning against the wall in the entryway, a samisen and a violin hanging on the wall. . . . So, I said to myself, here are two individuals who must share a complete devotion to music. I realized that though Nishimukai knew the path well, he was hardly likely to make the trip to the station on his days off unless there was a special reason, and that his trekking up the mountains every other day was in some way related to those musical instruments.

"Horito, do you play too?" I asked.

"Yes." Horito spoke clearly and firmly, with none of the shyness displayed by Nishimukai. "Yes, Mr. Nishimukai is my teacher."

"Won't you please play something for me?" I urged.

"Well, I'm not very good at it, but. . . ." Horito was about to begin.

"No, no, that won't do at all. It's nothing for him to listen to." Nishimukai the teacher covered his face with his hands in embarrassment and simply would not let Horito play.

"You wouldn't play for me the day before yesterday when the geisha came, would you?" I said.

Of course, I didn't have to bring up this incident at that point, but my longings for her and the town were such that I couldn't help it. "Naturally you may not feel like playing when a geisha like that sings. . . ."

"No, that's not it at all." Nishimukai spoke as though he were apologizing from the bottom of his heart. "I felt self-conscious because she's a first-class geisha in these parts."

"Which geisha are you talking about?" Horito struck a coquettish pose as he asked.

"Miss Yumeko. She and Kotaki are considered outstanding around here." As he said this Nishimukai thrust forth his short little nose.

"Oh, don't be so modest, play," I urged him again.

"Why shouldn't we play?" Evidently Horito was quite eager to begin. He spoke in a low voice and tugged at the sleeve of his teacher.

"All right, then. But please, Sensei, don't laugh. You understand that we're very poor at this."

It took Nishimukai a considerable amount of time to make up his mind. But once they stopped talking and started to perform, they played one piece after another without tiring. They played so much that in the end I got bored. Horito played only the violin, while Nishimukai switched instruments continuously. For the first piece, he had Horito help him carry in the koto from the entryway.

The sight of Nishimukai, who suffered because of the shortness of his nose, and Horito, who struck coquettish poses as a woman would, carrying in an instrument like the koto, which seemed to have no visible connection with them, was more than comic, it was eerie.

"It's a little out of tune. Will you help me tune it?" Nishimukai had asked Horito to assist him. Turning the side of his short nose toward me and splaying his arms and legs like a carpenter at work, he tightened the strings and moved the bridges up and down the face of the koto with a hand as deft as a young girl's; yet he looked more like a stagehand handling a prop.

Noting that the koto seemed to be an Ikuta, rare in eastern Japan, where the Yamada type was more popular, I asked, "Say, is that an Ikuta?" "Yes, it's an Ikuta. Oh, you know a lot about the koto, don't you?"

And to my, "I didn't ask her, but I'm sure that the geisha Yumeko we met the other day said that she plays an Ikuta. . . ."

Nishimukai replied, as he tuned his instrument, "Quite likely she does. Her teacher is probably the same as mine, a music teacher who comes here from the Kyoto area once every three years and stays and teaches for six months at a time."

All the while we talked, Nishimukai was busy tuning his koto, making adjustments here and there among the thirteen bridges, and Horito, nearby, was testing the strings of his violin, setting up a nickel-plated music stand, and doing the various other things that had to be done before the performance could begin. At last, at Nishimukai's "Hatsu!" the violin and koto duet, "Lingering Moonlight," began.

In bearing and in appearance, Nishimukai seemed a totally different person. Nothing remained of the man who earlier had carried the koto into the room or the man who had been adjusting its strings. The madcap expression, the short nose, the inordinately heavy brows, the back arched like a cat's, all escaped notice. As the old saying goes, "There was nothing but the music." The player as well as the instrument, the cheap old koto, had ceased to exist. Of course, making a special effort, one might still have seen the upper half of Nishimukai's body and his wildly agitated fingers racing in circles, monkey-like, on the strings of the koto, and his disciple Horito, the violinist, usually so concerned about cutting a graceful figure, bent over his sheet music, his small, womanish body rocked into disarray by the wild movement of his bow hand. But all in all it was truly marvelous to behold. On top of a snow-covered mountain in the thatched watchman's hut of an electric generator station, far from any other human habitation, two youths were literally dancing with their musical instruments like characters in a Namiroku novel.[10] Or, if you prefer, two youths were bewitched into complete abandon and submission to the music of magical instruments left behind and forgotten on the mountain a long time ago.

As tobacco smoke filled the room I opened wide the sliding panel in the corridor. Looking westward in the direction of On-take, I saw that the rapidly sinking sun had turned the icy snow on its top and on the peak of nearby Norikura a rosy red. Nishimukai was playing a west country song on the samisen. As I listened to the melody, my desire to be in the town at the foot of the mountain grew stronger, and I became agitated. I waited for the moment when he would pause, and said, "Mr. Nishimukai, it's gotten rather late. Shouldn't we be going back? If you have time, I'd like both you and Mr. Horito to come to my inn. We can call Kotaki and Yumeko, and you can play for all of us."

At first, Nishimukai held back as usual, reluctant to accept my invitation, but eventually he agreed to come; it was decided that Horito would ask Nakao to take over his shift so that he could come too. There was no need to take along the samisen since the geishas could provide one, and they could borrow a koto from either Yumeko or the daughter of the Heart of the Lake Pavilion restaurant, who was a fellow music student of Nishimukai's; and there were sure to be places where one could borrow a violin or two, so Nishimukai took only the *shakuhachi* flute, which he inserted in his obi under the cloak. Horito donned a large, baggy inverness that he had borrowed from Nakao, and the three of us trudged down the mountain road to town. I was most eager to see the town again and to see Yumeko, and at the same time, not knowing when I would come back, I couldn't help but regret having to leave behind the sight of On-take and Norikura bathed in the light of the sinking sun, now rapidly disappearing behind the mountains encircling the lake.

About halfway down the mountain, Nishimukai called, "Sensei . . . Sensei . . . may I ask you a favor?"

It sounded as if he were having difficulty talking about something that was worrying him.

"It's about Horito. . . . He can't see himself working as a watchman at the generator station for the rest of his life. . . . It's understandable, isn't it? He's only nineteen years old. He wants very badly to go to Tokyo and study music under a better teacher. He's willing to work as a houseboy in some teacher's home, or he could join some musical group as a junior member. In fact he's willing to do anything. Sensei, you know so many people, could you please help him find a suitable position? . . ."

"I don't know all that many people, and I don't know any musicians, really, but I'll keep my eyes and ears open. But don't depend on me too much, please. What about you, Mr. Nishimukai? Don't you feel like going to Tokyo?"

"Yes, sort of." As usual he looked embarrassed. "I would go anytime if I could, but I am a lot older than Horito, and I'm really a seal engraver . . . but I'd certainly like to go. . . ."

The path took a sudden turn, and the lake and the mountains on the far side of the valley that had been hidden for a time spread out before us again. Sorry to have to leave Ontake and Norikura, I said half jokingly, "You wouldn't be able to see the mountains if you went to Tokyo."

"If I could go, I wouldn't mind even if I couldn't see the mountains," he replied with complete seriousness. When we came down the mountain, we went first to my inn to bathe and rest, and then because it wouldn't do to play music in my room, we went to the Heart of the Lake Pavilion for our dinner party. Nishimukai and Horito invited Yumeko, of course, and Kotaki of the House of the Three Springs to the Heart of the Lake Pavilion to play with them that evening. Why do I make it a point to mention the name of the geisha Kotaki, you ask?

Today, four years after that evening, through some strange karma, Kotaki has become my wife. And now, as then, my love for Yumeko, whom I loved more than any other woman in the world, and who had a one-year-old child at the time, is just as strong. (Yumeko's child is probably already four years old.)

The following year in April Kotaki came down from the mountains of Shinano to Tokyo to become my wife; it was the year of the big festival held every seven years in Suwa to honor the Shining Deity, the deity of the grove surrounding the shrine that I saw from my room on the third floor of the inn, through the two round windows facing south.

When you entered the shrine precincts, surrounded by cryptomeria trees, and went around the main building to the back, you came on four large cryptomeria tree trunks stripped bare of limbs and bark, standing upright in a rectangular formation. Those four pillars were replaced in May of every seventh year, when a festival was held to commemorate the event. And since it happened but once every seven years, not only the whole town celebrated, but people came from miles around; even those who had only heard the name of the deity came. They came with their guests, wore festive dress, brought festive food, and all sorts of other festive things.

Yes, even an outsider like me could see what excitement this festival generated.

It may be that I just failed to notice, but, normally when I looked out the round window on the south side, it seemed that aside from a few people who took shortcuts across the shrine yard or an occasional baby-sitter or a child who came to play, hardly anyone ever set foot in the cryptomeria grove by the shrine. But now, although the grove and the area behind the shrine appeared to be the same as before, I never failed to see people there. Lately, five or six men wearing livery coats, shoes, and felt hats had been walking in the grove, examining the trees. On another occasion, a party of government officials, dressed in Western-style clothes and accompanied by three policemen, were walking to and fro on the grounds, discussing something very intently. Then, on each of the five or six street corners visible from my west window, I noticed long chests of varying shapes and sizes decorated with strips of white paper.[11]

According to the head clerk, they were there for the Parade of Chests, which was held during the Pillar Festival. Each ward in town had a chest, and each village had several apiece, which the inhabitants decorated to suit their own distinctive tastes and then paraded through the town on their shoulders. Sometimes the line of chests extended as far as two or three blocks. And from my west and north windows I could see the two hundred factory chimneys belching forth black smoke day and night. The mill hands, male and female, were probably working far into the night to get time off during the festival.

Toward the end of the day, in fact, every evening, I heard coming from below my third-floor window a dozen or so strange voices singing in unison a strange song that resembled a workman's song.[12] Because of the height of my room (as high as a pagoda), and the roofs of the town, and the darkness, I could not clearly distinguish the figures moving about down below. It seemed that the villagers who had come to town for the festival, which took place but once in seven years, were rehearsing their roles in it. Those who were supposed to carry chests suspended from poles were carrying chests on poles, those who were supposed to sing were singing, and so on. And then there were the townspeople. I had seen them a number of evenings already, mostly tradesmen, coopers, carpenters, and fishmongers carrying spears and chests suspended from poles. They devoted their free time to rehearsing their roles in the daimyo's parade, which was considered the main attraction of the festival.[13] And there was the bonfire in the shrine grove, which I saw one evening looking through the round window on the south side, and the clamor that rose from the people gathered around it.

There simply was no way to ignore this gala event. Each and every conversation in town was about or shifted in no time to that topic.

The head clerk of the inn said to me, "Sensei, even if you return to Tokyo, I'll be sure to wait for you to come back in May, and I'll reserve this room for you. In May the geisha will be five times as busy as they are now, especially the ones you've been patronizing, Yumeko and Kotaki. They'll spend about five minutes at a party of regular customers, but if they don't know the customer . . . he, he, he, he. I'm joking. Naturally they'll stay with you ten or twenty minutes even if they're wanted elsewhere."

"Will you be staying on for the festival?" the postal employee whom I had come to know by sight asked me. "It comes but once in seven years, so it's bound to be a big affair. The last time we celebrated it I was just a runny-nosed kid of fifteen; my father was still alive then. We were managing all right, and I was planning to go to Tokyo to attend a university; I never dreamed that I would end up working for the post office; I'll be thirty at the time of the next festival, and who can tell what will happen in the meantime."

Indeed, I thought to myself. . . .

At the last festival, Yumeko, who is about the same age as this postal worker, was probably still an apprentice geisha. Who could have foreseen then that she would be the mother of a child at the time of the next festival?

Every seven years these townspeople are given the opportunity to reflect on the past and think about the future. Seven years may seem like a long time, or it may seem to pass by all too quickly; folks may spend those years happily or miserably, and they may see the festival three times, or five times, or seven times, but the inn clerk, the postman, and the geisha will all die before they have seen it ten times.

And as I passed by the public bathhouse I overheard: "Miraculously no one was hurt this time when they cut down the trees." "That is unusual, isn't it? The last time Kanzō the cotton dealer was killed. Then there was that big fight. I hope that there won't be another like it this year. . . ." "Where are the pillars now?" "In Arimoto. Yesterday a group of fellows from Arimoto came and said that the pillars would get there today. . . ."

When I returned to the inn and questioned the clerk about what I had overheard, he explained that already for about a month now, representatives from the various towns and villages had been going to a spot some nine miles into the mountains to select four appropriate trees, which they would cut down and drag to the top of a cliff known as the tree-lowering cliff. From there they would lower the trees to the foot of the cliff. (Since there are about nine miles of mountain path to the cliff, it takes the better part of a day to come and go there from the villages and towns in the foothills, which left them only about an hour in which to do their work.) Then, once the trees have been cut and lowered down the cliff, folks from the village closest to where they land (which is about two miles away), and others who want to participate, tie ropes around the four tree trunks and drag them from village to village. They leave them a day or two in one village before they haul them to the next and finally, sometime in May, into Suwa, in time for the festival.

And in the midst of all these activities, that's when it happened.

Kotaki and I were both already thirty years old, so we obviously did not talk about love like twenty-year-olds, nor was there a formal engagement; to put it vulgarly, it was a bit like a cracked lid being put on a broken pot.

I left Suwa the following month, after a stay of nearly two months, and a week after I had returned to Tokyo, she joined me, and we became man and wife. In other words, it was in May, the month of the Pillar Festival, that *it* happened.

It is said that the deity who, every seventh year, makes people offer him cryptomeria trees cut deep in the mountains is not satisfied unless he has seen human blood flow, either when the trees are cut, or when they are dragged through the different villages, or at some other point during the festival—a fierce deity indeed. I did investigate this legend and found that not one but two deities are enshrined in two different places—that the one located in Shimo Suwa is the deity of the Lower Shrine and that the so-called Upper Shrine lies six miles to the east of Shimo Suwa. These two deities are a married pair known as Tateminakata-no-kami and Yasakatome-no-mikoto, who long ago dwelled together in the Upper Shrine, but they separated after a quarrel, and the wife, Yasakatome-no-mikoto, moved into the Lower Shrine. And from that time on, also according to the legend, any couple married during the year of the Pillar Festival is sure to divorce, so naturally such marriages have been discouraged. Yet that's when we got married. . . .

Toward the end of April—or was it the beginning of May?—I had to go back to Tokyo on business. The inn clerk tried to detain me, saying, "The Pillar Festival is but a few days away, couldn't you postpone returning to Tokyo until it's all over?" "There are exactly ten days to go, so I may well make it back in time. No, I'll make sure to be back," I replied, and left the inn for the railroad station.

It was a rainy evening, and the Tokyo-bound train was already there waiting as my ricksha pulled up. I clambered aboard, put my bag on an empty seat, and through the windowpane watched the entrance to the small waiting room. Thirty seconds to a minute elapsed. And then just as the departure whistle blew and the train started to move, I caught sight of two women in the doorway closing their umbrellas as they hurriedly walked toward the train. I hastened to the car's platform. The two women—Kotaki in front and Yumeko behind her—were coming through the ticket gate. "Thank you for coming to see me off. Good-bye," I called to them. Rain was falling between us, and there were railroad employees moving to and fro, blocking their way. Kotaki gazed at me with her large eyes and bowed. Half hidden behind her, Yumeko bowed, and before they had time to raise their heads, my train had picked up speed and disappeared with me, into the rainy night.

I shall never forget that moment.

Although we had not said it in so many words, Kotaki and I had agreed that she would visit me in Tokyo shortly. Not only that, but by then our relationship was already quite intimate. As for Yumeko, whom I had known before I knew Kotaki, and whom I loved with all my heart, and for whose sake I had come to love this town, and on whose account I came to this town again and again, with her I had made no arrangements and had no special understanding—I had never even really talked to her. In fact, we had never said anything beyond that which polite strangers would say to each other.

I pressed my face against the cold glass of the train window, and as I strained for a glimpse of the lake and the mountains shrouded in the night rain, from the bottom of my heart rose a cry: "Ye gods take pity on me!"

Is love of the kind I feel for Yumeko not to be realized in this world? Could the dualism of which the ancient philosophers[14] spoke as the bane of humankind be as the love I feel for Yumeko, on the one hand, and the love I feel for Kotaki, on the other? Ye gods, help me!

Thus I left the mountain lake, passed through Kaigane, slipped through the Sasago-Kobotoke passes, and arrived home in Tokyo the next morning. But ten days later I again boarded the train at Iidamachi for Suwa.

During the next ten days I was in Tokyo I received four letters from the mountain town: two from Kotaki and two from Horito (nothing from anyone else). Those from Kotaki were, in short, love letters in which she told me that she was lonely and had practically stopped working and wanted to come to Tokyo soon to talk things over with me. Horito urged me to come back for the Pillar Festival, saying that it was sure to be a rare experience for me and that although he didn't want to press me, he was sure that I would find it very interesting. Although Horito had written twice inviting me to come, for some reason there had been no word at all from Nishimukai.

That night at Iidamachi I felt as if I were under a spell; I had to board that train. And about that very same time, unbeknownst to me, of course, a telegram from Kotaki was delivered to my house. She wanted to tell me that she would visit me the following morning.

I arrived at my inn and that same night saw Yumeko (getting together with Kotaki had to wait for another day); we were having our usual desultory conversation when a telegram came from home, informing me that Kotaki had arrived in Tokyo during my absence. I replied, by telegram, that I would extend my stay another day. The following day was the day of the festival when the pillars of the Gracious Deity would be pulled into town.

In the past I had rarely ventured into town except to go to the post office, and this may have been because of my innate, almost pathological timidity, but now with rumors all over town, so I thought, about my relationship with Yumeko and Kotaki (if only those gossips had known the true state of affairs), my need for privacy was such that despite the fine weather I raised the hood of my ricksha on the way from the railroad station to the inn, and I remained all day long in my room on the third floor. But then, I did not have to go out to learn that there was a big celebration afoot: the sounds coming from the mountains, the mood, the behavior of the people, the atmosphere in the inn, all were so many telltales. And when I cautiously opened the round window on the south side, I beheld the ordinarily drab-looking shrine grove in all its once-in-seven-years finery. There were red-and-white and black-and-white awnings all over and so many tightly packed exhibition tents and vending booths that they literally buried the cryptomeria trees from view. In the evening the whole area looked and sounded almost like a battlefield. Gas lamps, electric lights, hand lanterns, and bonfires were blazing all over, and all sorts of sounds intermingled into awesome noises: the thumping and jingling of the carnival (which had been going on for several days already), the folk ballads, the musical accompaniment of an exhibition of Heaven and Hell, the sacred music of the shrine dances, and so on.

One had to be deaf and blind not to know that there was an extraordinary celebration taking place in this town. It could be seen and heard not only from the round window on the south side, and from the windows on the north and west side overlooking the town, but from the windows in the east corridor, the ones facing the mountains, as well. The smallest of houses and the meanest of huts in the mountains were now visible, decorated as they were with flags and lanterns. And paths, before invisible, and where I would never have imagined them to be, were now clearly marked by numbers of gaily attired children and grown-ups cheerfully walking to and from town.

All this gaiety and to-do outside was, alas, in sharp contrast to the way I felt. I was far from happy at the thought that Kotaki had gone to Tokyo during my absence to discuss our wedding plans. I was, in fact, overcome by a feeling of utter helplessness.

My outlook on life had been free, unhampered, full of hope, until I met her. From that time on, it grew gradually dimmer and narrower, until I felt as if I were in an endless tunnel. Or to use another metaphor, as some poets would, while outside the town was celebrating, a funeral procession was passing through my heart.

I had come here in search of mountains, lakes, a town, a dream . . . and here I was looking down at the town from my third-floor window and feeling as though I had fallen into a black hole. That is why I informed no one of my arrival, not even Horito or Nishimukai. I told only one person—Yumeko.

"You don't go out at all, Sensei, and yet you took the trouble to come here. Why is that?" The clerk handed me a pair of old-fashioned binoculars that he carried in a black leather case that hung from his shoulder. "They're not very good, but please go ahead and use them. Over there. . . . They say that the daimyo and his retinue will come down the road that passes right in front of us. . . ." Intending to be my guide, I guess, the clerk sat down beside me on the sill of the west window. "Look, over there on the top of the slope, you can already see a group of them shouting, 'Clear the way.' The points of their spears are already visible."

Indeed, a group on foot, dressed as attendants and shouting "Clear the way," came dragging their staves. Next came spear bearers and men carrying chests suspended from poles. But I could not see too well because they were coming down a road that led straight into an area hidden from my view. Moreover, as I said before, I felt quite glum, and so I really did not get much pleasure from seeing the parade. The clerk—more for his own sake than for mine, it seems, for he was deeply involved in the spectacle, and evidently enjoyed it, and seemed to assume that I shared his enthusiasm—commented on how unbecoming those costumes were on people nowadays and explained that the man heading the line was a rowdy blacksmith, quick to pick a quarrel, who had become an influential man about town, and that the second spear bearer was almost sixty, an old-timer who was carrying a spear in the Pillar Festival for the fifth time. As he went on talking, he excused himself every now and then and took back the binoculars that he had given me, and he did that so often that, in the end, it seemed that it was I who had lent him those binoculars, rather than the other way around.

When he realized that for some time I had been anything but cheerful, he tried to console me: "I believe that Yumeko will come anytime now. I'm sure that's what she said on the phone an hour ago. Although the geisha are busier today than they are at New Year's, knowing that it was to your room she was asked to come, Sensei, I am sure she'll be here any minute."

When I could use the binoculars, I not only tried to watch the daimyo's procession but ever so often shifted my attention to what I could see of the town. Besides the inns, shops, theaters, and office buildings, there were private houses that opened onto the street, and I could see the carpets spread on the floor, the standing screens, the people drinking sake, the *go* players gathered around the *go* boards, the people singing, the people shouting, the townspeople and the people from the surrounding countryside, the old folk and the children; in short, I could see all sorts of people enjoying this great festival. I could see them larger than life through those old-fashioned field glasses.

What attracted my attention most, however, were the geisha, who, today, first class and third class alike, with their hair in the *Shimada*-style coiffure and the long trailing skirts of their crest-embossed kimonos tucked up, eclipsed everyone else in the crowds on the streets and in the houses. And I wondered if Yumeko was somewhere among them. And I thought about Kotaki, too, who with her haughty demeanor well befitting her status of foremost geisha in town, would certainly have stood out from all the others had she been here.

I wondered what she was doing in my house in Tokyo while I was away.

"Sensei, the lord is coming!" the clerk shouted in my ear. Excuse me, may I borrow the binoculars for a moment?" And as he held those field glasses to his eyes, he shouted his admiration:

"Splendid, splendid. Altogether as I imagined. When he's dressed up as an adult, he looks just like his father."

"Please let me have a look too." I took the binoculars from him and looked in the direction where he pointed. Although the spear bearers, the servants, in short, all the attendants were adults, the daimyo himself was a twelve- or thirteen-year-old boy, and instead of riding in a palanquin, he alone rode on a horse.

Before I had a chance to ask who the boy was, the clerk said, "In this town the daimyo is always the son of a wealthy family. This one, Sensei, is the son of the father of Yumeko's child, which means that Yumeko's child and that boy are half brothers. Take a look at his glittering eyes and flattish nose. Isn't he the spit and image of his father? It costs a fortune to sponsor one's son as the daimyo of this festival. He's probably taken off two or three kimonos already; it's a good showing for the father when the son can remove layer after layer of kimono and still display another magnificent one underneath. Those kimonos alone cost a considerable amount of money, but that isn't the half of it. See that child leading the daimyo's horse by the reins? That child comes from another town, but he still has to outfit him, and on top of that, he has to tip all the people who make up the retinue; no one but a very wealthy man could do all that."

Need I say that I didn't want to listen to the rest of his story? I carefully wiped the lenses of the binoculars with a handkerchief and took a good look at the mounted child daimyo, who had removed several gold-brocade kimonos and was now bare to the waist. A hard-to-define emotion that was neither jealousy nor hatred welled up within me, and I imagined myself to be the legendary Wind God.[15] In fact, if I had had a big wind bag like his, I would have opened it on the spot and released a wind big enough to blow away the child lord and his horse. I would have blown away that child daimyo with the innocent look—who most certainly wasn't innocent—with that flat nose screwed into the sky and that powder-covered, simpering face of his, which he turned hither and yon whenever someone called out to him. I would have blown away that boy with his thrust-out chest who had slipped out of and let fall around his hips endless layers of gold-brocade, damask, and crepe kimonos each time he passed in front of somebody important. I would have blown away his horse too, and his attendants, and the town and the spectators.

Even so, it's good to know that no one else knew of the existence of this would-be Wind God who entertained such incongruous and rebellious thoughts.

Eventually the daimyo's procession quietly turned the corner to the left and continued along the road to the Shrine of the Gracious Deity. Once they had turned the corner, one by one they disappeared from view below the eaves of the silk floss shop to the left of the intersection.

For hours thereafter I heard the noises of the festival, borne by the wind, coming from all directions.

I regretted having come. What must Kotaki be thinking as she waited for me in my house in Tokyo? I didn't know how busy Yumeko was, but why had she not even shown her face? What if? . . . No. Could it be that she didn't come because she had heard that Kotaki was not at the festival because she had gone to my house in Tokyo? With my thoughts in turmoil, I wanted to take the earliest possible train back to Tokyo; then I changed my mind and decided to try to see Yumeko just once before I left, and so having worked myself into a state of nervous agitation, I stood at the west window and gazed at the heavens.

When I say that I gazed at the heavens, I mean that I intended to take in the distant scene of the tranquil mountains without looking at the town. There were no clouds in the sky that day, yet, probably because of the haze that settles on the cold mountain country in spring, I couldn't see Ontake or Norikura no matter how hard I strained my eyes. Then a maid appeared in the doorway.

"There is a Mr. Horito here to see you. Excuse me, sir, but could you come to the foyer? . . ."

I went down to the foyer wondering how Horito had learned that I had come (he probably heard it from the clerk—I had forgotten to ask him not to tell anyone that I was here) and curious to find out what Nishimukai was doing. Horito, as he was wont to, bowed coyly, like a woman, with both hands neatly placed over his knees; and then without any preliminary greeting, he announced: "Sensei, the pillars will be passing by any minute now, and unlike the daimyo's procession, you will not be able to see them well from your room here, so please, won't you come to the company building? I saved a seat for you, and I'll take you there. Please. . . ."

He seemed determined to take me, despite my repeated refusals; I didn't want to go at all lest Yumeko come while I was out, but he wouldn't be put off, so I gave in and let him lead me away.

His company building was less than half a block from my inn, and we arrived in no time at all; along the way we had the following exchange: "What is Mr. Nishimukai doing? I haven't heard from him at all. Is he in the area?" "Yes, he's here." "Is he at the company office?" "Yes. . . ." Horito led me to their yard, which was surrounded by a black log fence of the sort one sees at old barrier checkpoints, and introduced me to a clerk into whose keeping he entrusted me.

"I'm going up the mountain for a little while. Mr. Nakao and I are taking turns working half-day shifts because of the festival."

He left in a great hurry without listening to what I was about to say.

Soon a hubbub of voices rose from the street, and the clerk with whom Horito had left me came up to me and said, "The pillars are going to pass by, so I'll take you to your seat." Like the substation on the mountain, this office consisted of a shabby building standing on the far side of a bare plot of land two hundred yards square and enclosed by a fence. That is to say, one passed through a gate bearing the name of the company and crossed an empty yard to get to the company building. I forgot to mention this before, but there was a cloth screen spread parallel to the fence, about two yards distant from it, which I had found strange, but now, as the clerk led me across the empty yard, I saw that there were a number of chairs arranged in rows between the black log fence and the red-and-white cloth screens. The idea was for people to sit on those chairs with the curtain behind them and to look, through the spaces between the pickets of the black fence, at the pillars being pulled along in the street. With the clerk's help I secured a seat at the end of a row in a corner. And when I sat down next to him, I saw a host of people pulling at two ropes to which they clung like ants, as elementary school children would playing a game of tug of war, except that in this game the two teams were pulling in the same direction. And as they pulled, they sang a song, pausing after each stanza. It was a sort of workman's chant that sounded familiar. Indeed, I had heard it earlier, during the festival rehearsals. And as I listened more closely it seemed that there was someone in the rear leading the singing, for each time the crowd pulling the ropes stopped singing one verse, a single voice far in the rear was heard singing the next, and as soon as he stopped, the crowd immediately repeated it in unison.

I asked the clerk seated next to me, "Are the pillars attached to the ends of those ropes?" "Yes, that's right." He said no more, but looked straight ahead, pushing his face between two fence pickets to take in as much as he could of the rope pulling in the street.

When the pillars were hauled from village to village, they were pulled by youths of different villages in turn; but today, all the young people from all the villages in the vicinity of the Shrine of the Gracious Deity had turned out to participate, so it took a surprisingly long time for the length of required ropes to pass by the spot where we were watching. The pillars were coming closer . . . very gradually.

At first I had the impression that there was one single person leading the singing, but I discovered that in this long line there were over ten subordinate song leaders placed at intervals along the ropes. These subordinate song leaders, dressed in white in the manner of Shinto priests, moved in a line between the two ropes, relaying the singing that was begun by the leader standing on the pillars, and, as the procession advanced, the young men pulling the ropes who were close enough to hear them joined in, and all sang in unison.

At last the pillars were right in front of us. With all the fanfare that accompanied the pulling, I had come to expect something else, but all I saw were four tree trunks lashed together to form a platform decorated with ritual strips of paper. I was disappointed by this bare simplicity and at the same time shocked when I recognized the man who was leading the singing. He was standing on a straw mat spread out on top of the raft and was dressed in the same priestly white as the subordinate leaders but cut a much more imposing figure when he waved his paper wand as if he were conducting an orchestra. His voice had a familiar ring to it when I first heard it in the distance, but I was too preoccupied then to give it another thought, and now he was right in front of me.

"It's Nishimukai, it's him. . . . Let's call him, shall we?"

That's what the company employees sitting beside me were saying to each other, but I didn't need them to identify Nishimukai for me as he stood on the straw mat at the end of the raft singing with his mouth wide open and beating out the rhythm with his wand as mechanically as a doll. The rest of his body was stock still as if nailed to the spot. Even as he passed us he remained in that dream-like trance without so much as a glance at his fellow workers at the electric company, and it seemed as if he would remain that way forever.

According to the clerk sitting next to me, various people had been nominated for the role of head song leader, but about ten days before the festival, one of the men was called away on business, and the others were found wanting for one or another reason, and finally Nishimukai was chosen.

This came about as follows. One evening Nishimukai was drunk, and as he unsteadily made his way through town he sang the pillar song (he must have picked it up somewhere). This attracted the attention of someone, who had him investigated, and so it was learned that he had a good family background, was fairly well educated, and, most important, had always been very fond of music. When thereupon he was asked to try out for the role of song leader, uncommonly shy as he was, he tearfully refused many times, but when the organizers insisted that all he had to do was come to rehearsals, he couldn't refuse anymore.

So he went once, twice . . . and impressed all and sundry so much with his singing and other talents that they forced the role of head song leader on him.

And now, it was said, the townspeople were congratulating themselves for having made such a fine choice.

The clerk, his face wedged between two fence posts, could not take his eyes off Nishimukai as he mumbled to himself, "He is very good; his very shyness gets him in that trance; he sings with such zeal, indeed with real ardor."

During all this time, waving his wand as he sang, Nishimukai and the pillars slowly inched their way past us.

Even had I not been acquainted with Nishimukai, I would have had nothing but good feelings for that song leader, just as I would still have wished to be the Wind God to blow away the child lord I saw an hour ago even had I not known who he was. Nishimukai did not thrust out his chest or bare himself or cast simpering glances at the crowd as that child daimyo had done. He looked neither to the right nor to the left. As if possessed by a deep feeling of gratitude and obligation—in a trance—he waved and waved his wand as he sang and sweated heavily. His voice, which he had once described as terrible because of his short nose, had the perfect timbre and resonance for this workman-like chant, the pillar song. It really touched people's hearts.

As I watched him inching by, a thousand rope-pulling people echoing that voice in measured cadence, the area between my eyes began to twitch. And as he gradually disappeared in the distance I was overcome by an emotion I can't describe. I felt neither sad nor happy, neither solemn nor gay, but there was a lump in my throat, and everything looked blurry.

Three calendar years have passed since then.

So, did we, who dared tie the knot of matrimony in the year of the Pillar Festival, escape the wrath of the deity? It is said that no one that foolhardy ever did.

According to some outward appearances it may seem so. We are still living together, peacefully. Yet that deity may have reserved for us a far more dreadful punishment than divorce. True, from the time we started living together as husband and wife there was a bond of mutual affection between us. Yet, as before we were married, whenever given the chance, my heart went out to Yumeko, my wife's sister-geisha, who remained in the mountain town.

And this surely is one of the ways in which that deity avenged itself.

As for my wife, granted she had been able to return to Tokyo, where she was born, after thirty long years of patient waiting. And granted that she was now a married woman, not the mistress of the man she was living with, and (this may seem immodest for me to say) her husband was not a man she need be ashamed of, and all this was certainly nothing to be sneezed at.

Yet her husband was in many ways as a stranger to her. Since they were married she had not once walked by his side or sat across from him more than two hours in one day, except when he was sick. She didn't know whether he loved her. She didn't know what he thought; he never talked about his work or what he did when he went out. And to make matters worse, she had of late begun to regret leaving her mountain town—which she had left with the intention never to return. It seemed to her that life had been more enjoyable then and more predictable. She not only had been an independent geisha but had managed a geisha house.

Surely this anguish and regret were other punishments that that deity had meted out to us. But alas not the worst.

We had been married three years and did not have a single child and probably would never have one. In other words, although we led a fairly comfortable daily existence, the deity had denied us a future. And of all the punishments this was the heaviest to bear.

I believe it was in the fall of that same year, the year of the festival, that one fine day, to my astonishment, I found Nishimukai standing in the doorway of our home.

"What a surprise! When did you come to Tokyo?" I asked him after I had led him into the parlor.

He was as bashful as ever but managed, "I've been here for about two weeks."

On returning to Tokyo I had written to him. I told him that I had made a secret trip to Suwa to see the Pillar Festival, that Horito got me a seat in the courtyard of the Electric Company where I could see him very well, and I complimented him on his performance. Instead of a reply from him I received a letter from Horito informing me that he had been scolded by Nishimukai, not only for writing to invite me to come to the festival when he knew full well that Nishimukai would disapprove, but especially for going so far as to arrange for me to see him perform. After that letter communication between us had stopped.

"What is Horito doing?" Instead of asking Nishimukai directly why he had come to Tokyo, I broached the matter indirectly. I first asked him about Horito, who had said that he wanted to come to the capital to study music.

"Horito, . . ." he said weakly, "Horito was transferred; he has gone to Shimajima and is very unhappy there."

"Shimajima? Do you mean the Shimajima at the gateway of the Japan Alps?"

Then I gradually shifted the conversation to Nishimukai's situation. "Well then, where are you staying now?" I asked. Judging from his appearance, his coming to Tokyo had not been very rewarding; he was uncommonly despondent, and his clothes were anything but neat.

"Living in the country became pretty dull, and there was someone who used to work in our shop in Kai who came to Tokyo and is now doing well in Yotsuya. I'm staying with him. After living in the country for six years, I just got sick and tired of it. . . ."

The seal engraver in Yotsuya with whom he was staying had once been an employee in his father's shop and had apparently received help from his father, and Nishimukai was now relying on this person to help him out. Although he did some work for him, he was clearly a superfluous member of the household and was living with him as a dependent and feeling extremely uncomfortable about the situation. But as before when I met him in the mountain town, he did not come out openly and talk of his plight or the sorrow or pain that he felt. Instead he talked about lying around day after day up there on the second floor, and about how he got used to boredom to the point of discovering its flavor, and about how even Mount Fuji, which he could see from the window of his room, could become interesting if one stared at it long enough; but he added that since he had made up his mind and left the country, well, he intended to stick it out; he didn't know how things would turn out, but whatever happened he would stay. He told me all this haltingly and leaving much unsaid.

Knowing how he felt, I was anxious not to embarrass him, and so I didn't say anything about the Pillar Festival. He didn't say anything about it either. He left after about an hour, but as he was saying good-bye at the front door he set down a package wrapped in newspaper. "This is a little unconventional, but please accept it," he said as he ran off. Later, when I opened it, I found five packs of National Pride cigarettes, neatly wrapped in paper and tied with a gift-wrap cord, and a small packet similarly wrapped in paper and bound with a gift-wrap cord. The smaller packet contained an ivory seal, engraved with my name, that he had made himself.

After that, in that same year, he visited me three more times. Each time on his way out he left a present wrapped in newspaper; it was usually a practical gift, like a bar of soap or a towel. Each time he seemed strangely embarrassed. He could never have used the phrase, "This is only a humble token . . ."—especially in the ostentatious way in which some people frame it.

Another time he said, "I wonder if a person like me could write; I'd like to try, I wonder if it would be all right? . . ." When I said, "Surely it's all right to try if you feel like it," he reacted as if he had been granted an extraordinary privilege and kept repeating, "Oh, thank you, thank you." But I never saw anything he wrote. When I asked him, "Are you playing your musical instruments? . . ." he said, "No, I'm not up to that sort of thing right now."

The second time he came—it was four or five months after his first visit, I believe—he told me, "Horito quit his job at Shimajima and returned to Suwa." When I asked, "Is he working at Suwa?" he said, "No, he's not. He's in a fix, he's out of a job. Right now he's taking orders for engraving seals. He sends the orders on to me to fill. I give him a commission for each one, but it's not much. Horito is really having a hard time and, probably like me, doesn't feel like making music these days. He imagines that all he has to do is come to Tokyo to get a good job. And he keeps writing to me about it again and again. And I keep writing back that for a person who comes to Tokyo from the country there's nothing to do but become a robber or a beggar. And so he's angry at me because he thinks I'm being spiteful and don't want to help him. Sensei, what could he do in Tokyo?"

I noticed that he now looked far more dejected than the first time he came and that his clothes were dirtier. Until now I couldn't tell from his face how he felt: cheerful or depressed, pessimistic or optimistic. For the first time, I saw plainly that his face was not that of a happy man. The whole of it as well as each individual feature seemed to be weeping: the carelessly parted hair, the thick brows, the short nose, the short, thick moustache under the nose that made him look like a white-collar worker, or was it an artisan? . . . And then again the whole of his crying face appeared to be laughing.

On New Year's of the following year he informed me, on a New Year's greeting card, that he would be moving. In parentheses along with his name he wrote that in about a month's time his new address would be in care of such-and-such a person in Ushigome. That was his way of announcing that he would leave the seal shop in Yotsuya to begin a new life in a rented flat.

Later on when he came to visit me he looked much more depressed than the time before and very emaciated. "A person like me," he said, "cannot live where there are no mountains. It's the same as with plants; there are some that grow in the fields, some that grow by the riverside, and some that won't grow at all unless they're in the mountains. Human beings have their places where they can live and where they can't live, don't you agree,

Sensei? I'm so bored now, I spend my days walking around Tokyo. It's quite a feat to walk that much every day. My wooden clogs are all worn out. . . ."

"Sensei, you know that one can see mountains even from Tokyo." Nishimukai was becoming unusually talkative. "Sensei, did you know that on a clear evening all the mountains from Mount Fuji to Mount Hakone are visible from Ueno park? Of course, this is the best time of the year for seeing them. . . . Sensei, if you walk toward Tabata, you can even see Mount Tsukuba. The first couple of times I saw it, I wondered what mountain it was, and I asked passersby, but no one could tell me. But the third time I got as far as the area around Tabata station— you probably know it, that place where they put up a fence on one side of the street around a big hole?—well, there was a sweet-sake vendor who was unloading his wares, so I stopped for a drink, and as I was drinking and looking at the mountain he told me what it was. Sensei, from there you can see not only Mount Tsukuba but the Nikkō and Chichibu mountains as well. Sensei, don't you think that the Chichibu mountains have something in common with the mountains in Kōshū? Of course, I haven't seen them all that often, although I went to Ueno a number of times . . . and you know, Sensei, each time I went there I wanted to stop at your place but was always afraid of bothering you. . . ."

Indeed, given his character, he probably did stay away each time out of fear of imposing on me. He told me that on three occasions he came all the way to my house only to turn back because shoes belonging to guests of mine had been left in the entryway.

He went on talking about mountains but said nothing at all about the seal shop in Yotsuya, or why he was renting a flat, or what he was doing. But from bits of information here and there, I pieced together that he was in pretty difficult circumstances. And yet he continued to talk about nothing but mountains.

Hardly aware of it, I was myself drawn into his discussion about mountains and said, "Do you know that the Kōshū mountains are visible from the vicinity of Tokyo?" He drew closer and asked, "Really, Sensei? Really? Where?"

I had heard that they could be seen from within the city limits, from Mount Atago and from several other spots; I did not know much about those places, but I did know that the three mountains on the northwest side of the Kaigane range stood out in clear relief, like heaps of sugar, when seen from the inside of the train on the Keihin line as one approached the Rokugō river plain near Kawasaki, and I knew that one could also see them if one got off the train at Kawasaki station. When I told him that from within the moving train for a while the mountains appeared to be running along the house tops and the tree tops, he leaped from his seat in surprise and joy.

None of my other friends talked about mountains with such interest and enthusiasm, and for this reason alone, being with Nishimukai was never disagreeable, no matter how busy I was with work. But I also appreciated his extreme bashfulness, the elegance of his behavior, rare in a man from the provinces, and the goodness of his character. But there was another, more important reason why I welcomed his visits, and that was because he brought new information, which he had no doubt received from Horito, about that mountain town. And news about the mountain town necessarily included news about her (my beloved Yumeko). But although I use the words *new information,* in effect, fewer changes had taken place there (in the mountain town and in her life) than occurred in a single day in the city where I lived. In short, the news was information along the order of Horito's recent meeting with the clerk of such-and-such an inn who asked to be remembered to me, or Horito's passing by the House of Dreams on an errand on the morning of a certain day in a certain month and seeing Yumeko drawing water with her sleeves tied up, or Horito catching sight of Yumeko holding up the hem of her skirt as she emerged from the Heart of the Lake Pavilion the night before, or word about a variety show from Tokyo with song, dance, and magic tricks, now at the local playhouse. To tell me these things, he waited for the moment when my wife was not present and did not forget to lower his voice a notch; he did not talk when she was around.

When he had met her before in the mountain town, she had been nothing more than a geisha past her prime, and when he saw her next in my house in Tokyo, she was suddenly my wife; but he was as respectful as though she had been my wife from the day she was born, and when he addressed her, or referred to her, it was always, "Mrs." this, and "Mrs." that.

But I needed no more than what he told me to imagine all those scenes more vividly than if I had seen them. Yumeko . . . her kimono sleeves tied back as she went to fetch water at the community well in front of her house, on the top of the hill, her slender figure bent under the weight of the heavy water buckets. Yumeko holding her skirts as she emerged from the Heart of the Lake Pavilion, her sad eyes downcast. The smell of the mineral water of the communal bathhouses overflowing into the streets. Mountains all around, covered with snow.

According to what he wrote on the first postcard (he sent me two, two months apart) he did not wait three days, after I had told him, to go to that place on the Keihin line where one can see the mountains of Kai, his home province. On the second postcard he said he could not see them anymore because of the spring haze, and that made him more unhappy than if he had been separated from a loved one.

It seemed that he had tried to see them and had failed a number of times already.

No matter how clear the day was in Tokyo, once he got to the Rokugō river area the sky was blue only directly overhead, while the sky on the horizon in the northwest, and probably in all other directions as well, was thick and cloudy, white as milk. He also reported that one day he asked a farmer in the field and was told that the mountains cannot be seen this time of year.

About a month later I received another letter from him sent from a town in Kōfu. He had at last returned to his hometown in the mountains.

At this time of the year, the snow on the three mountain peaks of the Kaigane range was melting, while the snow on Mount Nōtori to the south remained to give that mountain its famous bird shape.[16]

He told me that he had been staying for about a month at his father's house, where he spent each day looking at mountains; every three days or so he could see Mount Nōtori, the part of the Kaigane range that he had not been able to see from Rokugō. He said that he intended to go back to Suwa, where he had lived for six years, but that he still didn't know what he would do once he got there; at any rate, he was having Horito look for a house for him, and he invited me to visit if I ever went there; and then, almost as an afterthought, he mentioned that the day before he had received a letter from Horito informing him that Yumeko was pregnant again and would quit working as a geisha in the near future.

I shot bolt upright in the middle of the room with the letter clutched in my hand and said to myself, If she is pregnant and quits her job, she will be inaccessible to me as surely as the Kaigane range disappears from view when spring comes to the fields of the Rokugō river, and until she gives birth and returns to work as a geisha, I will not be able to see her again no matter how often I board the train at Iidamachi.

I haven't mentioned this before, but actually a situation developed that, ironically, would have prevented me from seeing her anyway.

After the Pillar Festival three years ago, unbeknownst to my wife, I went to Suwa about four times together with a friend who had lots of free time on his hands.[17] One night, on our third visit there, my friend and I, together with Yumeko and one of her geisha companions, rode to a nearby town in an automobile to see a movie. The next day there was an article in the town's newspaper insinuating that we had gone there for illicit purposes. As a result I was forced to leave much sooner than I had intended.

In the novels that I write for a living, I have on occasion used as a model a woman who resembles Yumeko, and so she would have eventually come under suspicion and incurred the displeasure of the father of her child, that is, her present patron, even if the newspaper incident had not occurred. But apparently she was all the more severely rebuked by him because of the article.

Not long thereafter she sent me a clipping of this newspaper article together with a letter in which she asked me, if I had any feelings for her, to please publish a statement saying that our relationship had in no way been improper.

Because of the letter, my wife found out that I had gone to Suwa, and it made her very angry and jealous.

When I finally had to admit to myself, after trying again and again to deny it, that Yumeko's letter was a final good-bye, I was dumbstruck with sorrow. There is no figure of speech that can express the sadness I felt, though I had never slept by her side or talked of love to her. I loved her more than anyone else.

The fourth time I went to Suwa, I traveled alone and shut myself up in the room on the third floor. Every day for three days I went round and round the room, going from one window to the next, all the time wondering whether I should try to see her. . . . Finally I left without calling her.

Each time I saw Nishimukai Kanzan, who was still in Tokyo, I talked about having gone there, but I didn't say a word about what had happened between her and me.

So even if I had worked up the courage to take the train from Iidamachi, could I have seen her? It certainly wouldn't have been as easy as going down to the Rokugō fields on a clear winter day to view the Kaigane range. More likely, my journey would have been as fruitless as Nishimukai's coming to Tokyo.

A person like me can find pleasure in sadness, can enjoy himself in the midst of grief, no matter how difficult the circumstances in which he is placed, as long as he has enough leeway to dream. So as long as she was a geisha in that town, no matter what the situation was, no matter what kind of relationship we had, even if I didn't actually go there, or, having gone, I had to come back without having seen her, as I did the fourth time, I could still take pleasure in my hope. And that's why Nishimukai's news that she would quit working as a geisha because she was pregnant (with the child of the man who had reproached her and made her write that letter to me when our innocent outing was misinterpreted and publicized in the newspaper) came as a tremendous blow. It was like being beaten with a stick out of a comfortable nap. (As silly as it may seem, sleeping is my one and only consolation in this troubled, transient world.) And I stood stock still in the middle of the room, clutching his letter as if I were imitating some actor when the curtain goes down at the end of the play. And then I had a tremendous urge to go and see her, to go to the mountains at once without a moment's delay!

PART 2

Spurred on by my passion to go to the mountain country and to see her, I had thrown some things in a suitcase, put on my hat, and already had one foot past the gate, when I was stopped cold, as if I had suddenly found myself at the edge of a raging, rain-swollen river and knew that if I took another step I would fall in. . . . It was the memory of her farewell note. . . . It doused my burning feelings as with a water pump. . . . I went back to my room as dogs sometimes retreat to their kennels with their tails between their legs.

As you know, I am a novelist and at that time had already written several novels that were essentially about my relationship with her.

After I had made travel plans only to abandon them immediately, I was feeling pretty depressed sitting in my room; there was no one to whom I could complain or appeal for sympathy, so, intending to sing myself a little lullaby as it were—this is a shameful story—I took out those novels and began to read them.

On learning from my friend Nishimukai Kanzan who wrote from his hometown in Kai province that she whom I loved with all my heart was pregnant with her second child and would soon stop working as a geisha, I resolved on the spot, as I stood there with his letter in my hand, to go to Suwa before she quit, even if it meant traveling all the way to that distant province and then being refused when she realized who the guest was who was inviting her to his room. (Since I couldn't know what would come of it, I decided to leave it up to the gods and to go.)

Then one day passed, and yet another, and it wasn't as if I had forgotten about going, but even if I had brushed aside all the worldly affairs that kept creeping up, the memory of the parting letter I had received from her was like a lid clamped over my feelings, and so day after day went by, and then a month, and then two months had come and gone.

Borrowing a metaphor used to describe diseases, I can say that the feelings of love such as I then experienced had become chronic. They were awakened, not only by stimuli that were visible to the eye and apparent to my conscious mind, but also by stimuli that I didn't notice and couldn't understand. At night as I tossed and turned on my mat, unable to sleep, or suddenly in the middle of a crowded streetcar, as I was holding onto the hand strap, or as I gazed up at the sparkling stars in the sky on my way home late at night—at all times and under all kinds of circumstances, when I least expected it, those feelings manifested themselves with prickling aches and pains. And when I saw the shapes of mountains rising in the distance above the horizon in between rows of houses, or received a letter from Nishimukai, or glimpsed a woman who resembled her, the symptoms became acute, and I had to endure the agony a twenty-year-old goes through.

I waited and waited in vain. There was not the least bit of news about her in the letter that came from Nishimukai, who had finally returned to Shinshū. It was his first letter since he had returned to Shinshū from his hometown in Kai.

This time he had gone not to Suwa but to the town of Okaya. There were at least two reasons why he couldn't go back to Suwa: the lack of suitable housing and the fact that, after leaving Suwa for distant Tokyo with high hopes, he was ashamed to sneak back like a thief. Though Suwa was dearer to him than his own hometown, it had turned into a place where he could not walk in broad daylight anymore, and after consulting with Horito, he had decided to move to Okaya. He told me that Okaya was a town where the lamplight flickered as in the shadow picture town, which I had seen at night from my favorite west window on the third floor of the inn in Suwa. It was a very good place, but a strange place, for though it was referred to as Okaya village in the census register, it was populated by over fifty thousand men and women who worked in the silk mills. He and Horito had decided to live there together, and neither of them had found a way to earn a living yet.

I wrote to him asking whether he ever went to Suwa, whether he had heard anything about Yumeko, and whether she had already stopped entertaining guests; I asked him to find out anything he could about her, even to have a person he could trust investigate for him if need be.

On the back of the envelope of the following letter I received from Nishimukai there was a handsome rectangular seal affixed, which read "Goose Lake Music Institute," and alongside the seal, in small letters written with a pen, was the name "Nishimukai Kanzan." His handwriting was awkward; the strokes were as thin as silk threads. He wrote that he had secured some financial backing and had started a music school. "Goose Lake," as I probably knew, was another name for Suwa lake; someone had given them the name "Goose Lake Music Institute." "'Music Institute' is a strange name, isn't it?" he asked. They had about fifteen students, and Horito, who was the assistant teacher, spent every other day trying to recruit more. He also asked me to come and visit him, and that is about all he said in that letter.

My reply was a short one, I wished him success in his new endeavor and wrote very little else. Even if I had asked him directly, could he have given me the information I wanted: news about that certain person in Suwa? I knew that he could not afford to see a geisha even once a month, and the private affairs of a particular geisha were not everybody's business, even in that remote mountain country, where everybody was supposed to know everything about everyone else (as I had formerly been inclined to believe). I am convinced that not a single mill hand, male or female, in any of the innumerable mills in Okaya knew so much as the name of the geisha who lived in the neighboring town and whom I loved with all my heart. But then Nishimukai had mentioned in his letter that Horito made the rounds every other day trying to recruit new students, and he would surely hear this and that about her by and by and let me know. So I decided to be patient for the time being and not ask about her anymore.

About a month later another letter came from the Goose Lake Music Institute; thinking that this time there would be something in it about Yumeko, I opened it at once, but it was about Sunday, the day before yesterday (they took a day off from practice every third Sunday), when he and Horito had gone to Shimajima, the place to which Horito had been transferred by the electric company in Suwa. Living there was a man, a former colleague of Horito's, who had climbed more than thirty mountains in the Japan Alps. So they had decided that they would take an extra day off from the institute and have him guide them as far as Kamikōchi, provided their legs would hold up and they otherwise felt up to it. But instead of Kamikōchi, he had led them all the way to the top of Tokumoto pass. Nishimukai had proposed that they turn back more times than he, Nishimukai, could remember. Horito had not tired that easily, in spite of his girlish frame; in fact, he had joined the guide in urging Nishimukai on (literally almost pushing him up the mountain) to go as far as the pass from which they could see Hotaka—and so they had toiled up to the pass.

After they had labored so hard to get there, the entire side of Hotaka that they had gone to see was swathed in thick clouds; it looked like a ghost, and it roared (the peals of thunder sounded like roars). The two others said that it would clear up, and they waited at the top of the pass for nearly an hour, but instead of clearing up, monstrous clouds gradually spread out in their direction, and so finally his two companions were forced to listen to him, and they all scurried down the mountain to Shimajima. They had almost reached Shimajima when they were doused by a heavy evening shower. "We often used to say to each other that mountains are to be seen and not climbed, didn't we?" wrote Nishimukai. "I believe that strongly. Yet because it was the first time in all my life that I actually climbed a mountain, I was so elated at the prospect of coming face to face with a mountain like Hotaka that my heart was thumping by the time we got to the pass. And it turned out that in the end we could not even see it. —Going to see a mountain is a bit like going to meet a professional woman, isn't it? . . ."[18]

This time, there was a note from Horito enclosed with Nishimukai's letter. It consisted of three lines of greetings and best wishes for my health in the hot summer.

Needless to say, Nishimukai's story about climbing the mountain made me happy, but the fact that he had not written a single line about her after such a long interval left me sighing.

In reply I wrote that people in my profession do not work according to a monthly schedule, nor do we have to sit at home like shopkeepers; ours is a so-called pleasure business, and to outsiders it may look like we play every day, but there is no work as unsettling, that makes one so fidgety, that makes one feel as though one were constantly pursued by a dream. But of late I have been loafing around every day, and every night, waiting days on end, not accomplishing a single thing, and so I read the story about climbing the mountain with great interest and pleasure. If I could just relax and calm myself, I might manage, but in this intense heat, I feel as though I were being assailed by the manuscripts I owe a certain magazine. Things have become unbearable. At one point, I thought of taking a trip to some cool place where I could write, and I got out my suitcase; but then, no, I said to myself; if I were to go off somewhere, I'd fall behind in my work, and so I changed my mind and put my bag back in the closet. Even if I were to travel to my favorite place, my favorite room on the third floor of the inn with windows on all sides would now (after what she wrote) be off limits for me. I am in such a state that I hardly know how to answer when people ask me what I do every day (Nishimukai didn't know why that third-floor room was now inaccessible to me, like some so-called forbidden chamber, but in my great unhappiness I mentioned it just the same); this was the sort of thing I wrote in my letter, and after writing the date and his name, I added, "You haven't heard any news about Yumeko, have you?" And as I wrote this, I blushed.

There was no answer from Nishimukai, but about ten days later, on the same Goose Lake Music Institute stationery, I received a letter from Horito penned in the same thin silk-thread-like strokes as Nishimukai's. (Had Nishimukai's influence spread to the shaping of his handwriting too?)

At that time I wasn't thinking about Yumeko. I hadn't received a letter from Horito since the time after the Pillar Festival, and I wondered why he was writing to me. There was no salutation or greeting of any kind; it began abruptly with, "The night before, when I went to Suwa on a business matter, I saw Yumeko in front of the gate of the Kakuya inn, where you always stay, coming down the hill." He said that he had a feeling that I had come to Suwa, and he thought of asking her, but though he knew who she was, she seemed not to remember him and walked by him rapidly. She must have been close to term, yet if one didn't know that she was pregnant, one could hardly tell by looking at her. Of course, she hid it by the way in which she held the hem of her kimono skirt in her left hand, and her obi was tied in a way to cover up most of it. In fact, she didn't look pregnant at all, but according to what folks say, it's over five months now, and as pregnancies go, high or low, hers was a high one, and deliveries in such cases are difficult. That was what he wrote.

The letter made me at once both extremely happy and extremely sad. For a long while all sorts of pictures flashed back and forth in my head, and it all seemed to me—of course, being in love I was more foolish than ever—that among all the women, born of women, no one was made to look as beautiful by sadness as she. In my novels, I have already written, far too many times, that she was not especially beautiful; rather, her facial features and her figure, and all other aspects of her physical being, which on the whole fell quite a bit short of the common standard of beauty, seemed to have been made to express sadness. Gentlemen, please do not laugh at me for what I say and have said several times already: among women born of women, I have never seen one who could, as she did, refrain from loudly voicing either joy or sorrow, from bragging, from concealing things, from talking about herself or other people. People will speak ill or well of others, well or ill of themselves, and this may be because such confessions give them relief from their afflictions. And there is practically no one, man or woman, who does not do this. Only she (the one I am talking about) doesn't do it. In this respect she's one in ten thousand. And this quality alone would entitle her to the respect and admiration accorded to "genius," even if she were to give birth to ten boys, even if she had a propensity for theft, or wetting her bed at night.

And I proclaim loudly and clearly to all that it was this character trait of hers that made me love her so.

Once again I decided to leave immediately to go and see her. But not only was there the letter that separated us (the fact that I loved her and she did not love me back didn't matter that much). . . . There was a web of tangled, complex emotions. . . .

Then, I realized that although her condition may not be apparent, if she were pregnant, she would most probably refuse to see me, and, disheartened, I returned to my desk. And so despite my intense longing, I couldn't go back to that mountain town of hers until winter of that same year.

That summer, not counting a couple of evening showers, it rained only twice in fifty days.

Why do I mention this?

Well, every day, for fifty days, without missing a single day, as soon as the sun went down I set out with my walking stick for a certain café in Kyōbashi ward. And during that entire period I recall taking an umbrella instead of my walking stick only twice.

To get to this café you had to turn off the main street onto a side street too narrow for even a ricksha, then turn into a back alley, where all sorts of businesses, law firms, mail-order offices, trading houses, and the like, were crowded together in dimly lit buildings. In one of those buildings was the café. A strange location indeed.

Aside from an occasional drunk who lost his way, or couples who wanted to avoid walking on the main street, I could not imagine any customers. In the summertime, to let air in, the glass door was replaced by a reed screen three feet tall attached to the door frame two to three feet off the ground by a mechanism that made the screen open with a squeak, then automatically bang shut, so that if you walked outside, crouched down, and peered under the screen, you could see the table and chair legs. They were of course inanimate legs; rarely would you have seen the legs of customers.

Now I have to tell you about an unusual weakness of mine. Once I start something and begin to enjoy it, I have a tendency, or, rather, a bad habit, of indulging in that one thing exclusively.

Readers, it will not do for you to take me too seriously.

Allow me to cite an example of my weakness. I am chronically constipated, and my constitution is such that I can't stay healthy unless I take medicine. Till recently I got along by taking any medicine that happened to be around, but then something happened that led me to investigate each and every kind of laxative available, to find the one best suited to my condition. I sampled all the different Japanese laxatives on the market, all the American brands, the German brands, and the French brands that I could find, and compared them.

And now I wonder if this weakness of mine is fickleness rather than zeal? . . .

Anyway, around that time, finding flies to be extremely dirty and annoying, I felt that I had to eliminate them somehow. In the beginning I was irritated by the disagreeableness of those beasties that came flying at me, but in the end I began to take an interest even in such trivial things as going from corner to corner looking for them and hearing the sounds they made when I caught them. So I began to collect not only mechanical spring-operated flycatchers, but old-fashioned flyswatters, bow-shaped fly guns, glass fly bottles filled with vinegar, bamboo bark pasted with lime, American-manufactured flypaper, fly powder, and every other kind of fly-catching device that I laid eyes on. Nor did I overlook an unusual ad for a fly-suction tube, also called a fly-catching tube, that appeared in the newspaper one day. According to that ad, with the conventional fly-catching device one generally has to wait for the flies to gather before one can catch them; in other words, these are passive kinds, although occasionally among them one does find a more active kind, such as the flyswatter, with which one attacks the flies; but to use it one must wait for the fly to alight, and it is useless if the fly lands on a spot that is too high, or in a corner, or on a soft surface, or upside down on the ceiling; in contrast, our extendable glass fly tube with its funnel-shaped end is a device with which you can suck in flies, no matter where they alight, simply by compressing the rubber bulb at the lower end. The Japanese housewife who suffers from lack of physical exercise can, with one of our fly tubes, also compensate for her lack of physical exercise as she eliminates noxious, unsanitary flies and thus indirectly as well as directly promote her health. Therefore, we recommend it especially for the middle-class housewife.[19] That was the gist of the ad. And I felt that I would be able to catch flies with that trap, and it was moreover a novel way of catching them; what pleased me especially was the phrase "compensate for lack of physical exercise," for though I am not a housewife, I work at an occupation that leads to a want of exercise. I wrote down the address of the place that sold the fly trap on a scrap of paper, and that evening I walked around Kyōbashi ward looking for it, and that's when I discovered the café that I mentioned before.

A rather early riser, I am usually out of bed by seven. After I get up I eat, read the newspapers, leaf through a magazine, and then eventually confront my work. Yet I am generally tired and yawn before I manage to write two or at most three lines, so I put down my pen and pick up the fly tube and begin chasing flies all over the room and from room to room all over the house. And when I come back to the room where I started, I find that I've spent approximately five times more time catching flies than writing.

While the fly tube is of course not as effective as advertised, it is still the most appropriate way of catching flies when they're on the ceiling, or on the windowsill, or in other places where you have to look up to catch them. Of course, one can also use the fly tube when they are on the straw mats, or the lid of the rice bin, or the tabletops, or in other readily accessible places, but it isn't much fun. For trapping flies in places like these I take out the old-fashioned fly bottle, which is a jar with a narrow neck and a wide bottom filled with vinegar. When the fly enters the jar, it has nowhere to go, so it drops to the bottom, which is filled with vinegar. Usually I lure the flies to the jar by placing something sweet on the lip. A glass device that they enter on their own accord when they fly to it is what I call a passive fly trap; but I devised a more active method, namely, stealthily transporting the jar to where they're resting and catching them by placing the mouth of the jar over them. I am extremely keen on catching them this way.

After twenty or thirty minutes, when I am tired of catching flies, I return to my manuscript and write two or three lines; but when I just can't write at all, I pick up a book (any book) lying near at hand and read five or six pages; and if I'm about to fall asleep over the book because of the heat, or fatigue, and a fly comes zooming at me from somewhere and lands on my face, I get up at once and go after it, now with the fly tube, and now with the fly bottle, from room to room, from the kitchen to the bathroom, looking in every nook and cranny, treading softly as a burglar. But when evening comes, without fail I lay down the fly-catching equipment, set down my pen on my manuscript paper, no matter how pressing the work may be, and leave the house as though I had some very important business to attend to.

Every evening of every day, like a weasel on a well-trod path, I board the same trolley car, slip down the same side street, and open the same screen door to enter that back-alley café. That's where I met and befriended Ichiki Naokichi.

Ichiki Naokichi patronized that café before I did. It opened about a month before I began going there, and I am told that Ichiki started going there about half a month before I did. And by a strange twist of fate, the friend who took Ichiki to the café for the first time was a middle school classmate of his and an employee of the S company, which advertised the fly tube that I had been looking for when I accidentally discovered the café. Yet what may make this story look even more like an elaborate fabrication is the fact that Ichiki's friend, the employee of the S company, invented the fly tube, and the text of the advertisement, which I had read with great interest, had been drafted by Ichiki himself.

"If that contraption were selling any better, I would be better off too, I would be getting a share of the profit," said Ichiki ruefully.

"Why are you always alone, doesn't that inventor ever come here?" I asked.

"Well, that. . . . He first brought me here, and for about a week we came here together every night. He's no longer with that company. . . ." And, being a man of few words, Ichiki said no more. But later, after we got to know each other better, he told me that, having invented the fly tube, his friend talked the owner of the café into selling it there and then borrowed funds under various assumed names and lent out the money without telling anyone about it; and that is why he was hiding out from everyone, including Ichiki.

But, as I said, that is what he told me much later. In the beginning, for a week or ten days at least, we saw each other every night, but each time our eyes chanced to meet across the tables we quickly looked elsewhere; neither of us spoke a word of greeting; indeed, there was between us something almost like a feeling of hostility.

He had a solemn air about him with his large, protruding eyes. He scarcely spoke even to the waitress when he summoned her for something, and then whatever he said, he said without a trace of a smile. In a word, I had never seen a man who seemed so unapproachable. But as I noted earlier, he and I were just about the only customers in that café in the evening. Aside from the two of us, once in a great while a clerk or an errand boy from one of the neighborhood trading offices or mail-order houses stopped by on his way home from the public bath, or before going home to bed, and ordered an ice cream or a soda; or a strolling couple from one of the local houses of assignation dropped in on the spur of the moment. Of course, you couldn't get a meal there. The menu was limited to ice cream, soda water, syrup-flavored coffee, and four or five brands of Western liquor. What was strange was that although I went there every day, I had seen the proprietor no more than two or three times. The only people who were always there were a sleepy-looking, bleary-eyed waitress and a man about thirty dressed in white, Western-style clothes who was always reading some sort of storybook and who was in charge of dishing out the ice cream and pouring the soda water. As if by prior arrangement, both were quite unfriendly, even curt. But one thing I noticed that seemed even stranger was that for a small, dirt-floored establishment that had only five tables and that was almost always empty and quiet, there seemed to be a lot of people upstairs in what was apparently the proprietor's living quarters. When I say that there seemed to be a lot of people upstairs, in fact, every evening I saw a number of well-dressed men walk, one by one, through the café, nod briefly to the man dressed in white, and enter the room in the back, where there seemed to be a staircase leading to the second floor. What was the proprietor doing? Were those people his friends? At any rate, that's what gave me the impression that there were always a lot of people in the room upstairs over my head. Once I asked the bleary-eyed waitress, "Is the proprietor's apartment upstairs?"

"No, it's farther to the rear. I don't know for certain, but I believe that some other people are renting the second and third floors." Her tone was rather equivocal. I didn't question her any further.

How on earth did Ichiki and I come to talk to each other in such a place? I don't remember the first time it happened, but as two castaways on a desert island will eventually speak to each other and become intimate, no matter how reserved and bashful they may be, so he and I (and we were taciturn by nature and shy as close-lipped people often are) began to talk to one another and drew closer together as time went on.

As I said before, from the time I got up in the morning until evening I was always at home, exerting myself at my work, the writing of sentences. It was hot, and I wasn't making any progress, and on top of that I had to entertain, not only newspaper and magazine people who were sent to urge me to finish my assignments, but young people who wanted to write and sought the advice of an established author. But I avoided some of the latter by having my wife go to the door to tell them that I wasn't receiving anyone because I had to meet a deadline for a writing assignment but that if it were convenient, or if they wished to, would they please go to such and such a café in Kyōbashi, where I would be sure to be that evening after eight. I felt abashed as I eavesdropped on the exchange at the doorway between my wife, who, though reluctant to do this, explained that I couldn't see anyone, and the caller, who received her explanation ever so politely. But on most occasions I soon enough put my manuscript aside and, using in turn the fly tube and fly bottle, worked up a sweat as I stalked the flies that landed on the candy bowl, hunted down the horseflies clustered in the corners of the ceiling, and went after the bear flies as well as the little flies. I didn't get tired when I caught flies, but I tired rather easily when I worked on a manuscript, so that for every fifty flies I caught I wrote barely one page. And when a day spent in this sort of activity ended, I lay aside my manuscript paper, pen, books, and dictionaries, all the tools of my trade, and put away the bottle, the box, and all the other instruments for catching flies, and took off like a weasel down the same road for the café in the back alley of Kyōbashi ward.

Usually Ichiki arrived twenty or thirty minutes before I did and was sitting at his regular place at a table in the corner, staring dead ahead with a blank expression on his face and puffing away at his cigarette, usually Golden Bat brand, as though it had neither taste nor odor. Had his goggle eyes been focused on the paintings on the wall, or the vase of flowers on the table, or the sidewalk outside the door, it wouldn't have made any difference, for he saw nothing. His expression was completely vacant. Yet what attracted me most were his eyes. In a word, they were the eyes of a person deep in thought. His was the look of a detective, or a stockbroker, or a philosopher, or of someone, no matter the profession, who worried. I often wondered what kind of work he did.

On the fourth day after I had begun talking with him I learned that though we had attended different universities and were a year apart, we had studied the same kinds of subjects. I had been in the literature department, and he was a graduate of the philosophy department. As we gradually became more intimate, from time to time he aired his grievances. "Nowadays, unlike before, people in literature, no matter how obscure, can somehow make a living by translating or writing literary essays; but in philosophy there is still no way of earning money. Could it be that I'm too awkward or lack the skills? I've tried several times to write literary essays and popular prose, but the magazine publishers just won't accept them. . . ."

"Excuse me for saying so," I said, "but I seem to remember seeing your name several times in magazines. . . ."

"Oh yes—I do write once in a while." Then glowering as if he were angry and as he was wont to do, he said, "But even if I wrote gossipy news of the sort published by the coterie journals, no magazine other than a second-class one would accept it; and then there are no magazines that will publish anything philosophical even if written by people quite a bit more distinguished than I am. You know, and this isn't funny, I don't average five yen a month for what I write, yet by some twist of fate I happen to like philosophy so much that I can't live without it. If I could write about something more fashionable like economics or social problems, it would be easier to make a living, but as luck would have it, those things don't interest me in the least."

Now, may I remind you that Ichiki never said everything he had on his mind all at once? He would let me go on talking and reply with one word to every ten of mine, and he spat out the words as if he were angry. Including all the meaningless expressions and sounds, if what he said were written out, it wouldn't come to much more than a line, and it took him all of three days to say it, and that is no lie. So I would like you to know that, to save time, I compressed into the above what it took him three days to get out.

For a long time I assumed that, as a specialist in philosophy, Ichiki Naokichi could do nothing but philosophize and as a result earned less than five yen per month. I didn't know about his other, more important "job." It isn't that I failed to notice that his dress was quite stylish for a philosopher. But the unlined kimonos that he wore directly over his bare skin that summer did not make him look particularly prosperous, and I never saw him wearing a half coat, or a hat, or socks, perhaps because of the nature of the place where we always met.

One time when I happened to arrive before him, I fell to talking with the weary-eyed woman who was the café's only waitress; when she said of Ichiki, "He's probably a stockbroker," I thought she was guessing at his profession from his appearance. "Why do you say that?" I asked. "He used to go to the stock exchange quite often with Mr. Akagi." "Mr. Akagi? . . ." "The Mr. Akagi of the fly tube," she said.

So that was the man who first brought him to the café, his middle school classmate who invented the fly tube and then later disappeared.

Actually, his main work, besides philosophizing, was trading on the stock exchange. And I was quite surprised later on when I heard from his own lips that it was not Akagi who introduced him to stock trading but the other way around. Ichiki Naokichi had been dabbling in stocks for quite a while before he enticed his former classmate, whose whereabouts were now unknown, to try his hand at it. So his household, which consisted of his wife and three children, was supported, not by philosophy, but by speculating on the stock market.

"You may think that I like gambling," said he. "Not so; mine is an eminently unconventional nature, and so except for playing the stock market, I hate gambling, as opposed to Mr. Akagi of the fly tube. He isn't interested in any game, be it cards, chess, sumo wrestling, or baseball, unless he can wager money on the outcome. Yet he didn't know that one can play the stock market until I told him so. When I think about it, this seems quite strange. I don't know where he is now—probably gambling somewhere, trying to make a living at it."

He related all of this in fragments, a sentence at a time. Ichiki himself seldom went to the exchange. He had taken Akagi there several times to teach him about it and had gone several times thereafter at Akagi's urging, but ordinarily he conducted his business by mail, as one might expect of a philosopher. He got his information on stock prices from the evening newspaper and then communicated his decisions to his broker by special delivery postcards—a way of doing business that may not be all that surprising if it's done by a person who trades but once or twice a month, but Ichiki was supposed to be making a living at it.

And what else did Ichiki do during the day while I was at home catching flies and writing at the rate of one page of manuscript for every fifty flies killed?

Unlike me he was a very late riser; it was always around one in the afternoon when he got up. During the summer, because he sweated easily and profusely, he could neither read nor write, and so, when he got up, he ate a brunch and then, rain or shine, set out from his house in Azabu for the used-book quarter in either Kanda, Hongō, or Ushigome. He had divided the used-book stores of Kanda into three sections, and considered those of Hongō and Ushigome as making up one section each, and every day from around two in the afternoon until evening he browsed in the stores of one of those sections, so that he returned to the same section every sixth day. Now, while he managed to scrape together enough money to go to the café every night, according to what he said, he couldn't afford to buy the books he fancied and went from store to store simply to take in the book scenery. In the beginning he used to buy a couple of books now and then, but nowadays he couldn't buy anything. In the beginning too he used to skim each and every book he laid his hands on, doggedly from cover to cover, picking up where he had left off the day before. Now, he pulled books off the shelves wherever he happened to stop while meandering about in the stores, opened them at random, read half a page here and another there, and imagined the rest. And so by calling into play his fancy, much more than he would have otherwise, he turned reading into an unsurpassed delight. And what kinds of books did he read? Well, he managed to limit himself to three types: books on philosophy, his specialty, books related to his work on the stock market, and books about mountains, which pleased me most and made me feel closer to him than ever.

As I go on in this manner some of you inattentive readers who forgot what I said earlier may imagine that, every evening when we met in the café where we were the only customers, all we did was talk and talk and talk on, exchanging all sorts of confidential information. Nothing is further from the truth; as I said before, I am anything but a talker, and he, among men of few words, is certainly the least talkative. In fact I don't believe that we spoke more than a single word every ten or even twenty minutes. And no matter how hot the evening, we seldom had something cool, like ice cream or soda water, but always ordered hot tea, so that the man in white Western clothes who was in charge of serving the liquor and boiling the water had to go to extra trouble for us each time. I don't know when, but it became our habit to sit on chairs facing each other at a table in the farthest corner of the room.

And so the summer passed, and it became fall, but that didn't change the pattern of our lives at all. Both he and I continued to go to the café in Kyōbashi at the end of each day. What did change was the length of the days, which grew shorter as the season advanced, so we began going there earlier. As for my daytime activities, since there were fewer flies, when I was not writing, I looked at photographs of mountains, read books about mountains, and studied maps of mountainous regions. But I spent most of the time, five times as much time as I spent writing, immersed in daydreaming about mountains and Yumeko. As for Ichiki, every other day he wrote a philosophical essay and then thought about it, and on the other days, following the pattern he had established over the summer, he continued to work his way through the used-book store districts. And at the end of the day we met in the café. Any third party seeing us from the outside would have been amazed by the dull regularity of our lives. The life of a clerk at city hall was probably less monotonous.

I believe it was in the very early part of October. . . .

(I didn't say anything, but I remember that I was surprised when Ichiki the fashionable philosopher, who prided himself on wearing light, unlined kimonos next to his skin, without any undergarment, showed up one day in a lined kimono.)

One evening, when the screen door of the café had already been replaced by the usual glass door, and Ichiki and I, sunk in silence, were leaning back in our chairs, half-emptied teacups before us, I thought I heard someone outside the door. I turned in that direction and caught sight of a human face peering through the glass. I found it strange that though the face and the footsteps came to a halt together, the door did not open. Was I imagining things? It looked like a small, white face. I couldn't make it out clearly because the interior was lit and the outside was dark. I felt sure that I had seen it before, so instead of turning away I raised myself off my seat and concentrated on looking in that direction. The person outside seemed to have recognized me; the door opened with a squeak, and who should appear but Nishimukai's friend Horito.

"Good heavens!" I shouted in surprise.

Horito blushed a little in embarrassment; his face, neither young nor old, looked as it had when I saw him some years ago, and he walked toward me as he used to, with the same womanish gait.

"When did you come? What? . . ." I started to say, then instantly caught myself. I remembered the time when he and Nishimukai and I had come down the mountain together from the generator station and Nishimukai told me that Horito wanted to go to Tokyo and asked me to find him a position in an orchestra or a place as a houseboy in a home where he could study music. And I remembered waiting over two or three months for news about the mountains from either him or Nishimukai and how annoyed I was when I didn't hear from them. But then when I think about it, I had better reasons for being ashamed of myself for being so selfish than I had for being irritated at them for not writing more often. I wrote to them because they lived in the same town as Yumeko, to whom I couldn't write directly. When I inquired about their well-being, it was Yumeko's that I had in mind. It was news about her, not them, that I wanted. And so when Horito suddenly stood before me, I didn't see him but saw through him what I wanted to see . . . and I was very happy.

When I questioned him, he told me that he had arrived in Tokyo several days ago and had tried to see me yesterday, but my wife came to the door and told him that I was busy writing during the day, so would he please go to such and such a café in Kyōbashi in the evening, where he would be sure to find me. So he had come to the café that evening, and I didn't know till then that he had already tried to see me because he had come right in the middle of the ten-minute period when I was working like the devil and my wife, who didn't want to disturb me just then, forgot to tell me about his visit.

"Where are you living now?" I asked.

"In Suga-chō in Yotsuya ward," he answered.

"Oh, the seal shop where Mr. Nishimukai worked?" I interrupted. "You haven't become a seal engraver yourself, have you?"

"No, the other day it was arranged for me to enter the School of Oriental Music in Kanda ward," he said with a self-satisfied air.

"Is that so? That's very good. I'd like to hear more about it later," I replied, and then I introduced him briefly to Ichiki. At some point, the conversation turned to mountains. Unlike Ichiki, Nishimukai, and myself, Horito didn't have any particular love of mountains, but he was born in Kiso in Shinshū and had lived in Suwa and at Shimajima, so he had no difficulty joining our conversation and answering our questions. Moreover, he gave us information about things we weren't even aware of, and as he got used to our company, he became gradually more loquacious and talked more than either of us.

Horito told us that in the summer there were hordes of mountain climbers in Suwa and that therefore it was anything but restful; in fact it was chaotic. But since all those people had left, now was the perfect time for us to go. And he added, "It's still like summer here, isn't it, Sensei? In Shinshū the mountain peaks are already covered with snow, and the air is so brisk at night and in the morning that the old folks have begun to use their foot warmers."

"Yes, it would be a good season for people like us who enjoy seeing mountains to take a trip there," interjected Ichiki, who had been listening silently for about thirty minutes while we talked.

His words moved me. That instant the mountains of Kai, the mountains of Shinano, their shapes and their towns, all those things that I had not seen for a long time stood before my mind's eye with the moist freshness of a landscape seen through tears.

"We should take a trip to Shinshū, shouldn't we?"

"Yes, indeed." Ichiki replied with an enthusiasm that was rare for him.

"What is Mr. Nishimukai doing?" I asked Horito. "You haven't said anything about him. . . ."

"Oh, yes," he replied. "Mr. Nishimukai is the same as always. . . . Yes . . . he's still playing his musical instruments."

"Has something happened?"

"Yes and no. . . . Nothing in particular. . . ." Horito was evasive.

I felt that something had happened. And that evening when I left Horito, I invited him to come and visit me the next afternoon, and he said that he would stop by on his way home from school. As I walked home alone that autumn evening I couldn't think of anything else but what might have befallen Nishimukai—what might have happened in that town and how she was faring. . . . Was she well? . . . Was she still a geisha? . . . I couldn't get rid of those preoccupations even on the following day, so I decided to put all thoughts of work out of my mind and yield to them, but in a positive way—not expecting the worst, waiting for Horito to tell me.

Horito called on me the next day punctually at three o'clock and started, at once, to tell me that he had heard that Nishimukai had a wife who left him some six or seven years ago. She, apparently, fell in love and ran off with an itinerant actor just about the time when she was despairing over the prospects of Nishimukai's seal-engraving business, that is, when she saw the rest of her life with Nishimukai as one of unending poverty.

Five or six months thereafter Nishimukai closed up the seal-engraving shop and entered the electric company's training school. But as soon as he started working at the generator station, his runaway wife, who somehow got word of his whereabouts, started writing to him at his new address.

Of course this was all hearsay, but Horito, who had befriended him shortly after Nishimukai joined the electric company, had learned quite a bit about this situation firsthand.

While he did not suspect, at the time, that the woman who wrote to Nishimukai from Tokyo and his former, runaway wife were one and the same person, he found out about it later on.

Nishimukai went to great lengths to get money to send to that woman, but he never talked about those letters, not even when asked about them. But one fine day. . . .

Nishimukai had returned to his hometown and was teaching music, rather successfully, and living with Horito (Nishimukai had taken him in when Horito was jobless, without prospects or resources, in other words, completely down on his luck) when, one fine day, a not altogether respectable-looking young woman—she didn't look like a geisha either—came calling on him in a ricksha rented at the railroad station. That woman was Nishimukai's former wife. And she moved into Nishimukai's place that very day and has been there ever since.

At first she was rather subdued, even docile, but it didn't take her long to revert to her old willful, egotistical ways and push the timid Nishimukai around as she had done in the past. Nishimukai felt ill at ease living with her in the presence of Horito, whom she did not like. He was of course literally Nishimukai's dependent, so Nishimukai became increasingly apologetic about Horito while at the same time trying to shield him from her ill temper. Horito, caught in between, sometimes tried to mediate their quarrels. I shouldn't say "their" quarrels, though, because she was, invariably, the aggressor. She relentlessly abused Nishimukai with the foulest language imaginable. Horito remembered especially one night when he had to listen to it all through the wall that separated his quarters from theirs.

So, listening to this and that, after a while Horito had a pretty good picture not only of their present relationship but of their past. She, apparently, had worked in a silk-thread factory and had known quite a few men before she married Nishimukai. And even after she was married, and up to the time she ran away with the itinerant actor, she had had a number of affairs. And it is safe to assume that she wasn't without male companionship after she ditched her traveling actor—or did he ditch her?—and went to Osaka—or was it Nagoya?—and finally came back to Tokyo.

What she did to earn her living during that time, of course, only the gods know.

Nishimukai, as I have said before, spared himself no trouble to get and send her the money she requested in her brazen, heartless letters.

"Could he do such a thing if he were not in love? He must be in love with her, don't you think so, Sensei?" Horito said to me. To which I replied, "No sentimentality, no love could inspire such behavior. Indeed, as I listen to you I cannot help thinking that Nishimukai is a great human being—in some ways."

That wife of Nishimukai's must be pretty hysterical. At any rate, after listening to Horito's account of her behavior, it was very hard not to draw that conclusion.

As we continued to talk about it a few more events came into clearer focus. For instance, Nishimukai's going to Tokyo was not entirely motivated by his desire to establish himself professionally; that runaway wife of his was behind it to quite an extent. And it was she who enticed him—so Horito believed—to leave the seal-engraving shop in Yotsuya. At any rate, when he did so and rented a flat in Ushigome, she refused to live with him. No wonder he looked so dejected around that time. It must have been because of her that he wandered about looking at mountains. He must have been weeping inwardly all the while. And he must have talked about mountains simply to avoid confessing his troubles. He could have confided in me, for instance.

Although it became increasingly uncomfortable for him to stay there, Horito withstood all that commotion and strain fairly well for about three months. It was much harder on Nishimukai. Having to watch both his wife's behavior and the growing discomfort of his friend, he became more and more constrained and upset. In fact, he reached the point where he misread the score when he gave his music lessons—something he had never done before. And one time, when that woman threw a fit in the back room, he hid himself for over two hours while four or five of his students were waiting for their lessons. They became confused and impatient and left one by one, so that when he finally came out to meet them they had all gone. And so it went on day after day until his reputation was completely ruined.

Then, at a time when that wife of his was out of the house, he talked to Horito in private, saying: "I am truly sorry for having caused you to be embroiled in this awful situation and extremely grateful for your contributions to the success of the music school. But if you continue to stay, you'll end up like me. You're still young, so why don't you go to Tokyo as you've always wanted to? You have put up with my wife's selfishness for quite some time; and it was absolutely pointless. I pretended not to see it, I couldn't admit it to myself, but now I am convinced that you should leave. So, how about going to Tokyo? I know the owner of a seal-engraving shop in Yotsuya; I'll introduce you to him. And there's a school in Kanda that's fairly easy to enter, so please go. I'll pay for your meals at the seal shop and the monthly tuition at the music school. As for spending money,

I'll write to the shop owner about it, but you talk to him too; you can earn it at the shop running errands or something. But when I send you money, you must not write to acknowledge it, and if something unforeseen comes up, write to me through one of the people who come to the house; you can put your letter in a double envelope and send it to Mr. Nagai at the clock shop, for instance. No, no, there's no need to stand on ceremony; that money will come from the tuition fees of the students you've worked so hard to recruit for me. No, you mustn't feel obligated to me on any account. It's enough that I should suffer on account of a woman like my wife. I made a mistake when I married her, and I'm resigned to my fate; but there's no reason why you should have to share my bad luck. No, no, it's nothing to feel thankful about. Indeed, it is I who should be grateful; please study for the two of us. . . ."

And so they wept together like two women. And to tell the truth, as I listened to Horito's story I felt a stinging in my eyes, and though I tried to hold it back, eventually I had to cry.

From that time on without fail, about every other day, or every three days, Horito's small, womanish figure appeared at the café in Kyōbashi where Ichiki and I met. The striped double-threaded cotton kimono that he wore on his small frame was fashionably long-skirted and hid his geta; his obi was, for a man, tied immoderately high over his chest, and when he bowed, he never failed to tilt his neck slightly and place both hands next to each other over his knees;[20] his every gesture was so much like a woman's that the bleary-eyed maid sometimes muttered behind his back, "What an unpleasant person. He's just like a woman—how odious!"

According to what he said, although she was over six months pregnant, Yumeko, my beloved, was still working as a geisha in that mountain town at the time he left. When, however, I mentioned that I wanted to ask Nishimukai for more information about her, Horito was alarmed. He told me that a letter in which questions were asked about the activities of a geisha would be sure to make Nishimukai's wife extremely suspicious and unhappy. As with all hysterical wives, her suspicion was easily aroused. She would believe that Nishimukai had a questionable relationship with some geisha and would not only closely watch him when he read the letter but forbid him to answer it.

What he said was a greater blow to me than if I had heard that my food supply had been cut off. I was dumbfounded and sat there facing Horito, speechless for over five minutes.

By that time Ichiki and I were as intimate as if we had been friends for over ten years. As I have repeated so often, in the several novels in which I proclaimed my relationship with her, I had altered the facts and fictionalized over half the events that I described, but in spite of the addition of a good portion of novelistic fancy, I had expressed my innermost feelings so honestly as to make myself appear foolish. Ichiki, who had read my novels, every so often asked me about the woman in the mountains, as if it were a joke. And I told him in the same tone, jokingly, the truth that lay in my heart. And when he said to me, "I'd like to come along the next time you go to those mountains," I replied, "Of course." "Whether I meet her or not, it's too embarrassing to go there alone, so I should be pleased if you were to accompany me."

And in this same manner, as if he were telling a joke, Ichiki talked to me, from time to time, about his lamentable situation. Putting together the disconnected statements he had made over a period of several days, it seemed that during the last six months he had suffered loss upon loss on the stock market. Not only had he lost his wife's inheritance, with which he had set up his operation, but he had borrowed money as well. He had had some gains, but when balanced out, his losses were always greater than his gains. His wife's capital had disappeared in less than two or three years, and despite the money he managed to borrow from her relatives and friends, he had reached an impasse. No one would lend him anything anymore. He couldn't, of course, declare a profit, but neither could he declare a loss; he might be subject to punishment. Why? Well, he had for years already been living off borrowed money that he was supposed to invest; that is, instead of making the borrowed money grow for the benefit of the lenders, he had used it to keep his three children, himself, his wife, and a maid in food and clothing.

"Indeed, my market activities add up to neither gain nor loss," he concluded, with a smile that put creases on either side of his mouth.

From the end of autumn he skipped coming to the café every fifth, fifteenth, and last day of the month. Curious about why he was staying away precisely on those days, I asked him. He answered, quite simply, "Because the bill collectors know that I come to this café." And then he asked me, "Aren't we going to take a trip?" and, "Where should we go?"

He had, of late, hardly talked about anything else. Yet he had to put these questions in as halting a manner as ever. Since I too was eager to travel (I hadn't gone anywhere since spring), ignoring Horito, we took the Japan Ministry of Railroads map, which was hanging on the wall, spread it on the table, drew our heads together over it, and talked about the trip we planned to take as excitedly as middle school students would.

"Have you ever been to a place called Mount Minobu?"

"No, I haven't."

"I heard that if you climb Mount Shichimen, which is next to Mount Minobu, you can see the Kōshū basin and get a good view of the Kōshū mountains. . . ."

These were some of the things we said to each other.

Was it two or three days later? We were at the café. Having nodded to each other, exchanged a few words, and then seated ourselves across from each other, we had already fallen into a state of absentminded reverie when Ichiki took out of his pocket a sheaf of manuscript paper neatly tied together and wordlessly pushed it toward me. Wondering what on earth this could be all about. . . .

Leave Tokyo, 1:00 P.M. Spend the night on the train. Arrive at Fuji approximately four the next morning. Change trains. Arrive at Mount Minobu around seven o'clock the same day. Thirty minutes to go to Sanmon, four miles away, by ricksha or horse-drawn carriage; automobiles also available. Arrive at Kuonji temple on Mount Minobu around eight o'clock the same day.[21] Mount Shichimen approximately fifteen miles from Kuonji temple. Spend the night at the Shichimen hall on top of the mountain. Leave Mount Shichimen at six o'clock the next morning. Arrive at Minobu at noon. Lunch. Leave Minobu at 1:00 P.M. Enjoy the scenery of Fujigawa river from a carriage or ricksha or from an automobile; anticipate arrival at Kōfu that evening. Leave Kōfu by train the next day at noon. Arrive at Tokyo Shinjuku station in the evening. The train fare from Tokyo to Minobu is eight yen, twelve sen. The breakfast on the train is forty sen, the tea eight sen; the total is eight yen, sixty sen. From Minobu to Sanmon, ricksha fee, one yen. Round-trip fare to the Fujigawa river bridge, ten sen. Lunch on Mount Minobu, one yen, fifty sen (tea included). Overnight

> lodgings on Mount Shichimen, three yen, fifty sen.
> Lunch in the town of Minobu, two yen. Carriage fare
> from Minobu to Kōfu, approximately eight yen (not
> certain). Overnight lodgings at Kōfu, six yen (tea and
> maid service included). Kōfu. Geisha's fee, anticipate
> six yen. Kōfu to Tokyo, three yen, ninety-two sen.
> Lunch (box lunch on train, tea included), forty-eight
> sen. Miscellaneous expenses, ten yen.
>
> Total: fifty-one yen, ten sen.

This was, roughly, what had been written in a neat hand
without a single erasure. A rough map of our itinerary was attached to the last page of the manuscript paper.

As I wondered when this grave-looking researcher in philosophy, this laconic stockbroker, had found the time to write this
down and why he had done so, I had to make quite an effort to
keep a straight face.

"What is this item, the 'geisha's fee' at Kōfu, next to the
overnight lodgings expenses at Kōfu?" It wasn't that I couldn't
guess, but I wanted to make sure, so I asked.

"That's for a geisha. I thought that one would probably be
enough," he answered without smiling.

"Oh, payment for one geisha, is it?" I replied, also with a
straight face.

We talked about how interesting the road would be from
Minobu back to Fuji river and how grand Mount Shichimen
would look from Kōfu, but at no time had either of us proposed
to translate the plan into action. Ten or fifteen days later we
talked again.

"It's said that if you go to Ontake in Kōshū and from there
to Shimokurodaira plain and Masatomi, in that order, the

panorama at Tokusa pass is magnificent; Mount Kinpu is right next to it, and from there you can see Mount Fuji in the distance."

"We could probably climb a mountain like Mount Kinpu."

"Oh, no, don't they say that mountains like Kinpu and Kokushi and Kobushin are the most difficult of all to climb?"

Three or four days after this conversation, Ichiki brought in another sheaf of manuscript paper on which he had neatly outlined an itinerary and estimate of our expenses; he also brought a map, which he silently spread out on the table before me.

From about that time, Horito came to the café less and less frequently; in the beginning he had come practically every other day, and then once every fourth day; of late he came but once a week, and he hardly ever called at my house in the daytime. On one of the rare occasions when I met him at the café, I asked him, "How is school?" "Well, it's not terribly interesting," he replied in a small voice.

In the beginning he had been so grateful and pleased just to be in Tokyo enrolled in a music school, something he had never dreamed possible when he was in the country; and now, in no time at all, his attitude had changed so drastically. Of course, one could interpret this change as backsliding, or one could consider it a sign of progress. It seemed to me that Horito had at times applied himself energetically to his music studies but that, though he could with his talents have made a living in the provinces, as Mr. Nishimukai did, he did not have a clear idea of what it meant to earn a living in Tokyo. And like many young men his age and in his position, he expressed uneasiness about the future, complained about having to live almost as a dependent at the seal shop, and inquired how much money he would need to live in the cheapest sort of boarding house in Tokyo. In short, he seemed pretty unsettled.

One evening—it was already winter—Ichiki and I were sitting across from each other at the square table, with a cracked porcelain brazier on the empty chair beside us. As was often the case, we didn't talk. I kept gulping, like a horse, quantities of black tea, and Ichiki, who smoked four packs of Shikishima cigarettes a day, was blowing smoke like a chimney. The bleary-eyed waitress, who had brought me a fresh serving of tea, said as she stirred up the coals in the hibachi, "That person, what was his name? The womanish man, Mr. Horito, hasn't been around at all lately has he?"

"No, he doesn't seem to come anymore. He probably found a better place elsewhere," I said. "This sort of place doesn't suit a young man like Mr. Horito."

"Oh, do you mean to say that the two of you are old men?"

"No, we're middle-aged. But then to come here one has to be not only middle-aged but oddballs as we are."

Ichiki, who had been silently puffing away till now, turned to me. "Horito came to my place two or three days ago, you know. I was still sleeping when he came."

Of late Horito hadn't come to see me, so I wasn't all that pleased to learn that he had gone to Ichiki's house. "Is that so? Has he changed any?" I asked.

"No, not really. But it seems that he's leading a pretty fast life these days."

I imagined that we would be discussing Horito for a while, but Ichiki being Ichiki, the conversation petered out in no time, so I broached another subject. Pointing to a bulky, paper-wrapped package that he had put on one of the corners of the table, I asked him, "Did you buy another toy today?" "No," he answered.

Why did I ask him that when I saw his package? Well, every third day, although he was very poor then, he came to the café carrying a package with something he had purchased, not for himself or his wife, but for his children, always toys for the children. Also, depending on how he felt, he brought with him to the café either his oldest child, who was nine, or the next to oldest, who was seven, or the youngest, who was four, much as I took a particular walking stick from my collection to suit my mood on a particular day.

All his children, the two boys and the girl, had big, shining, bulging eyes as he did, and they were gentle and, except for the girl, already as taciturn as he was. Ichiki spoke so little even when he was with his children (and he was very fond of them) that one could hardly notice the difference between the times he came to the café with them and the times he came with a package instead.

At another time he said to me, "When I read your novels, I get the impression that you are absolutely carefree."

"Carefree because I have no children?"

"Yes."

"I thought that it must be nice to have children," I said, and since it was still summer, I added, "If I had children, I wouldn't spend so much time catching flies."

"If you seek enlightenment, children surely are an impediment."

"So I am better off catching flies after all?" I said this in jest, but he, as straightfaced as ever, countered, "Even fly catching can become a spiritual discipline if you keep it up long enough. Bodhidharma[22] had to sit on a rock for three years. There is a saying, don't you know, that children are a burden in any possible world, past, present, or future. Not only children, but any possessions, anything that is dear to you."

"Yes, but aren't children our most valuable possessions?"

"Your walking sticks also seem to be pretty valuable." When he said this, there were wrinkles in the corners of his mouth, and he smiled for the first time, and as he continued, "Yes, walking sticks may be barriers to enlightenment," he guffawed. "Ha, ha, ha, ha."

But after a while I felt quite melancholy. That conversation about children had conjured up images of Yumeko, the geisha, now pregnant with her second child, eyes downcast, demurely sitting by the foot warmers in her own home or in a guest's room, for in those mountains people were already seeking out the warmth of their foot warmers. And I thought of how trying her life was, and then I was reminded of the desolation of my own childless house. Ichiki may have had a point when he compared my life to the way of the Bodhidharma, but when I considered that my wife and I had nothing more valuable than walking sticks to tie us to this world, I was overcome by a strange feeling of loneliness.

Then there was the time when Ichiki, that philosopher, remarked, "Indeed, you don't have my kind of burdens, but how about Yumeko, that person who is all over your novels—you are romantic, you know. Isn't she what is most valuable in your life?"

"You've got me there." I probably said this smiling the way he did, with creases on either side of my mouth. But in fact, had he said this or not, I would have been thinking the same thing. And this may seem childish, but children sometimes die, and one falls out of love, and couples do divorce, but until I die the kind of feeling I have for her there in the mountains will never disappear, even if she has a dozen children, or becomes somebody's concubine, or dies. . . .

I hadn't heard from Nishimukai in the mountains for several months when I got a letter that read, "It has been a very long time since I last wrote. Are you all right? I hope you are well. It seems that we shall have an extremely cold winter this year; I believe that the lake will be completely frozen in another month. There also seems to be much more snow on the mountains than usual. Do you sometimes see Mr. Horito? I would also like to go to Tokyo. The enclosed appeared in yesterday's newspaper; I cut it out to send it to you."

The clipping, a small piece of paper with hardly a paragraph on it, was stuck in the bottom of the envelope, and I hadn't seen it at first. The five- or six-line announcement was sandwiched between two other articles and printed in that small, faint pica so common in country newspapers. It read: "Geisha retires. Suwa gay quarters geisha, Yumeko, daughter of the House of Dreams, twenty-three years old, submitted her notice to retire. Reason: 'little drum.'" The style was obviously clumsy and disagreeable, yet for a long time it didn't occur to me to tear it up; it's not that I doubted the rumors I had heard or disbelieved what I had learned from Horito and from Nishimukai, but seeing the announcement in faint, blurry pica print, I felt as though I were being forced to listen to a last verdict, and for a while I was pretty dispirited. "Little drum"—what did the words mean? Swollen belly? The words that affected me most, however, were "twenty-three years old," right below her name, just like in the reports of robberies and drownings. She was twenty-one when I first met her; therefore, it was only natural that she should be twenty-three now and, in forty more days when the year ends, turn twenty-four. Yet I not only felt that there was quite a difference between twenty-one and twenty-four but also worried that being the daughter of the House of Dreams, as the newspaper article said, that is, practically the mistress of the house, and having two children, and being twenty-four, she may decide never to work as a geisha again. On top of that, should I decide to go to her mountain town, I couldn't even hope to see her from afar anymore . . . walking by, holding up her skirts. . . . With her big belly she most probably doesn't leave her house, doesn't venture a step outside. So all I could accomplish would be to make myself more miserable yet.

That evening, when I met Ichiki at the café as usual, down-playing my feelings as much as possible, and in as indirect a manner as possible, I related to him the terribly shocking experience I had had that day. His reaction, as usual, was laconic and measured. While I began to feel uncomfortably self-conscious as I went on and fell silent, he, using the simplest words possible, at the slowest possible rate (breaking the silence once every five minutes, then three times every ten), remarked, "Not even your ideal woman can withstand the attention of the newspaper reporters, can she?" and, "That reference to her age, twenty-three years, is unpleasant, isn't it?" and, " 'Little drum' is a curious expression, isn't it?"

I was beginning to feel the strain and was trying to find a way to change the subject when he broke the silence again with, "When you reflect on it, our positions are reversed, aren't they? Your anguish is more philosophical, while mine is more novelistic. . . ." He smiled. His smile was infectious. I smiled. After another pause of two or three minutes, he said, "Let's take that trip, not just talk about it." He sounded quite excited.

"By all means, let's. I've been wanting to go somewhere, any-where, for quite a while. But where should we go?" I asked.

"Well. . . . Don't be shy. How about Shinshū?"

I was "shy" about it but of course approved wholeheart-edly. "Yes," I said. "The snow in the mountains is probably already deep, and they say that the cold is especially severe this year. . . ."

"But going in the summer to Shinshū, the so-called snow and ice country, is so prosaic; isn't it more interesting to go in the winter?"

"You're right," I chimed in, hiding my joy as much as I could.

I'm sure that it took Ichiki less than a week to make up an itinerary for a trip to Shinano, complete with expense estimates. (I remember well . . . because I remember so well the evening we debated the pros and cons of this and that about the trip . . . we debated as we never did before.) It read:

> Leave Iidamachi, 11:00 P.M. Plan to arrive at Kiso Fukushima, the next afternoon between one and three, depending on the weather; get off at Shiojiri and stroll about for approximately an hour and a half. View the Northern Japan Alps. . . .

We lost our sense of time as, with the zeal of elementary school boys planning a school outing, we pored over Ichiki's manuscript paper. His characters were well formed in every detail. He must have corrected and recopied his first draft several times over, as a conscientious student would.

According to his plan, we would first enjoy the winter sights of the Kiso highway from the train window and spend the night at Kiso Fukushima. Then we would return to Matsumoto, and go as far as Ōmachi on the narrow-gauge railway, and spend one or two nights there. He went on to say, "On the way, we'll pass Hotaka, Yari, and Ariake, and then when we arrive in Ōmachi, Shirouma and all the other mountains will probably be white with snow, won't they? I'll bet the scenery will be so bright it will hurt our eyes. You have a real academic knowledge of mountains, so you probably know that the one called Ariake is supposed to be a truly splendid mountain. And you know the poem by the monk Saigyō that goes, "I want to travel that lonely road and see Mount Ariake in the West in Shinano."[23] People like the monk Saigyō really walked a lot, didn't they?"

I had never before seen him so excited and talkative.

"Well, then, we'll return to Matsumoto from Ōmachi, spend one night at the Asama hot springs, and, depending on circumstances, we might spend one night at the Akakura hot springs at the foot of Mount Myōdaka—but we'll probably go to Akakura another time—and then we'll go to Suwa.

> Arrive in Suwa 5:10. Stay as many days as we want. Lodgings fee not fixed; geisha's fee not fixed. Arrive Iidamachi 5:21 P.M.

"At last I'll get a chance to see Yumeko, that geisha I've known through your novels for so long." Ichiki seemed quite excited, which was so rare for him. "She's retired now, isn't she? At any rate, I'm delighted to go to that province, to that town you are so fond of," he continued.

So we had decided on where to go but still had not decided when we were going. Maybe we could have decided that too had we remained at the café until 11:30 as we usually did, and then maybe not.

I sat across from Ichiki facing the door at an angle, so that when I happened to glance in that direction, I saw a strange man on the other side of the glass pane beckoning as if he had an urgent message. For me? For Ichiki? I didn't believe that it was for me. I alerted Ichiki. He took a look, then with another glance gave me to understand that he didn't know the man. When we both looked at him at the same time, he pulled back at once. After a while, feeling uneasy, I looked up, and there he was again, motioning as insistently as ever. Now, I must say, that man made me feel quite uncomfortable. There he was in a deserted back alley, late at night, his face half hidden by darkness, peering and gesturing at me from behind a glass door. I could hardly pretend not to have noticed him or his hand signals, so I gathered up my courage and went to the door. As I opened the door, the man outside, about two yards away, continued to beckon to me. I saw at a glance that he was swarthy, goggle eyed, wore a hunting cap and a tight-sleeved kimono, and was determined to lead me somewhere with his hand signals. I grew more apprehensive by the minute yet resolutely took a few steps in his direction, and, at that moment, it occurred to me that he could be a detective. But what could a detective want of me? I felt more and more queasy.

As it turned out, the man *was* a detective. He showed me his badge, led me out of the light under the eaves of a nearby house, apologized for his rude behavior, and explained that the second floor of the café was used by a host of gamblers the police wanted to apprehend that very night. Everything had been carefully planned, but they were anxious that no harm should come to innocent bystanders. So could I go back in the café and, without telling him why, get Ichiki to leave with me as if we were going home as usual? Our leaving the café would be the signal for the police to move in. . . .

All this was quite shaking; yet even more unsettling, although one might expect it of a detective, was the fact that he knew both our names, and he let me know it by mentioning them again and again.

As he went on talking, I also noticed here and there, under the eaves of houses and other dark places, a number of policemen standing ready as if for a rice riot.[24] The chin straps of their hats were pulled down, their sabres were tied down to prevent them from rattling, and, perhaps most impressive, they all wore gaiters and straw sandals. I had never seen them so outfitted and armed, so ready . . . not even at political rallies or labor strikes.

At the signal that the operation was about to begin, countless numbers of them moved forward as stealthily as crawling flies.

I was shaking. Get Ichiki out of the café and flee this place with him was all I could think of. I signaled my intention to the detective and was on my way when, on a sudden impulse, I retraced my steps to ask him if I should warn the bartender and the waitress.

"Not on your life," he chided me. "They're in cahoots with them. You and Mr. Ichiki just come out of there together without saying a word, please."

As I returned to the café, I recalled that the bartender had indeed looked strangely alarmed a few minutes ago when the detective peered through the door and beckoned me, and when I thought about it, he had looked frightened when Horito peered through the door the first time he came to see me.

By that time I was so scared I didn't want to go inside, so I opened the door just a crack and called, "Mr. Ichiki, Mr. Ichiki!" Ichiki came with a suspicious look on his face, and scurrying right behind him, as if he were pursuing Ichiki, was the white-uniformed man from behind the bar. I was startled. Without thinking I retreated a few steps. And as Ichiki came through the squeaking door with the white-uniformed man right behind him, literally in the twinkling of an eye, the detective leaped from the darkness where he had been hiding and grabbed the bartender by the arm.

At that moment all hell broke loose. The police had moved in from all directions.

If I hadn't known what was going on behind all that ruckus and racket on the second floor—timid as I am—I would probably have been petrified with terror.

It seemed that most of the gamblers had instinctively fled to the back door, but there were surely more policemen there than in front where we were. Five or six of them were now on either side of the roof. One of the gamblers jumped off the roof and was caught. Another was caught in the foyer of the café. So together with the waitress and the bartender, who had been caught before, we had witnessed four arrests. That was enough.

On shaky legs we made our way to the foot of Kyōbashi bridge, where, in a daze, we bid each other a listless good-bye.

I felt as if I were in a dream.

Later I heard the astonishing news that Ichiki's middle school friend Akagi was one of the gamblers who had been arrested that night. Akagi, the inventor of the fly trap, whose whereabouts were supposedly unknown. I recall that when I heard the story, I spent at least an hour trying to imagine what kind of man that Akagi was.

It was sometime after the twentieth of December when Nishimukai suddenly appeared at my front door. He looked so haggard I was shocked. Before he was thin because he was undernourished; now he looked as if he had been wasted by a broken heart, and he wore a new kimono I had never seen on him before and carried a Western-style umbrella.

"When did you arrive?" I led him to the parlor, asking him the usual polite questions.

"I got here yesterday morning at five."

"Oh, then you spent last night at the seal shop in Yotsuya?" I asked.

"Yes. . . ."

"Did you meet Horito?"

"Yes, I did." He sort of twisted his arm around his neck in embarrassment, something I hadn't seen in quite some time. "Sensei, you probably know a certain Mr. Ichiki. When I went to Yotsuya yesterday, right after I arrived, I was told that Horito had left a month and a half ago and was now staying at Mr. Ichiki's house in Azabu."

"What? . . ." I had heard that Horito had seen a lot of him recently, but . . . I was dumbfounded. Nishimukai didn't seem particularly surprised.

"He was somewhat like that in the country already, he played around, but never stopped studying for all that. But after coming here it seems he got much worse. He gave up his studies altogether. Tokyo is a frightening place, isn't it?"

"Did you go to Mr. Ichiki's place?" I asked.

"Yes, I went there before coming here, but I didn't meet Mr. Ichiki. He was still sleeping. . . . I understand that you have never been there yourself, have you? It's a very big house, you know. I heard that there is an eight-mat room, a six-mat room, and a four-and-a-half-mat room upstairs; I met Horito in the six-mat guest room. He was very upset. He said he was ashamed to see me. That shows that he's still good at heart. He acted like a woman. When he saw me, he hid his face in his sleeve and burst out crying.

"He told me he stopped going to school three months ago, and now, even if he wanted to, he couldn't go back; he hasn't paid the tuition. It seems that his playing around in Tokyo started when he was invited out by the workers at the seal-engraving shop in Yotsuya. But those workers' playing time was limited to the few fixed holidays they had, whereas he, much as any student, had lots of free time; all he lacked was the money. That's where the original arrangement for him to earn spending money came in. . . ."

When Nishimukai came to the important places in his story, he looked embarrassed, as though he were talking about himself.

Of course, Horito was quite clever in ways; he had learned to carve seals in the country by imitating Nishimukai, and in Tokyo he began by engraving three-character and other kinds of simple seals during some of his free time to earn spending money. But as he spent more and more time playing, his need for money increased to the point where he gave up his music lessons and finally stopped going to school and carved seals from morning to night. The people at the shop wondered, Did he come to Tokyo to study music or to carve seals? At any rate, he had reversed his priorities, put the cart before the horse, so to speak. He now worked all day long, as fast as he could, to earn as much as he could to pay for his nighttime activities. Meanwhile, living at the shop became more difficult; the workers disliked him; even the women he patronized began to treat him with contempt; there was no way out but to ask Ichiki if he could stay at his house.

"Apparently Horito went to see Ichiki quite often, although he rarely called on me. It's strange, isn't it?" I said.

"I said the very same thing to Horito"—Nishimukai sounded as constrained as ever—"and he told me that you intimidate him and that it was therefore difficult for him to visit you. Sensei, what sort of person is this Mr. Ichiki?"

"What kind of person? . . . He's impossible to describe in a few words," I said, embarrassed.

"Well, he most certainly must be a kind person. I'm truly grateful. As I said, I wasn't able to meet him today, but will you allow me to accompany you when you visit him?"

"Yes, certainly, we'll go together. By the way, do you think Horito will go back to school after all?"

"Well, when I saw him today, he said that he wants to go back to the country. . . ."

"And how about you?" I don't know how many times I wanted to ask him that. But when I finally did, he changed the subject. Had he done that because he knew what was really on my mind, or did he do it without thinking? I couldn't tell.

"Sensei, four or five nights ago I felt quite depressed, so I went to Suwa, I hadn't been there for ages, and to the Heart of the Lake Pavilion to drink. As you can imagine, in no time it was past ten, and I was pretty drunk, but I still had some time left before the train would leave for Okaya, so to sober up I went for a walk. I wandered about aimlessly for a while, then went north past the Kado house, then walked several hundred yards on the road that goes past the House of Dreams to the generator station. As you know, there is a ravine to the left of town by the lake; well, the wind that came whistling up from down there went right through my bones, even though I was drunk. Shivering, I headed back to town, and as I passed the House of Dreams I noticed that, for some reason, the front door had been left open. As you know, that house is built in a somewhat unusual way. There's a small garden immediately inside the gate, then there is a four-yard or so frontage as houses on a theater stage have, and from the road one can see four papered panels leading into the interior. But you know, Sensei, I have never seen the paper on those panels except in tatters, and this may well be because of the child who is living there. At any rate, as I passed by, there was Miss Yumeko's child clinging to the door, peering through the holes in the paper, and screaming. Whether he was crying because Miss Yumeko was out on an errand somewhere or because the grandmother wasn't there, his screams, forgive me for saying so, were inhuman. Aaahr . . . aaahr, aahr . . . he sounded like an animal. That's all there is to my story . . . but that child, Sensei . . . they say that he'll be four years old at the beginning of the new year, and he still can't talk, all he says is aaahr . . . ah. . . ."

As he got ready to leave I happened to ask him again, "Where is it that you are staying? Oh yes, I remember, you said Yotsuya, didn't you?" "Yes, that. . . ." He sounded embarrassed but added, "I'll come to see you again soon, if I may. And Horito said that he would come soon too to apologize."

On his way out, as if intending to leave a souvenir behind, he put a package wrapped in newspaper on the foyer floor. "By the way, this. . . ." And before I knew it he was gone. It was a typical gift of his: half a dozen handkerchiefs of very good quality and two containers of face powder, each item wrapped separately in white paper and tied with a gift cord.

Two days later Horito came. He hadn't called on me for a long time and had gone to live at Ichiki's house without telling me. At first, he seemed quite uncomfortable. He looked more diminutive, more deferential, more womanish than ever before, but recovered soon enough his usual composure, a sort of blend of brazen loquacity and utter obsequiousness.

"Sensei, I heard that Miss Yumeko has stopped working. Of course, that's to be expected, she has been with child for seven or eight months already, but she'll be working again next summer. After all, she's still quite young, and the person she calls her mother is very strict if not cruel. She'll be working again indeed!"

What he said made me very happy.

Wanting to change the subject, I asked, "Have you seen Mr. Nishimukai recently?"

"Yes, I saw him today before coming here."

"Where is he staying? In Yotsuya?" That question was only to make conversation. I had already asked it of Nishimukai himself.

"No, he's more circumspect than that. He is afraid that his wife will come after him. He is staying at the Koshinkan, a rooming house in Shinjuku. And because he doesn't like rooming houses, he said that he is going to look for a room in Ushigome where he rented a flat the last time he was here."

"You say that his wife is after him? . . ." I was really surprised. "Mr. Nishimukai dislikes his wife and has run away from her?"

"Yes. He said that she has made his life unbearable and that he won't go back. In truth, who could put up with such a wife? As he said, he lost a number of his music students of late because of her. And I believe that to be the main reason why this kind, long-suffering man took such a drastic step."

"Well then, did he come to stay in Tokyo for a while?"

"No, I don't think so. He says things here are not at all the way they are in the country . . . and if his wife found out that he is in Tokyo. . . ." Horito placed his sleeve over his mouth like a woman and lowered his voice. "This is about all I know. . . . But then, his wife intends to run away with a traveling magician whether Mr. Nishimukai is in Okaya or in Tokyo. And this man, a certain Matsudama Saitenbo, who, for the past months, has been traveling all over the country performing magic tricks and curing illnesses with hypnosis, said that he would come back to Tokyo after the new year.

"It seems that Mr. Nishimukai came to Tokyo pretending that he wanted to live here, when he really wanted to go back to the country, go back to his job at the generator station, which, by the way, is now called the XX Electric Company. They ran an ad in the newspaper recently advertising a new stock issue. His getting hired there is practically decided already. It may turn out that I'll go back myself. Mr. Nishimukai is worried about me and told me that if I agree, he has already asked a former music student of his, who is now an officer of the company, for a job for me. That way it's almost certain I'll get it."

"That's good news, isn't it?" I said. But that glib-tongued twenty-year-old chatterbox moved to another subject before I had half a chance to get the full measure of all that befell Nishimukai. And Nishimukai is very dear to me.

"Sensei, this is changing the topic, but Mr. Ichiki's household is really different, you know," he began. "I really shouldn't talk like this about the man who has helped me, but that family seems to be in real trouble, you know. Are all households in Tokyo like that one, I wonder? Your household of course is different, but a household like Mr. Ichiki's. . . . They serve fine foods and give the children whatever they want. And at first, they seemed to me to be able to afford luxury perhaps undreamt of by even the rich, people with incomes of ten, even a hundred thousand yen; but lately certain callers have made me change my mind. Five, perhaps ten, I don't know exactly how many, but there's not one among them who isn't a bill collector." It reminded me of the saying, 'In the city one lives on borrowed money.' And when those duns are told that the master of the house is asleep, they come to an understanding among themselves so that at least two or three of them are ready to pounce on him when he wakes up. They are a hard-nosed lot. But then, as you know, Mr. Ichiki's not the talkative type and usually dismisses them with, "Please wait a little longer," or, "It's inconvenient right now," or, "I'll see to it soon," and leaves the house, not to return before midnight. The duns who come after he has left have to talk to his wife, and she, unlike Ichiki, is very ingenious, you know. But this can't go on, can it? The way I see it, they are barely a misstep away from having five or six liens on their property all at once. Mr. Ichiki has been playing the stock market a lot, but of late, his brokers have refused to take his orders. And I wouldn't be surprised if by year's end the Ichikis are completely ruined."

And finally that year too drew to a close, and on the first day of the new year we boarded the train at Shinjuku.

At first I planned to leave the night of the thirtieth of the last month of the old year, but various business affairs interfered, and I had to postpone the trip for two days. Ichiki had to go to a rooming house for the day of the thirty-first because he could on no account remain in his own house, so he went to the Koshinkan in Shinjuku where Nishimukai was staying. He didn't go into details, but he had arranged for Horito to watch the house. His wife and three children left the same day to spend the new year in Gifu, their home prefecture.

So on the night of the first the three of us, Ichiki, Nishimukai, and I, were heading for the mountains. Nishimukai had promised to go back to Shinshū to secure jobs for himself and Horito at the XX Electric Company and to summon Horito by telegram as soon as he had done so. On the other hand, we, Ichiki and I, had no other purpose than to enjoy the journey, which according to plans was to take us from Kiso Fukushima to Ōmachi, from Ōmachi to Matsumoto, and then from Matsumoto to Suwa, the town I loved.

"And if one or the other town appeals to me, I intend to stay put for a month or two," said Ichiki. "That's what I intend to do too, I don't want to go back to Tokyo for a while," I said.

Horito was the only person on the platform at Shinjuku that night of the first to see us off. Yet he barely managed to say good-bye to Nishimukai and me, he was so busy talking to Ichiki.

They held forth in low voices with earnest miens. It was probably about Ichiki's house, which was about to be seized, what had happened the thirty-first, and what Horito was supposed to do. Anyway, when I asked Ichiki after the train had left the station, "Will everything be all right with your house?" he simply said, "I have been done in, as expected."

"Done in? . . ." I asked.

"In other words, I'm under pressure from private quarters, the government isn't involved," he said, and smiled with tiny wrinkles in the corners of his mouth. "Well, tomorrow morning at about dawn we should reach Kasuga. That is, if we want to see the mountains, we'll have to get up at dawn, so let's go to sleep early."

"Let's," I said.

We bid each other a good night, and each of us, Ichiki, Nishimukai, and I, retired behind the blue curtains of our respective berths.

As I lay in my narrow bunk in the swaying coach, images of Ichiki, Nishimukai, and Horito, and of my wife, and of the woman I loved, and of the town to which we were going began to whirl in my head like figures in a battle scene. When I dozed off, they vanished as shadows in a clearing mist, and when I woke up, I sat up in my berth and felt as lighthearted as an innocent child.

Wondering what the weather would be like the next day, I put on an overcoat and went to the observation platform of the train to look out the window. There, unexpectedly, I ran into Ichiki. For some unaccountable reason, we both felt embarrassed.

"You haven't gone to bed yet?"

"No, I slept already. . . ."

"The berths on this train are really hard and uncomfortable, aren't they?"

"Stars in winter look so cold, they're so clear, aren't they?"
"The weather should be nice tomorrow."

After that exchange we went back in the coach, climbed in our bunks behind the blue curtains, and again bid each other a good night.

As the train rolled on, I napped, then woke up, then napped again, and woke up again, and each time I woke up I felt better, knowing that the mountains were getting closer. The thought of seeing the mountains of Kai again as soon as dawn broke made sleeping difficult. Each time I opened my eyes, I looked at my pocket watch, which hung suspended from the baggage rack. (Ichiki and Nishimukai probably had similar experiences.) I had been waking up and dozing off again and again, but when I woke up for good and looked at the watch, it was exactly five o'clock, and I didn't want to stay in bed any longer, so I quickly got up, dressed, and hurried to the observation platform to look outside. It was still as it had been in the middle of the night; stars glistened in the darkness. Then I returned to the coach to use the washbasin. As I came out of the washroom, I was startled to see Ichiki again; that habitual late riser was already up and about as well.

Each of the berths in the coach had a blue curtain stretched before it, and there was no sign that any of the other passengers were awake. At six o'clock, Nishimukai appeared in the smoking car, where Ichiki and I were sitting. He greeted us with a "Good morning, everyone."

Never before had I waited so impatiently for a winter night to end. Every so often I got up and went to the observation platform. Judging from the chilly air and the speed at which we were moving, I was sure that we had reached or were close to that place in

Kai where the gradient increases as the railroad approaches Shinano. At last the long-awaited dawn broke. Because ours was the first train to pass that way since nightfall, the tracks, on which the evening dew had frozen, squeaked incessantly under the wheels. The window, of course, was completely clouded over, as if the glass had been ground and rubbed, and we couldn't see anything outside; I tried to open it, but it wouldn't move. I entered the bathroom and then the washroom and tried to open the windows there, but they wouldn't budge. Then I ran out again to the observation platform, where Nishimukai and I joined our strength. With one hand we each grasped the iron railing so that we wouldn't tumble out and with the other hung onto the door leading to the outside. It too was frozen shut, but by straining all we could, we managed at last to open it.

Dawn had spread a golden hue over everything, and the sky and the snow-covered mountains of the Southern Alps literally leaped into view. It was a startling sight. But the very instant we opened the door, painfully cold air poured in like water, and my all-important glasses clouded over in a flash. Thinking that they would soon clear up as they did when they clouded over with steam, I waited, but to no avail. When I took them off, I discovered that my breath had condensed and then frozen on the lenses.

With Ichiki on one side and Nishimukai on the other to shield me from the wind, I eventually managed to wipe them clear and so beheld the scenery before me.

The jagged, leaning peak of Kai-Komagatake shone as huge blocks of ice do, whereas, beyond it, Okusenjō, Jizō, and Hōō[25] looked like small chunks of ice and seemed to be jostling one another to align according to height, as soldiers getting ready for inspection. Farther back yet on the border of Suruga province, where the sky was still rose colored, there was Mount Fuji, dyed purple exactly as in the woodcut prints.

Next we tried the door on the right. It was as difficult to open as the other one had been, but as it opened there stood Yatsugatake, deep blue, yet covered from its peak down with snow that looked like granulated sugar.

"We're here at last!" I cried. "Wonderful!" cried Ichiki.

And the train sped on to Shinano . . . to Shinano. . . .

Notes

Part 1 of "Love of Mountains" *(Yamagoi)* was first published in *Chūō kōron* in August, followed by "Love of Mountains, Continued" *(Yamagoi-zoku)* in the same journal the following month. The epigraph appears in "Shiromine sanmyaku no ki" (A record of the Shiromine mountain range) in vol. 1 of Kojima Usui's *Nihon Arupusu*. It was taken from *Heike monogatari* 10.6 ("The Journey Down the Eastern Sea Road"), in which is described the journey of the defeated Heike captain Shigehira along the Tōkaidō to Kamakura, where he is to be handed over to his enemy, Minamoto Yoritomo. Traveling eastward, past countryside he knows he will not live to see again, he catches sight of snowy peaks stretching far to the north:

> Snowy peaks appeared far to the north; and upon making inquiry, he was told that they were the Shirane Mountains in Kai. He expressed his feelings in verse, restraining tears:

oshikaranu	*I do not desire*
inochi naredomo	*to cling to this wretched life,*
kyō made zo	*yet, most happily,*
tsure naki kai no	*I have survived to behold*
shirane o mitsu	*the Shirane Mountains of Kai*

(*The Tale of the Heike,* trans. Helen Craig McCullough [Stanford, Calif.: Stanford University Press, 1988], 337.)

1. The Chūō main line (Chūō honsen), a national east-west rail line. Today the Chūō line leaves for Suwa from Shinjuku station, but in 1923 the departure point was Iidamachi.
2. That is, *kamisama,* Shinto deities.
3. A *tokonoma*: a recessed alcove in a formal Japanese sitting room used for displaying flower arrangements, scrolls, and pottery.
4. In place of permanent walls and hinged doors the Japanese room features sliding wooden frames with panels of pressed paper *(fusuma)* and translucent paper *(shōji).* These structures enhance the feeling of airiness and luminosity enjoyed from the high elevation.
5. Such personifications of wooded mountains were common in traditional Japanese literature. Haiku poets often read human expressions in the various aspects of mountains. Mountains were said to "smile" in the spring (*yama warau*) when they put on green color and radiated the joy of the season. They "dripped" in the summer *(yama shitatari)* with blue and green. In the fall they "adorned themselves" *(yama yosou)* with gold and red makeup and gorgeous clothes. In the winter they removed their garments and "slept" *(yama neru)* under snow. (*Yamayama jiten,* ed. Kondō Nobuyuki [Tokyo: Taishūkan Shoten, 1988], 36–37.) In *Kyōchūkikō,* Ogyū (Butsu) Sorai describes pine trees "greeting him," Lotus Peak (Mount Fuji) "rising with a big smile," and the Spirit of the Mountain "making herself up" for his sake (*Ogyū Sorai's Journey to Kai in 1706,* trans. Olof G. Lidin, Scandinavian Institute of Asian Studies Monograph Series, no. 48 [London and Malmö: Curzon, 1983], 44, 86). A similar proclivity for miniaturizing and prettifying landscape can also be seen in the traditional literati arts of miniature landscapes, miniature container gardens, and the cultivation of miniature trees *(bonsai).* For a detailed history of this tradition, see Rolf A. Stein, *The World in Miniature: Container Gardens and Dwellings in Far Eastern Religious Thought* (Stanford, Calif.: Stanford University Press, 1990).
6. Shinto shrines are traditionally located in groves. Indeed, trees are believed to have been the original habitations of the *kami.*

7. That "certain European scholar" is most likely Herbert Spencer, according to Senbokuya Kōichi ("Yama no Bungaku to Uno Kōji," in *Taishō bungaku no hikaku bungakuteki kenkyū,* ed. Naruse Masakatsu [Tokyo: Meiji Shoin, 1968], 263–289).

8. The passage from *Kyōchūkikō* that the narrator quotes appears as follows in Lidin's translation: "Further to the right lies Mount Narada, and yet further to the right these mountains follow in succession: Nōtori, Nōushi, Hōō, Jizō, and Komagatake, which adjoins Mount Kinpu in the north. Thus the province almost looks up to Heaven from inside a kettle. The mountain which rises craggy and steep above the two Nō mountains is Shirane (White Peak). Its aspect is cold and forbidding. On its barren pate each winter snow falls first. Is it because it glistens white with no grass or trees covering it [that it has obtained the name Shirane]? And is this the reason why it enjoys such popularity . . . among poets?" (see *Ogyū Sorai's Journey to Kai in 1706,* 83).

9. That is, a *kotatsu:* a heating device consisting of a wooden frame constructed over a heat source and covered with a quilt to retain the heat. A flat board placed on top of the quilt enables people to drink tea or write letters as they warm their feet and legs. The *kotatsu* used in the Suwa region, described in the text, was the kind that was sunk into the floor to conserve heat more effectively.

10. Chinoura Namiroku (1865–1944; real name Murakami Makoto; also known as Murakami Namiroku) was a popular Meiji period novelist whose novels were popularly known as *bachibin* novels after the hairstyle worn by their chivalrous townsman heroes, in which the hair *(hin)* of the head is shaved in the shape of a plectrum *(bachi).* Koto music is central to the climactic scene in Namiroku's well-known *Mikazuki* (Crescent moon), in which a townsman commits suicide as he listens to a koto being played by a samurai-priest who inflicted a crescent moon-shaped scar on his body twenty-five years before. The reference to Namiroku in the context of Nishimukai's koto concert—Nishimukai, of course, plays with a plectrum—is a display of wit reminiscent of that found in *gesaku* literature.

11. The chests *(nagamochi),* similar to the ones used to carry provisions for the daimyo's retinue in feudal days, were originally used to carry food and clothing for the men who went into the mountains to

bring back the fir tree trunks used in the Pillar Festival *(Onbashira Matsuri)*. The chests were hung from a long, stripped Japanese cypress *(hinoki)* pillar, which was borne on the shoulders of three to six men, depending on the size of the pillar.

12. He hears a *kiyari,* a traditional woodcutter's high-pitched, wailing song heard throughout the Suwa Pillar Festival. The *nagamochi* parade was (and still is) one of the highlights of the Suwa Pillar Festival.

13. A reference to the daimyo's procession *(daimyō gyōretsu),* in which villagers dressed in Edo period garb march through the town—a popular event in many Japanese festivals. It is common for children to play the role of the daimyo in such festival parades, a practice rooted in the belief, some say, that *kami* are likelier to inhabit children and women more readily than they are adult males. For a discussion, see A. W. Sadler, "Carrying the Mikoshi," *Asian Folklore Studies* 30, no. 1 (1972): 112–113.

14. That is, Western philosophers.

15. Although the Suwa deity Takeminakata is a god of wind, the reference here is most likely to the traditional storybook Wind God *(kaze no kami* or Shinatsu Hiko no Mikoto), who is depicted wearing a tiger skin loincloth and carrying a big bag filled with wind.

16. The name *Nōtori* is written with the characters "farm" and "bird." Some mountains in Japan (e.g., *Nōuma,* or "farm horse") are named after the animal shapes created by the snow on their peaks. Such mountains were used as "almanacs" by farmers, who determined the time for planting from the snow patterns on mountain peaks.

17. In his critical biography of Akutagawa *(Akutagawa Ryūnosuke* [Tokyo: Bungei Shunjū Shinsha, 1953]), Uno describes the time he and Akutagawa went to Suwa and took Hara Tomi and another geisha by car to Okaya city to see a movie. They were seen by someone, who reported it to the local newspaper. Going to Suwa to see "Uno's dream woman" seems to have been something of a standing joke with Akutagawa, who liked to tease his "shy" friend about his "dream" in Suwa.

18. The majestic Hotaka range was once worshiped as a *kami* and from olden days was known as Hotaka Daimyōjin *(Yamayama jiten,* 59). Not only are mountains sometimes likened to women, but *yama*

no kami (the god of the mountain) is also used as an uncomplimentary term for a wife (*yama no kami* can also mean "the mountain ruler" or "the mountain wife"). The fact that some wives may be as fearsome and bent on controlling their households as mountain *kami* control the plant and animal life on their slopes is alleged to be one reason for the appellation (ibid., 39–40).

19. The passage is in the style of advertising handbills written by *gesaku* writers. For example, advertising a kind of beauty rinse, Ryūtei Tanehiko (1783–1842) writes: "Women should have a dazzling fair complexion—and as proof, just think how beauties are praised by comparisons to white jade or to snow. But some women are, by nature, sallow or dark. The sallow woman can borrow the hues of safflower or of [?; not clear] rouge and mask her pallor, but the darker woman who tries to conceal her complexion with powder wins the unflattering designations of 'starchface' or 'bark cloth.' The sorrier her lot! But just when all seems most hopeless—lo! a marvelous beauty rinse, its formula a secret in the family for generations. Simply mix it with bran and apply it: Your complexion will become fair and display a healthy sheen. It cures blemishes, freckles, and psoriasis; congenital birthmarks and the like gradually fade and finally disappear. It tightens the grain of the skin, and this eliminates the danger of sunburn in summer or chapping in winter" (Andrew Lawrence Markus, *The Willow in Autumn: Ryūtei Tanehiko [1783–1842]*, Council on East Asian Studies [Cambridge, Mass.: Harvard University Press, 1992], 114). Tanehiko also wrote advertisements for breweries, eel, confections, gourmet restaurants, drapers, excursion boat rides, *nori* seaweed, and dentures.

20. This is a woman's way of bowing; men place their hands along the sides of their legs.

21. Mount Minobu is a principal seat of the Nichiren (Lotus Sutra) sect. Kuonji temple, which Nichiren built in 1281 on Mount Minobu, is the site where the religious leader's ashes are enshrined.

22. Bodhidharma (Japanese, Bodaidaruma or Daruma, ca. 470–543?) is the Indian monk and twenty-eighth patriarch after Shakyamuni Buddha who, according to tradition, traveled to China and sat in meditation for nine years (a period known as *menpeki*

kunen, or "nine years in front of the wall"). He is a figure emblematic of determination and devotion.

23. On his journeys throughout the countryside, the medieval poet-monk Saigyō (1118–1190) composed many poems about his lonely existence and his aesthetic and emotional responses to nature. The name *Ariake* (dawn) evokes the image of the "dawn moon," the planetary body—a traditional symbol of the Buddhist law and Buddhist enlightenment—on which Saigyō composed many of his poems.

24. The so-called rice riots *(kome sōdō)* were violent protests against the inflated price of rice that arose spontaneously throughout Japan in 1918. An estimated 1–2 million people rioted, and 25,000 persons were arrested by 92,000 armed troops called in to suppress the riots.

25. Hōō (Phoenix mountain) is also written with the characters "King of the (Buddhist) Law," referring to Dainichi Buddha, who is said to have once caused an auspicious sign to appear on the mountain (see Lidin, trans., *Ogyū Sorai's Journey to Kai in 1706,* 90).

GLOSSARY

asobi: usually translated as "play," it may denote lying about; being idle; amusing oneself; doing something for pleasure; enjoying literature or painting; taking excursions; making music; boating by moonlight; dallying with geisha; drinking; tricking, dissembling, or telling jokes; and a number of other activities generally not associated with the obviously useful.

bunjin: a refined, cultivated person accomplished in the various arts, especially literary arts (including Chinese poetry).

bunmei kaika: "civilization and enlightenment"; a rallying call, disseminated by the popular press during the Meiji period (1868–1912) and urging the Japanese people to give up their old-fashioned, native traditions and adopt modern Western manners and customs.

chōnin: a class of townspeople (artisans, shopkeepers, and merchants) relegated to a status below that of samurai and farmers within the social system established by the Tokugawa government.

daimyo: the hereditary lord of a feudal domain *(han)* during the Tokugawa period.

dōjin zasshi (also *dōnin zasshi*): a magazine published by a literary coterie. Hundreds of *dōjin zasshi* were published during the Meiji and Taishō periods.

Emma (Sanskrit, Yama): The king of the eight hells and the judge who determines which hell the damned will live in, according to the nature of their crimes.

furoshiki: square cloths of various sizes and fabrics used to wrap and carry objects.

fūryū: translated as "elegance," the word implies elegance in a traditional poetic sense, with a deep feeling of appreciation for the beauties of nature, art, and poetry.

fusuma: a sliding panel, covered with thick paper, used as a room divider in traditional Japanese buildings.

gesaku (playful compositions): popular fiction of the late Edo and Meiji periods written in a light, noncommittal, often amusing manner for the primary purpose of entertaining.

geta: elevated flat wooden clogs.

gidayū: a dramatic narrative recitation style accompanied by samisen initially developed by Takemoto Gidayū (1651–1714) for the *bunraku* puppet theater in the Genroku era (1688–1703).

hakama: a split skirt worn by men on formal occasions.

haori: a full, cloak-like jacket worn over a kimono.

heimen byōsha (flat surface description): a guiding aesthetic concept proposed by the naturalist writer Tayama Katai (1872–1930) according to which the writer would strive to describe surface reality as objectively as possible and would suppress all subjective evaluation.

hibachi: a traditional metal or ceramic charcoal brazier.

honkaku shōsetsu: an "objective" as opposed to a subjective, personal novel, such as a *shishōsetsu.*

Hyottoko: a comic mask of a man's distorted face with a blind eye and pursed lips; a comic dance performed by a man wearing such a mask; a word used to disparage a man.

Ikuta: A style of koto playing that originated in the Kansai area during the Genroku era (1688–1703); the plectrum is rectangular in shape, and the player sits at an angle to the koto.

Jizō: the bodhisattva who protects roads and crossroads and serves as an advocate for the dead when they appear before Emma, King of Hell.

jōruri: an art of narrative chanting to samisen accompaniment named after a character in a narrative that became popular in the early Edo period, particularly in the Osaka-Kyoto region.

kami: Shinto "deity" or "spirit."

kanbun: classical Chinese accompanied by markers that enable the reader to read the text using Japanese syntax; *kanbun* was a standard way of writing and reading scholarly texts before the Meiji period.

Kannon (also Kwannon; Chinese Kuan-yin; Sanskrit Avalokitesvara): the bodhisattva of mercy.

kiyari: a traditional workman's song.

kokkeibon (comical books): a kind of literature that used elements ranging from the ordinarily laughable to the scatological to provoke laughter.

kokugo: "national language," that is, Japanese as it is formally taught in schools.

koto: a thirteen-string zither, about six feet long and placed on the floor while played; each string has a movable bridge, which is adjusted to vary the tones as it is played.

musume gidayū: gidayū performed by women.

obi: stiff, broad waist sash worn over a kimono.

onnagata: a female impersonator in the kabuki theater.

oshare: fashionable, up-to-date, stylish.

Ōshima: a handspun silk pongee produced on Ōshima island off the coast of Kagoshima prefecture in southern Kyushu; one among many kinds of pongee used to make men's kimonos.

Otafuku: a mask of a woman's face with a high, bulging forehead, swollen cheeks, and a flat nose; also known as Ofuku and Okame; used as a derogatory term for women.

otogi-banashi: a fairy tale.

rakugo: traditional comic monologue stories ending in a "drop" *(raku)* or punch line.

samisen: a traditional, three-stringed, banjo-like musical instrument with a twangy sound; used to accompany singing.

Satsuma linen (Satsuma jōfu): a linen cloth dyed an indigo blue; produced in what was formerly Satsuma (now Kagoshima prefecture) and in the Ryūkyū islands.

sensei (teacher): a term of respect used for teachers and others whom erudition and professional distinction have rendered worthy of esteem.

shakuhachi: traditional eight-holed (*hachi,* eight) bamboo flute.

shichiya: a pawnshop; during the Tokugawa period *shichiya* functioned as lending institutions for commoners, dealing primarily in clothing and items of personal use but occasionally also lending money against houses and even shops; there were 2,700 *shichiya* in eighteenth-century Edo and 2,400 in mid-nineteenth-century Osaka.

Shikishima: a brand of cigarette popular during the Taishō period, considered to be a high-class kind of cigarette, second only to the Funi brand.

Shimada: an elaborate chignon with puffed-out front, side, and back locks worn by geisha.

Shingeki (New Theater): a theater movement that specialized in the production of translated Western plays and modern Japanese plays according to Western principles of realistic dramaturgy.

Shinpa (New Wave): a theater that flourished briefly during the Meiji period; although it was intended to be a realistic theater, before long the acting style had reverted to the stylized posturing of the kabuki stage; it is remembered as a melodramatic experimental theater, a historical oddity that was succeeded by the Shingeki theater after 1905.

shitamachi (downtown): the section of a city where shopkeepers and artisans have their shops and homes.

shizoku: a term used to designate persons who belonged to the warrior caste before the feudal system was dismantled in 1872.

Takajima: a dark blue cloth with a waterfall pattern.

Takeminakata-no-kami: the male *kami* enshrined in the Kamisha or Upper Shrine of the Suwa Jinja (Suwa shrine); mentioned in book 1, chapter 36, of the *Kojiki* as the obstreperous younger son of Ōkuninushi who challenges Takemikazuchi-no-kami the thunder god to a wrestling contest, loses the match, and is chased from the Central Land of the Reed Plains to the shores of Suwa lake. Takeminakata-no-kami was worshiped locally as a *kami* of wind and war.

tsūzoku-teki: popular, as opposed to serious (literature).

ukiyo-e (Pictures of the Floating World): woodblock prints first appearing in the early seventeenth century and depicting primarily aspects of the social life of the urban classes; subject matter included courtesans, kabuki actors, bathhouses, and scenes of travel along the major highways.

Urashima Tarō: a legendary character, similar to the Rip Van Winkle of the West; in exchange for having saved its life, a turtle took Urashima Tarō to the palace of the Dragon King at the bottom of the ocean, where Urashima lived with the palace princess; on arriving home and opening the jewel box given to him by the princess, he discovered that his home village had fallen into ruins and that he had aged 300 years.

Yamada: a style of koto playing used to accompany singing and recitation that originated in Edo at the end of the eighteenth century; the plectrum is rounded, and the performer faces the koto while playing.

Yamanote: the upland districts where the better residential neighborhoods are typically located; the best-known Yamanote is that of Tokyo where the samurai estates were located during the Edo period.

Yasakatome-no-mikoto: the female *kami* enshrined in the Shimosha or the Lower Shrine of the Suwa Shrine. Believed to have originally been a minor lower grain *kami,* she is traditionally regarded as the consort of the *kami* of the Suwa Shrine, Takaminakata-no-kami.

Yoneryū: a pongee named after the city, Yonezawa, where it is manufactured and after its resemblance to pongee from the Ryūkyū islands.

yoriki: a police captain under the jurisdiction of a city magistrate *(machi bugyō)* during the Tokugawa period. The *yoriki* were from the samurai class but received comparatively low stipends.

yose: a kind of vaudeville hall dating back to the late Edo period, where *rakugo, gidayū, kōdan* (dramatic storytelling), musical performances, juggling, magic tricks, and other popular entertainments were performed.

Yūzen crepe (Yūzen chirimen): silk cloth made with very strong raw threads laid horizontally and shrunk with warm water to produce a crinkled surface, then dyed according to the *Yūzen* process; named after its mid-Edo period inventor, Miyazaki Yūzen, the dyeing method was one used to produce brilliantly colored patterns of figures, animals, and flowers.

PLACE NAMES

Akaishi: a mountain range in central Honshu, extending over Nagano, Yamanashi, and Shizuoka prefectures; known also as the Southern Alps national park.

Ariake: a beautiful 6,794-foot mountain on the western edge of the Matsumoto basin in Nagano prefecture, famous for the waterfalls on its summit; sometimes called the "Shinano Fuji."

Atago: a hill in Minato ward, Tokyo, north of Shiba park, famed for the long flight of stairs leading up to the shrine on its summit.

Azabu: a fashionable residential area in Minato ward, Tokyo.

Chichibu mountains: a mountainous region that straddles Saitama, Yamanashi, Nagano, and Gumma prefectures and part of Tokyo.

Chūō main line (Chūō honsen): a national east-west rail line linking Tokyo station in east Tokyo to Shinjuku station in west Tokyo and passing through Kōfu and Shiojiri to Nagoya.

Dōtonbori: a theater and entertainment district in Osaka built along the Dōtonbori canal.

Echigo: the name of an old province; corresponds to present-day Niigata prefecture.

Edo: the city (roughly equivalent to present-day Tokyo) in eastern Japan that was the site of the shogun's castle and the center of political power during the Tokugawa period (1600–1868).

Fuji (Fujisan): at 12,358 feet, Japan's highest and most famous mountain; the image of the graceful, symmetrical, snow-covered slopes of this conical, once sacred volcano has long been an inspiration for poets and artists; located sixty-two miles southwest of Tokyo, it could be seen on clear days during Uno's time.

Fujimi (Fujimi tōge): one of three passes linking the Suwa basin, enclosed by mountain ranges, to the outside world.

Ginza: the name given to the shopping area of a number of towns, the most famous of which is the Tokyo Ginza, extending about a mile in length, with hundreds of shops, boutiques, restaurants, drinking establishments, and department stores.

Hakone (Hakone-yama): a volcanic mountain (4,717 feet tall) on the border of southwest Kanagawa and eastern Shizuoka prefectures.

Hakuba (White Horse): a village in northwest Nagano prefecture on the slopes of Shirouma (White Horse) mountain.

Hinoharu: a village in northwestern Yamanashi prefecture located near the Yatsugatake range.

Hitachi: an old province; corresponds to present-day Ibaraki prefecture.

Hōō (Hōō-zan, "Phoenix mountain"): a mountain in northwest Yamanashi prefecture and part of the Akaishi range; also the collective name of three mountains named after bodhisattvas: Jizō (Jizōdake), Kannon (Kannondake), and Yakushi (Yakushidake).

Hotaka (Hotakadake): a mountain in the Japan Alps, on the border of Nagano and Gifu prefectures; of its four peaks, Mae Hotakadake (10,135 feet) was first climbed by Walter Weston in 1893, and Oku Hotakadake (10,463 feet) is Japan's third highest peak and the highest mountain in the Hida range.

Iidamachi: a station in Chiyoda ward, Tokyo; opened in 1895 and now used for freight traffic; when "Love of Mountains" was written, it was the starting point for what is now the Chūō line.

Japan Alps: the appellation given to three lofty mountain ranges located in central Honshu; with the exception of Mount Fuji, Japan's highest mountains lie in these three ranges, which are divided into the Northern, Central, and Southern Alps (regions known as Hida, Kiso, and Akaishi, respectively). The term *Japan Alps* was popularized by William Gowland, author of *Japan Guide* (1888). Gowland, a contemporary of Walter Weston's, worked at the Imperial Japanese Mint and was the first European to explore the Northern Japan Alps.

Jizō (Jizōdake): an 8,340-foot mountain, located in the northern part of the Akaishi range in Yamanashi prefecture.

Kabuto-chō: a district in Tokyo named after a shrine built on a mound in which armor (*kabuto*) was buried; another name for Nihonbashi; it became a site for brokerage houses after the Tokyo stock exchange was established there in 1878.

Kai: an old province, located in central Honshu, west of Tokyo; corresponds to today's Yamanashi prefecture.

Kaigane range: another name for the Shirane range in Yamanashi and Shizuoka prefectures.

Kai-Komagatake: a mountain on the border of Yamanashi and Nagano prefectures, in the northern Akaishi range; also called Komagatake and Kaikoma; it is to be distinguished from Aizu-Komagatake in Fukushima prefecture and Kiso-Komagatake in the Kiso mountain range in southwestern Nagano prefecture.

Kamanashi river: a river in western Yamanashi prefecture that originates in the northern Akaishi moutains and flows in a southerly direction.

Kamikōchi: a scenic valley in the Northern Alps in western Nagano prefecture and a starting point for mountaineering; surrounded by Yakedake, Hotakadake, and other mountains; made famous by Walter Weston, who described it in *Mountaineering and Exploration in the Japanese Alps.*

Kawasaki: a port city in northeast Kanagawa prefecture.

Keihin line: a private railroad company linking Tokyo with the industrial cities of Kawasaki and Yokohama; founded in 1898.

Kinpu-san: a 7,785-foot mountain between Yamanashi and Nagano prefectures; the highest peak in the Chichibu range.

Kiso: a region in southwest Nagano prefecture.

Kiso Fukushima: a town in southwest Nagano prefecture in the Kiso valley (Kisodani); a former barrier station on the Nakasendō.

Kobotoke pass: formerly a barrier station on the Kōshū Kaidō; now the Chūō main line passes through tunnels built under the pass; located on the border of southwest Tokyo and Kanagawa prefecture.

Kobushi (Kobushidake): a 7,449-foot mountain straddling the borders of Saitama, Yamanashi, and Nagano prefectures in the western part of the Chichibu range; source of the Chikuma river.

Kōfu: the capital of Yamanashi prefecture, about a two-hour train ride west of Shinjuku station in Tokyo; once the headquarters of the medieval warlord Takeda Shingen (1521–1573).

Kokushi (Kokushidake): one of the Chichibu mountains; it was once a sacred peak called Daitakesan.

Komagatake: at 4,428 feet, one of the seven central domes of Hakone-yama.

Komagome: a district in Shinjuku ward in Tokyo.

Komoro: an old castle town and former post station in the eastern part of Nagano prefecture; made famous as the setting of Shimazaki Tōson's *Chikumagawa Suketchi* (Chikuma river sketches, 1913).

Kōshū: another name for Kai province.

Kōshū Kaidō (Kōshū highway): one of the five official highways of the Tokugawa period (1600–1868), it began at Nihonbashi in Edo and went through Kōfu to Kami Suwa, where it joined the Nakasendō.

Kuonji temple: built by the medieval religious leader Nichiren on Mount Minobu in 1281; as the site where

Nichiren's ashes are enshrined it is a center of worship for adherents of the Lotus Sect.

Kyōbashi: a commercial section of Tokyo located near the Ginza.

Minobu: a mountain southwest of Kōfu in Yamanashi prefecture; site of Kuonji temple built by Nichiren and an important center of the Nichiren sect.

Nakasendō: one of the five major highways of the Tokugawa period; a mountainous inland road tracing a northwestern path from Nihonbashi in Edo to Usui, Kami Suwa, and Kiso Fukushima, then merging with the Tōkaidō at Kusatsu before reaching Kyoto.

Nikkō-san: volcanic mountains (the highest peak is 7,452 feet) near Nikkō city in Tochigi prefecture.

Norikura(dake): a 9,925-foot mountain, named after its saddle *(kura)* shape, located between Nagano and Gifu prefectures in the southern part of the Hida range of the Northern Japan Alps.

Nōtori(dake): a 9,038-foot peak in the Akaishi range of the Southern Japan Alps, located between Yamanashi and Shizuoka prefectures; named after the bird-like pattern formed by snow on its peak.

Okaya: a city in the Suwa basin; during the Meiji and Taishō periods it was the center of silk thread mills, where many adolescent girls from poor villages in Nagano and Gifu prefectures worked under near slave-labor conditions.

Ōmachi: a town in northern Nagano prefecture that serves as a base camp for travelers setting out for the Northern Alps.

Ōmi: an old province in central Honshu; corresponds to Shiga prefecture.

Ontake: a mountain famous for its beautiful cypress forests and alpine flora, located in the Kiso district of western Nagano prefecture; regarded as a holy mountain from the latter part of the Sengoku era (1467–1568); pilgrims (men only; women were not allowed to set foot on the mountain) climbed it to worship at the shrine on its summit; also called Kiso Ontake, after its location in the Kiso district of western Nagano prefecture, to distinguish it from other mountains called Ontake.

Rokugō river: the southern end of the Tamagawa river, located between Tokyo and Kawasaki city.

Sasago pass: formerly a pass on the Kōshū Kaidō; located on the eastern border of the Kōfu basin, it was a landmark that marked the boundary of Kai province; traffic now passes through tunnels bored through the Sasago mountains.

Satsuma: a former feudal province located at the southern tip of Kyushu.

Sendai: capital of Miyagi prefecture; the largest city in northeastern Honshu.

Shichimen (Seven Faces): a mountain range southwest of Kōfu city in Yamanashi prefecture.

Shimajima: a village west of Matsumoto city in Nagano prefecture located at the foot of the Northern Japan Alps.

Shimo Suwa: one of five towns located in the Suwa basin; a former post station on the Nakasendō and the site of the Shimosha (Lower shrine) Suwa shrine.

Shinano: an old province in central Honshu; corresponds to present-day Nagano prefecture.

Shinjuku: formerly a post station on the old Kōshū Kaidō and today a station and departure point for travel west on the Chūōline; also the name of one of the twenty-three wards of Tokyo.

Shinshū: another name for Shinano.

Shiojiri: a city south of Matsumoto city in the central part of Nagano prefecture; a former post station on the old Nakasendō.

Shiojiri pass: a pass in the Kiso range linking the Suwa basin with Matsumoto city to the north.

Shirane range: a mountain range consisting of Nōtoridake (9,925 feet), Ainodake (10,460 feet), and Kitadake (10,470 feet); located between Yamanashi and Shizuoka prefectures.

Shirouma (White Horse): a mountain in northwest Nagano prefecture named after the snow formations on its peak that resemble the figure of a horse.

Sōemonchō: the neighborhood in Osaka where Uno grew up; at the turn of the century, a district bordered by Dōtonbori to the south and the entertainment district of Minami Shinchi to the East.

Suihara: a town along the Akano river in south central Niigata prefecture.

Suruga: an old province; corresponds to the central part of present-day Shizuoka prefecture.

Suwa: a city in central Nagano prefecture; also called Kami Suwa; site of the Kamisha Suwa shrine and a favorite resort town for Tokyo writers and artists during the Taishō period.

Suwa basin: a graben basin located in central Honshu in Nagano prefecture; linked to the outside world by the Fujimi pass leading to Tokyo, the Shiojiri pass leading to Matsumoto city, and the Ueda pass leading to Ueda and Komoro; located in Suwa basin are the towns of Suwa, Shimo Suwa, Chino city, Okaya, Fujimichō, and Hara village.

Suwa lake: a 25-foot deep, 5.4-square-mile lake fed by snow runoff from nearby mountains; lying in the western part of the Suwa basin, its 11-mile circumference is dotted with hotels and inns, erected for the visitors who come to see the shrines and to enjoy boating and fishing in the summer and ice fishing and ice skating in the winter.

Suwa shrine: a double shrine *(niza issha)* consisting of a Kamisha, located south of Suwa lake, and a Shimosha, located north of the lake; the main deity enshrined is Takeminakatano-kami.

Tabata: a station on the Tōhoku main line; located in Kita ward of Tokyo.

Tenryū river: a river in Nagano and Shizuoka prefectures originating in Suwa lake and flowing southward.

Tōhoku: the northeast part of Honshu, comprised of Fukushima, Miyagi, Iwate, Yamagata, and Akita prefectures.

Tsukuba-san: a 2,628-foot mountain in Ibaraki prefecture.

Ueda: a city in eastern Nagano prefecture on the Chikuma river; formerly the seat of the capital of Shinano province.

Ueda pass: a pass leading from the Suwa basin to the cities of Ueda and Komoro in northern Nagano prefecture.

Ueno: a district in northeastern Tokyo and the site of Ueno park and Ueno zoo.

Ugo: an old province in northwestern Honshu; now Akita prefecture.

Ushigome: a district in Shinjuku ward in Tokyo, its name recalls the fact that it was once a place where cattle *(ushi)* were enclosed *(kome)*.

Wada pass: 5,022 feet high and located in central Nagano prefecture; noted for its great scenic beauty.

Yarigatake (Spear Peak): a 10,430-foot mountain on the border of Nagano and Gifu prefectures; named after its spear-shaped summit; the fourth highest mountain in Japan and the second highest peak in the Hida range of the Northern Japan Alps.

Yatsugatake: a mountain range on the border of Nagano and Yamanashi prefectures, it is the northern part of the Akaishi range of the Southern Japan Alps; the highest of the "eight peaks" *(yatsugatake)* is Akadake (9,509 feet); the range lies on the eastern edge of the Suwa basin.

Yotsuya: a district in Shinjuku ward in Tokyo and the first station on the old Kōshū Kaidō.

Yuzawa: a hot springs town in the southeastern Niigata prefecture.